A Funny Thing Happened On The Way To Her Brother's Shotgun Wedding

By Noreen Riley

"A Funny Thing Happened On The Way To Her Brother's Shotgun Wedding," by Noreen Riley. ISBN 978-1-60264-428-1.

Published 2009 by Virtualbookworm.com Publishing Inc., P.O. Box 9949, College Station, TX 77842, US. ©2009, Noreen Riley. All rights reserved. No part of this publication may be reproduced, stored in a retrieval system, or transmitted in any form or by any means, electronic, mechanical, recording or otherwise, without the prior written permission of Noreen Riley.

Manufactured in the United States of America.

This book is dedicated to my three sons: Colin, Timmy, and Patrick. I now know that the greatest moments in life come standard with ketchup on a chin, cleats that stink so badly they have to be left in the garage, the sound of the word 'Mommy', and the feeling of tiny fingers clutching my own. May this serve as a lesson that no one is strictly what they seem to be, no matter how closely you observe them. And that anything is possible, as long as you can dream it!

Acknowledgements

I couldn't have possibly written a book based upon the dynamics of close family and great friends without the true blessing of having both in my life. Granted, this is a work of fiction and none of the characters are based on any particular person, but the feelings I strive to convey are those that I feel on a daily basis, thanks to the wonderful ties I have to my own family and friends.

I'll start off by thanking my parents, Jay and Mary Frayne, for providing a lasting example of a strong and healthy marriage, which I use as a model for not only my fictional married parents in this book, but for my own real life marriage, as well. How blessed I was to have two people who believed in me right from the start. Just because I was born to them!

I'd also like to thank my brother, Jim Frayne, and sister, Beth Boland, for the crazy memories of childhood fun that continue even though we're all in our thirties! (And I have to admit some of the sibling stories do have a basis in real life...like a slight addiction to Jax on my brother's part and a go-cart mishap going down the Merlin Lane hill, to name just two.) And to Beth's husband, Dan, and Jim's wife, Lidia...you are most welcome additions to our family, and having lived with both Jim and Beth, I salute you.

Just because I can, and this seems like as good a time as any, I'd like to mention my love and admiration for some other family members that have always brought a smile to my face: Noelle Sullivan, Eileen and John O'Rourke, their three boys, Michael, Timmy, and Sean O'Rourke, along with their wives, Denise, Eleanor, and Kirsten, and Mary McInenery. Also Fr. Joe Finnerty, who has literally been there from the start; from when he baptized me, to marrying my husband and me, to baptizing our children. To the Ray cousins, what else can I say except we'll always have the Poconos? And thanks to Donna Bebb, who taught me the importance of wearing elastic waist clothing to all you can eat brunches, and Timmy Riley, for teaching me *NEVER* to name your mixed tapes "Kick Ass Mix". Many thanks go to my in-laws, Bill and Clare Riley, for helping to make their son the man he is today. I hope I'm able to do the same for the future wives of my three boys.

There are so many friends I have been blessed with from different times in my life that have always been there for me and have been some of my biggest supporters and cheerleaders that I'd be remiss not to name them. (Sit back, this is going to take a while!)

Thank you, thank you, thank you to my high school friends who *LITERALLY* screamed with joy when I first told them I was finishing this book. Who could ask for a better reaction? Marni McManus (thanks for the funny line!), Cindy Barban, Kate Tretheway (all early readers of the manuscript, all future PR reps for it), Courtney Dolan (famous for her tape recordings of *Dallas*, and whom I have been blessed to call one of my closest friends since we were the ripe old age of three), Regina Portsmore (who told me she had no intention of reading my manuscript until it was published, and she had complete faith that she would read this book), Heather Locke, and Jody Devaney have been my closest friends and staunchest supporters. (As well as some of their Moms who can now stop asking me, as they have for the past twenty years, "When are you going to finally write a book?" I'm talking to you, Mrs. Elias and Mrs. Clarken).

A big shout out to all the Scranton Girls, particularly, Lisa Lausten, Cynde Stacey, Stacey McGlynn, Susan Mark, Tara Langan, Margaret McConville, Megan O'Donnell, Karen McDonald, Leigh Melore, Colleen Reed, and Carol Roy. I loved every minute of my four years at the University of Scranton with you guys, not to mention the fifteen or so since we've graduated. As long as none of you decide to write your own tell-all book from those years, we're good!

Not too many people can say with certainty they were lucky enough to meet some of their closest friends as they aged. I can. Thank goodness my three sons have brought some wonderful people into my life based on the friendships they made. The women from the pre-school years at St. Mark's have filled my life with a ton of laughter and the sharing of pain. My once a month bunko crew has been a source of inspiration, laughter, wine (of course) and stolen dip recipes that I now claim as my own! And as each sports season rolls around, for any of the boys, I have no qualms stating I have always looked forward to laughing (and losing my voice) each week on the sidelines with the other Robbinsville parents, especially with those from the United soccer team and the Hillbilly Cheese baseball team.

To the fabulous Kristen Donato, as the *VERY* first reader (outside of my husband, Joe) of the earliest draft, who was able to make me feel like I had done something worthwhile and funny. As I've said before, you are one of my closest friends, and it's not just because you're married to my husband's best friend! This, of course, brings me to Tim Donato. You've given me quite a few laughs through the years and showed by example why I should always wear a bike helmet. Thank you for being as big a cheerleader throughout this process as your beautiful wife. Who else would have taken the time to make up a mock book cover and Amazon order form to show me what it would look like to order my title off their website? Before it was even officially done? Thank you both!

And to "My Brunner" as my youngest son, Patrick, calls Nancy Brunner. Quite simply, your friendship means the world to me! It's a gift I'll always cherish.

And, most importantly, thank you to my husband, Joe. Even though you asked constantly if Nate was based on you, I can't lie. He's not. He's not even a distant second to what you offer. Your humor, kindness, and intelligence are indescribable to anyone who has never met you, so I won't even try. Those that do have the pleasure of knowing you know what I mean. Plus, you're pretty easy on the eyes! And, aside from all the support and encouragement you've offered throughout this whole process, you've given me the greatest gifts I could ever ask for in life; our three boys, Colin, Timmy, and Patrick. I love you!

One

*O*h *my God, who the hell let the mariachi band into the apartment*, wondered Evie, her head pounding. Her mind raced, trying to figure out which of her friends could have possibly begun a relationship with salsa since last night.

"Please," she weakly called out from under her cover, "would you mind an awful lot if I asked you to just stop playing. Because I seem to have a bit of a hangover, and if I'm forced to get out of my bed, I think I might throw up, and I'd hate for any puke to get all over your lovely mandolins." No answer, but the music continued to play. She was sure this kind of music called for mandolins.

Great, she thought, *rude mariachi band members. I actually think it was quite nice of me to have the foresight to even think of their instruments.*

"Evie," her roommate Amanda called out from her room, sounding just as bad as Evie felt, "if you don't answer your goddamn phone, I'm moving out as soon as I can lift my head off this pillow."

My phone? Evie sat up in her bed wildly, her head swiveling around in search of the nuisance. Well, that might have been what she did in her mind, but in actuality she mostly just laid there and tried to move her eyeballs to survey the ground in search of her phone. Nights that included four bottles of red wine between four friends, and who knows how many martinis, didn't normally allow for mornings with lots of springing out of bed and head swiveling and such. This one was no exception. The noise seemed to be coming from inside the purse she used last night. The purse lay on her desk, which was across the room from her bed, basically taunting her with the upbeat and dreadfully loud music. Normally she complained about the cramped space she called her room, but this morning (And what the hell time was it anyway? Who would be calling her at such an appalling hour?) it felt like she lived in Versailles. It was simply insurmountable.

"I'm sorry, Amanda," she called out as loud as her throbbing head would allow. "I just can't get there...you may not believe me, but the Grand Canyon has suddenly sprung up in the middle of my room and my phone is on the other side. The chasm is huge and my bed is tipped precariously close to the edge. I'm afraid if I move, I'll mess up the delicate balance of nature and fall ass over tits into the deep abyss."

"If you used just a fraction of the energy you had to muster up for that ridiculous sentence, you could've answered your phone," Amanda called back. "And stop paraphrasing Helen Mirren. She's beloved on both sides of the pond and you don't do her words justice."

"Instead, whadda'ya say I just severely chastise whoever it was that called at such an ungodly hour. What time is it anyway? I can't see my clock."

"Let me guess...it's on the other side of the Grand Canyon? Ummm, eleven-fifteen a.m.," Amanda said. "Seriously, who would call you so early on a Sunday morning? And by the way, what the hell was up with that ring tone?"

———

It was close to one o'clock before Evie had a chance to check her voicemail. Not because she was busy up until then, but because that was the first time she ventured from her bed.

She pushed in her pin number and waited for the automated voice to tell her she had one new voicemail.

"Evie, it's me, Michael" boomed a recorded voice into her ear. She held the phone away from her at arms length, because keeping it any closer made her head start pounding again.

Michael was Evie's older brother and so difficult to reach, what with the six hour time difference between his home in London and hers in New York City, that she was seriously pissed off that she hadn't actually tried to answer the phone when it rang. Or sambaed. Also, the call would've been on his dime, which was always preferable to her racking up her phone bill.

"It's close to lunchtime for you, so I figured you would've been up. Maybe you went for a run or something," Michael continued, and abruptly stopped to snicker at his last comment. "Or more to the point, you're probably nursing a hangover and are cursing whoever is on the other end of the line. But seriously, Evelyn, when you get a chance could you call me? I need to talk to you. Bye."

That's curious, thought Evie. Michael rarely called her Evelyn. That treat was usually reserved for their mother or her older sister, Grace.

"Who was it that called earlier? Lucifer himself?" Amanda asked, suddenly standing in the doorway to Evie's room, looking like the proverbial cat having been drug through the mud.

"You look like crap on a stick, Mandy," Evie blurted out, taking stock of the makeup running down her face, disheveled tee shirt from last night obviously worn in lieu of pajamas, and hair that couldn't even begin to be described.

"You're a peach, Evie. I really appreciate having you in my corner as my very own cheerleading squad. So who was on the phone?"

"Michael...now I'm going to have to call him back. Maybe he's out to dinner with Charlotte and I can just leave a quick message and he'll have to call me back." Crossing her fingers as she dialed, she called him back.

"Michael Dunleavy," Michael's voice rang out in her ear. *Damn, he was in.*

"Hey, Mike, it's Evie. What's shakin' bacon?"

"You may be talking pork products, but you sound definitively downbeat. Hoping to catch me out, so you could leave a message and make me pay for the call?" he guessed correctly.

"It's because of that astute reasoning, that bank over there stole you from all of us here in the good ol' U-S- of A. Where, I might add, we could talk to you on a regular friends and family plan. Stupid Gringotts."

"Yeah, Evie, for the last time I don't work at Harry Potter's bank," Michael said mildly. "As cool as you think that would be," he hastily added, cutting off a nearly certain diatribe Evie would've launched into about goblins and witch currency, had she been given the chance.

"Listen, if you can promise me we don't have to talk about your refusal to believe I have not encountered–slash–stalked J.K. Rowling in my two years over here in England so you can get an autographed copy of a Harry Potter book, then I will call you right back so you don't have to pay for the call."

"Fair 'nuff. I'll talk to you in a sec."

Amanda had started to move away from Evie's door as she was hanging up the phone. "At what point, considering you are thirty-two years old, do you think it will start getting a little embarrassing for you to have your older siblings and parents call you back, so you don't have to pay for the phone charges, I wonder?" she asked idly as she walked away.

"Don't know. Haven't reached it."

Evie grabbed the phone as it started to ring. Michael started talking as soon as she picked up. "So I take it you haven't been swamped with freelance articles to write this month, considering the fact you don't call."

"Yeah, but Maura promised me a couple of things coming up for her in the next couple of months. So that should help the overdraft problem I've been accumulating," she hedged.

"Isn't Maura your friend who runs the catering functions at that shi shi hotel in midtown?"

"Damn your photographic memory, Michael. Thank God Mom and Dad seem to think she's a big time editor at one of the magazines I work with on occasion. I don't know why they haven't figured out that they haven't seen a by-line of mine in about three months, considering all the "opportunities" Maura throws my way."

"So, Michael," she continued, "all our pleasantries aside, do tell...what do I owe the honor of your early morning phone call to?"

"Ah yes. I actually have some happy news I wanted to share and I wanted you to be the first to know. Charlotte and I are engaged. I'm getting married!" His voice rose to an excited pitch, in a rather un-Michael like way.

It took quite a bit to shock Evelyn Dunleavy, but this qualified as a shocker. Her family always joked about Michael being the consummate bachelor and she was in no way prepared for this bit of news. Evie figured he was calling about yet another promotion, or frankly to say he was dating someone new. Michael never seemed to lack for female attention, considering he was blessed with dark, handsome looks, a great sense of humor, and a rather large bank account. None of the women he dated were ever able to get through to Michael, though, so they rarely were around for longer then a couple of months. And now he was going to marry Charlotte, a woman that no one in the family really knew at all. This would obviously be expected, since Evie's family lived on the east coast of the United States and Michael and Charlotte were in London.

Then another thought struck Evie. "Hey, wait a sec," she said. "You said I was the first to know...you haven't told Mom and Dad yet? Are you crazy?"

"Yeah, I was kind of hoping you'd do me a favor in that regard," Michael said quickly.

"Please don't say you want me to be the one to tell them, because that would be so gauche," she joked.

A slight pause on the other end of the line made her realize Michael was now pondering this approach and trying to figure out what kind of fallout could be expected with such an ill-advised maneuver. "Because I would never do it. It was a joke, so stop your mind from traipsing down that path."

"Yeah, I can just read the epitaph on Mom's grave now," he said. "Loving mother to three, had to find out about son's wedding via youngest daughter. Strain to her heart killed her. No, I was actually hoping you might have a chance to head home so you're there when I tell them."

"Alright, this has become very cloak and dagger-y and I'm not very good with this stuff. Why the hell do I need to make a trip out to Connecticut just so I can be there when you tell Mom and Dad? You're not making much sense, Michael."

"Well, there's actually some more good news that I need to share with you, and I was hoping my conversation with Mom and Dad might go smoother if I had an ally there, since I can't be there myself."

"Think band-aids, Michael. Hurts less if you just rip it right off."

"Charlotte's pregnant. I'm going to be a father."

"So you'll need me to schedule a stop at Grace's, too, then I suppose. I'll check the train schedule and get back to you."

———————

A couple hours later, Evie had set up a dinner date with her parents for Tuesday night at their house. She was able to do it without arousing too much suspicion, since she'd been known to have home cooked meal cravings before; but this time, instead of working it into her laundry schedule like she usually did; she worked it around Michael's work schedule. That left two days of her sitting on this huge piece of family gossip and no one in her family to talk about it ad nauseum with. It was time to call in the troops.

Two

E vie brought out four bottles of Michelob Ultra and plopped them on the table. It was Sunday night and they were about to go through a fair amount of these bad boys while she unloaded her story on them.

Amanda, now showered, looked remarkably like her old self and nothing like the crap on a stick Evie had likened her to earlier. Her short, blond hair was no longer sticking straight up, but rather in the kempt bob she always wore. She sported the usual Sunday hangover uniform of an old boyfriend's long sleeve tee, a pair of sweat pants, and no makeup.

Maura was the exact opposite of Amanda's casual look. Having just come from a catering function at the hotel where she was the events manager, she was looking quite upscale. She had on a beautiful pale, robin's egg blue suit (designer no doubt, Evie thought, since it fit her like a glove) and shoes that were the EXACT color of the suit, without looking too bridesmaidy circa 1988. Her long brown hair was swept up in a chignon and her large green eyes looked around Evie and Amanda's apartment when she bounded in the door. She held aloft another twelve pack of beer yelling loudly, "Did anyone call for reinforcements?"

Kelly, Evie's old college roommate who lived just a few blocks away from her and Amanda on the Upper East

Side, yelled from the kitchen, "Thank God you're here...the most we've been able to pry out of Evie was that Michael is officially off the market." Her head poked through the window cutout into the dining room/living room/den the other three girls were sitting in, and she added sheepishly, "I for one, am devastated."

Kelly came into the room, red hair in a ponytail, carrying the bottle opener and did the honors. "Let the Round Table discussion begin," she said simply.

"Alright." Evie said pragmatically. "Let's start at the beginning, shall we?"

There was silence all around the table, as well as exactly seven empties, by the time Evelyn finished rehashing her phone conversation with her brother.

Maura was the first to speak. "Well, that's a fine how do you do, huh? How do you think your parents will react?"

"That's the million dollar question, isn't it?" Evie answered. "The fact of the matter is no one in the family really knows her at all. I mean, they've been together for almost a year and a half, I guess, now that I really think about it. So I couldn't say he was exactly rushing into anything, or getting married just because Charlotte's pregnant. I've met her twice, which is once more than Grace has, I think. And last summer was the third time my parents met her. They've been over there a couple of times visiting Michael."

"What's your take on her, then, based on your two meetings?" Amanda asked.

"I don't even know if our first meeting could technically count as such, since it was so short. Michael and Charlotte were flying out to the West Coast to a wedding for one of his old college roommates and they had a couple hours to kill on a layover at Newark. He asked if I wanted to meet them in between their flights so he could introduce me to Charlotte, but honestly, I thought he just wanted me to bring a couple bags of Jax cheese doodles, because apparently Americans are the only folks on the entire globe that have the constitution to consume them, and he can't get them in England."

"I love Jax." Kelly threw out.

"I know, right?" Maura agreed. "If only they could figure something out with the orange residue...I'd eat them all the time."

"But they have," Kelly called out excitedly. They make an organic variety that's not bright orange. They're practically good for you."

Amanda got the conversation back on track. "Yeah, Kel, it's like eating a pile of broccoli. So-o-o...you met her at Newark, bearing Jax. Then what?"

"Well," Evelyn continued. "She seemed nice enough, I guess. Very posh British accent, I remember thinking. She was Eliza Doolittle after the professor got through with her. No *'enery 'iggens* coming out of her mouth. I thought she seemed a little stiff for Michael, but kind of chalked it up to the fact she was probably nervous meeting someone from Michael's family for the first time."

Evie thought back to that day in the airport just over a year ago to try to remember some more details to share with the girls. "She certainly travels looking very different than I do."

"Meaning," Maura said snarkily, "she possibly showers and dresses in something somewhat presentable, in order to not completely offend her fellow passengers on an international flight? That's preposterous."

"I like to think that I sometimes opt for substance over style."

"Sweetie," Amanda said, "you opt for something over style when you travel, I just don't think you could classify it as 'substance'."

"Back to what I was saying, if you don't mind. I think what surprised me the most was that she really didn't talk *to* me, if you know what I mean. I was standing right in front of her, yet she still turned to Michael and would direct any questions she had for me to him."

"What do you mean?" Kelly asked.

"Well, before Michael introduced us, she faced Michael and asked him, "So, what is it your sister does again?" I thought that was kind of odd. I mean, I didn't know if I should answer her myself, or wait for Michael to do it for me. It was sort of like having a translator even though everyone spoke the same language. Bizarre way to hold a conversation."

"So what about the second time you met her? When you went to visit Michael for that long weekend?" Amanda asked.

"That actually went a lot better. I don't know if it was because Grace was with me or the fact we were on her turf. Although while we were there she was away for work for two out of the four days, so it's not like we overdosed on her company or anything. This actually worked out better for Grace and me because we got to have some quality time with Michael. It's hard to make fun of his past girlfriends if the current one is at the same table. You'd be surprised at what an awkward bomb that can be."

"And you know this because..." Maura pried.

"I dropped one once. I made the mistake of mentioning a girl he had dated in college that I happened to be friendly with. I had run into her at a Starbucks and innocently brought it up and the girl he was with at the time thought I was trying to get her out of the picture. She actually said that, you know. 'What, are you trying to get me out of the picture? You want Michael to date his old girlfriend?' She pretty much sealed her own fate when she threw out the 'Well, we're together now, so you better get used to it' line. I like to remind him I saved him from a bunny boiler every now and then."

"Freakazoid, planet rock," Kelly added.

"So now I have to head to Connecticut to be sort of the phone buffer in case things go dreadfully wrong," Evie concluded with.

"I know I'm thirty-two years old and have lived on the east coast all my life, but do you guys know I still don't really have a clear view of where Connecticut falls in the grand scheme of the continental U.S.?" Kelly asked. "I mean, whenever we drive there, I feel like we drive through about twelve other states. One time, I swear I drove through Nevada to get to Greenwich. That can't be right, can it?"

Maura just sighed and shook her head. "This is why other countries mock us, ladies."

Three

E vie watched the gradual change in the landscape from the train window on Metro North as it turned from industrial to rural, almost without registering it. She was actually pretty apprehensive about how this evening was going to go. By the time she left her parents house, they would have found out that they were going to get a daughter-in-law, as well as a grandchild. And as her parents never ceased to surprise her with their reactions, she was unsure which way this one was going to go. She hoped it would be in such a way that they would laugh about it years later, saying to each other, "Why in the world Evie thought she should be there is beyond us." She was afraid, years later, they would actually be saying something like, "Thank God Evie was there. I don't know what would've happened if she hadn't been. She performed the CPR, you know, when the strain proved too much for both of us to bear." Evie had actually thought about purchasing smelling salts, but then decided that since she wasn't a Victorian lady-in-waiting, that it might be overkill. Besides, she had no idea what exactly they were and where one would purchase them. She settled on a big bottle of vodka. She figured they could toast their new extended family together if the reaction was one of joy, or they could drink to forget the fact that their son was going to marry a woman no one in the family really knew, who was going to bear them a grandchild they probably would not see all that often. Here goes nothing, she thought, as the train stopped and she disembarked at her parents' stop.

Evie scanned the faces on the platform, looking for both of her parents, as they always came together to pick her up. She wasn't quite sure why, just that it always happened. Then she heard her mother's familiar voice calling out from the far side of the platform, "Evelyn, darling, we're over here. Behind this giant of a man. Excuse me sir, I'm trying to get my daughter's attention. What are you, like 6'6"?" she added as an afterthought to the appropriately dubbed 'giant of a man'.

"6'5", actually," he acknowledged, not knowing whether or not to be insulted that a random lady at the train station had just referred to him as a giant.

Evie watched her father shake his head at the seemingly unstoppable chatter his wife, Rebecca, was spewing. He caught Evie's eye and smiled, then bent down towards his wife and indicated with a tilt of his head that Evie had seen them and was heading in their direction. Thomas Dunleavy steered Rebecca around her new friend and relieved Evie of her suitcase.

The sight of her parents looking like they always did reassured Evelyn. Her Dad, although no "giant of a man" was pretty tall himself, standing at six feet, two inches. Both Michael and her sister, Grace, had inherited his dark brown, almost black hair, although her Dad's had been turning more salt and pepper for a number of years now. They also were the recipients of his striking, coal colored eyes. The three of them had the coloring of their Black Irish ancestors, while Evie resembled her Mom's lighter coloring and shared her large blue eyes and lighter brown hair. Rebecca just spent more time in the salon making sure the gray hairs weren't popping up all over the place.

"Well, this is surprising," Thomas said to his youngest daughter. "Usually you have two rolling suitcases and a duffel bag full of dirty clothes when you visit."

"Oh, come on Dad. You make it sound like I only visit when I need unlimited use of a free washing machine." Both of her parents looked at her with one eyebrow raised, reminding her of The Rock. It was slightly disconcerting. "Alright, I'll visit more often without the dirty clothes."

They rode back to the house Evie grew up in in relative silence. Well, at least Evie and her Dad rode in relative silence. Her Mom kept the conversation flowing with tales from the neighborhood. Rebecca had just finished talking about the chili contest five couples on their block had decided to do. "So," she explained, "we'll all bring our chili over to Susan's house, in identical bowls, and we'll do a blind taste test. We'll write our favorites down and the winner will take home the kitty! Did I mention we're each going to throw ten bucks in a kitty?"

"Yeah. This contest is going to be a real gas," her Dad added for good measure and started to chuckle at his own joke.

"I think the potty humor is what I miss most about home."

"Then you should visit more often," her Mom said.

"I get it...visit more with less laundry. Check."

They got out of the car and headed inside where Evie took a deep breath to smell the lasagna that was warming in the oven. Her favorite. Her Mom continued talking about neighborhood events. "Did we tell you what's going on with the garden club?" she asked. She didn't wait for a response and kept going. "We're growing peonies right now, and they're simply lovely, if I do say so myself."

Evie thought back to the garden her Mom used to keep at the house. Or try to, in any case. It had mostly consisted of dandelions and renegade crabgrass and Evie tried to think of a diplomatic way to ask how things had changed so drastically that she was now growing lovely peonies. And where were the peonies anyway?

"I don't think I saw any peonies outside. Did I miss them?" she asked pragmatically.

"Well," her Dad said, looking at her strangely, "it is February, so that could be part of the reason you don't see any."

"That and we don't grow them at the house, dear. We use the community garden and greenhouse across from the library. That's where all the meetings are."

Her Dad finished filling in the blanks. "And to be honest, your Mom and I aren't really green thumbs, in case you don't remember. We mostly watch what the Taylor's are doing and putz around with them in their section. And to be even more honest, I don't really participate in the actual sowing, tilling or planting of the land. I really just go to sample the mint juleps they serve."

"Still haven't gotten over your embarrassing love of the girlie drinks, huh, Dad?"

"The girlie drinks are to be commended on their deliciousness."

She followed her Dad upstairs, who was carrying her bags to her old room. Her parents weren't the type to keep the kids' old rooms as sort of time capsules of their youth. The daisy wallpaper border no longer circled the room. Gone were the matching daisy drapes that had hung on the window. And, thankfully, no more cheesy Chip-N-Dale posters of oiled men, hanging on the walls. *I spent way too much time in that indoor flea market,* Evie chastised herself. In their stead were the soft greens and muted browns that reminded her of beach grass and sandy dunes. Shadow boxes of white painted shells were arranged above the bed. All that was needed for her to believe she had been transported down to the Jersey Shore was a lifeguard stand. She loved being in this room, and plopped herself onto the bed, wrinkling the clean, white duvet instantly.

"Evie, honey," her Dad hesitantly started. "I just want you to know that I've been a little anxious recently over your finances." He held up his hand to silence her as she started to protest, and continued on with what he had to say. "I don't think your Mom's picked up on this yet, but I know Maura isn't a magazine editor. She's your caterer friend. So, in case things are a little tight, I wanted you to have this," and he handed her an envelope.

Evie tried to give it back, but Thomas simply waved her off. "Just do me one favor. Treat yourself to something nice with it. Something you wouldn't necessarily get for yourself when you're watching what you spend. That's all I ask."

"Dad," Evie whispered in his ear as she gave him a hug, "This is so sweet, but you do know I'm okay, right? You don't have to do this."

Thomas laughed her off. "It's not like I just gave you a deposit for a house. Just a little something to have some fun with. Now, why don't we go downstairs and see if your Mom needs a hand with dinner. Just remember, this is between the two of us. No need to worry your Mom unnecessarily."

———

About a half hour later, Evelyn was helping her Mom make a salad while they waited for her sister, Grace, and her family to arrive. Grace and her husband, Jack, lived about ten minutes away from her parents, so it was easy enough to suggest they joined them for dinner without arousing anyone's suspicions that this night was going to

include a watershed moment for the family. Evie looked
at the clock for what felt like the fifteenth time in about
two minutes.

"Evelyn, dear, what's with the fascination with the
clock? You can't keep your eyes off it. Do you have to be
out of here by a certain time? Aren't you staying
tonight?" her Mom asked.

"Oh, yeah, Mom, I'm staying over...I'm just excited
to see Annie and Archie. It's been a while since I've seen
them." That was true enough, Evelyn rationalized to
herself. It had been over two months since she'd managed
to see her niece and nephew, and she knew no matter
what the night held the two of them would be able to
bring some laughter to it. It's what eight and five year
olds do.

"Well, it should only be another twenty minutes or
so. I told them not to get here later then six-thirty if they
could help it," her Mom informed her. "But now that we
have the kitchen to ourselves, I've been meaning to talk to
you. Your Dad is so bad with names that I don't think
he'd notice, but I do realize that your friend, Maura, is
actually the one in the hotel business, so it would
probably be hard for her to give you the writing
assignments you've been claiming she has." Evie looked
at her Mom sheepishly. "There's an envelope over there
by the phone that should help you out with your rent. Just
throw it in your bag so you don't forget it."

"Oh, Mom, you don't have to do that. I'm fine with
what I've got saved. I always keep a couple of months
cushion. You don't have to do that."

"I know I don't have to...but this is my mad money
and I can do what I like with it. However, I'm not going
to be one of those parents that say 'Use it for something
fun, like a new purse or shoes, or a fancy night out.' I
want you to use it for something sensible, like the rent or
your utilities. That's my only caveat, dear. Well, that and

let's just keep this amongst ourselves. I don't want your Dad to get all worried."

"And so it shall be obeyed. Thanks, Mom. It's unnecessary, but certainly appreciated," Evie said as she gave Rebecca a hug.

Evie realized with a start how nice it would be to have someone in her life that didn't want her to worry. It wasn't a typical thought and she didn't necessarily want it intruding on her again. She enjoyed the feeling of not needing or depending on anyone. *Shake it off, Evie*, she told herself. Thoughts like that could end up being very detrimental to your mental health.

It was only about ten minutes after that when they heard the car crunch along the gravel driveway. Evie and her parents went outside to greet them.

"Aunt Evie," both Annie and Archie screamed as they bolted out of the car door and went running into her arms.

"Hello, little urchins, it's so great to see you guys."

"Then I assume you brought a special treat for us to support that statement, right?"

"Annie, your vocabulary is frighteningly adult like. Dare I say it's better than your mother's?"

"No, you may not. But thanks for planting that little seed into her head," Grace said, following behind her children and giving Evelyn and her parents a hug.

"I don't know, Grace, Evie might have a point. The girl is obviously a linguist and I'm sure it's not too much of a stretch for everyone to conclude that she takes after her father in that respect." Jack looked around for support from everyone else. When no one responded he threw out, "Come on, people, I'm a friggin' wordsmith."

Thomas snorted at his son-in-law. "You had us until friggin'."

"The kids are still here." Rebecca told the two men. "With their two good ears each. Do you mind checking the bad language at the door?"

"Its okay, Grandma." Archie said, crinkling his freckle-spattered nose. "Peter down the block says friggin' all the time and Mommy just says to ignore him because he won't amount to much. I guess Daddy and Grandpa just won't amount to much."

"Out of the mouths of babes," Grace said, walking into the kitchen with her arm around Evie.

———————

"Dinner was delicious, Mom," Grace proclaimed as she pushed her chair back and started grabbing at plates to help clear the table. "Of course, any meal I don't have to cook is always special, so maybe I'm biased."

"No," Evie said. "I'll second the motion on delicious tasting dinners." She also started clearing the table, mostly so that the cheesecake she had brought with her could be brought out sooner.

"Have either of you talked to your brother recently?" Evie's Dad suddenly threw out. "We've been trying to get in touch with him for a couple of days and have only managed to get his voicemail. It's getting very frustrating."

Grace said no and Evie just went with that answer as well. Then she checked her watch, knowing that they'd all be talking to Michael in about ten minutes and this charade would soon be over. *Make that eight and a half minutes* Evie thought to herself when the phone rang. She surreptitiously made her way over to her bag and pulled out the bottle of vodka and brought it around to the table without anyone noticing. Her Mom looked at the caller id and just said, "Well, speak of the devil," before answering it.

"Michael," she chirped. "You must be working incredibly late, you poor thing. But your timing couldn't be better...the whole family's here for dinner. It's like you have a sixth sense to be calling tonight. Your ears might also be ringing since we were just telling the girls we haven't been able to reach you in a while, so this really is such a nice surprise. I'll put you on speaker and it'll be almost like you're here with us. As a matter of fact, I'll grab a photo of you and put it on the table. There we go. Ha. Just like old times."

Grace and Evie caught each other's eye on that one. Rebecca seemed to have forgotten what the actual "old times" were like. People yelling over each other to be heard, elbows on the table, and lots of whining about what the meal was. Selective amnesia her Dad called it.

"Hey, Mom. Hey everyone." Michael's voice sounded a little bit nervous over the speaker phone to Evie's ear. She wondered if she was the only one who heard it. It appeared so. "How are you all?" He didn't wait for anyone to reply before plodding on. "Actually, Mom, I'm not working late. Charlotte and I knew you guys would all be there tonight from Evie." All the adults turned to look at Evie, quizzically. "We have some important, happy news we wanted to share and figured getting you all together might be nice and make it feel almost like we were telling you in person." Without pausing for a breath, he continued. "You all know that Charlotte and I have been together for over a year and a half now, and I love her very much. She's my world. I know that sounds corny, especially from me, but I'm happy to say she's taken me up on my marriage proposal. We're going to have a new Dunleavy in the family!"

Evie quickly looked around the room and took stock of everyone's faces. Her parents were beaming from ear to ear, and her Dad actually looked a bit teary eyed. Grace and Jack started laughing and offering congratulations and Annie and Archie, feeding off of everyone else's joyous energy, were jumping up and down, but obviously not quite sure why. She breathed a sigh of relief. One down one to go.

"Is Charlotte there with you right now, Michael? Put her on. We want to welcome her to the family." Her Mom started barking orders.

"Yes, actually she is. I'll put the phone on speaker so we can both talk to you all."

Of course, the whole family started yelling into the phone at once with their well wishes, so Charlotte probably couldn't understand any of it, Evie thought to herself. Her Dad must've been thinking the same thing because suddenly he held up his hand and everyone in her parent's dining room stopped talking. "The poor girl probably can't understand a thing that's being said, since we're all trying to talk over each other. Charlotte, my dear, we are so happy for you and Michael. After our trip to visit you guys last summer, Rebecca and I said to each other there was a certain spark between the two of you. We're thrilled to welcome you to our family. May you enjoy a lifetime of happy moments with each other, with your children, if God so wills it, and with your friends...congratulations."

Evie couldn't help but laugh a little to herself. Michael couldn't have planned a better segue himself. He obviously thought so as well.

"Well, in that vein, Dad, we've got some more good news to share. You're not going to have to wait that long to find out if 'God so wills it' in the children department. He does. We're expecting a baby in six months. At the end of August."

This time there was just stunned silence as the family just sat there, trying to absorb that last bit of information. Evelyn was sure she saw actual question marks form over every single person's head at the table. They all stared at each other, like they were trying to figure out some sort of word puzzle that Michael threw out.

Grace was the first to speak. "I'm sorry, Michael," and she started to laugh a little nervously, "but it sounded like you just said you guys were expecting a baby in August. Did we hear that right?"

This time it was Charlotte who answered. "Yes, there's no problem with the line, Grace. Your brother and I are expecting a baby. I'm almost at the twelve week mark. We wanted to tell you all sooner, but felt we should wait until the first trimester was over, to be on the safe side. Obviously, we're thrilled about it and consider it quite a blessing. Michael even talks about how excited he is at the prospect of changing the baby's nappies, although, between you, me, and the table full of people listening on the other end of the phone, I think he might be overstating that last part a bit."

And that, Evie told her friends later, was all it took to change any doubts in her family's mind. Charlotte's voice, without any apologies, telling it straight, practically daring someone to say something negative about this little life growing inside of her.

"No one is going to call that child a shotgun baby, that's for shit sure," Amanda said later.

"What exactly is a nappie?" asked Maura.

"It's a diaper," Evie answered. "Which my Mom thought was just adorable. And that got her thinking about all the different phrases and words the British have for things that are different from the ones we use in America. So she's gone out and bought up every single *Bridget Jones* type book she can find so she can brush up on what amounts to the English language. Apparently she thinks she won't be able to follow too many conversations if she doesn't know her 'snogging' from her 'kissing.'"

"Ohhh, that's cute, though. It's like she wants to be able to speak with Charlotte in her native tongue," Amanda said.

"Dude, we just established that we all speak English. My use of the word 'dude' aside, which I can't imagine gets much airplay over in England, we shouldn't have any trouble communicating," Evelyn said.

"So what happened next?" Kelly wondered.

"It actually was pretty anti-climatic. I didn't even need to bust open the bottle of vodka. We basically just kind of guessed as to when and where they were going to have the wedding, that sort of thing. You know, making assumptions based entirely on conjecture, as opposed to any real facts. Family stuff."

Four

"Well," Kelly prodded. "Are you going to bring a date to the wedding?"

The two of them were standing in line at the ATM before heading to brunch to meet Amanda and Maura. Evelyn couldn't believe how quickly the past couple of months had flown by, making the wedding a little over three months away at this point. Charlotte had decided that it was more important for her to get married at a local castle she had always dreamed about getting married in, than to worry about how big her belly would be. The first available date the castle had was the end of July, which would make Charlotte about eight months pregnant when she walked down the aisle.

Evie turned her attention to Kelly's question. "And what boyfriend of record are you thinking I would ask? I haven't been with anyone in months."

"What about Brad? It's been a while since you've seen him, but you could always ask him if you needed a date."

Evie stared at Kelly in disbelief. "You obviously are suffering from selective amnesia, because there is no way I'd ever ask that shithead for anything. Let alone for him to accompany me to my brother's wedding!"

Evie shuddered at the thought of the last guy she had been seeing for a short time. Brad was a bartender at one of the trendy, new spots that Maura was forever dragging them to and he had caught Evie's eye immediately. Wearing the typical bartender fare of tight black tee shirt with tight (but not Ponch tight) jeans, they had made eye contact with each other for a good forty-five minutes before he came over with a martini for her.

"Thought you could use a fresh drink," he'd said plainly.

Points for not trying to come up with a cheesy 'shaken not stirred' reference, Evie had thought to herself.

In between serving the other patrons, Brad somehow managed to find a couple of minutes here and there to chat with her and after a couple more "fresh" martinis, she thought they were really hitting it off. So she wasn't that surprised when he asked her for her phone number and she gladly obliged.

It wasn't until their third date that she realized there wouldn't be any others. After a nice romantic dinner, Brad had suggested going back to her place. She had mentioned Amanda had gone on a girl's weekend away with a bunch of college friends so he knew the place would be empty. He quickly realized she hadn't mentioned this fact as a come on, but rather as a topic of conversation. When he had tried to move things along quicker than she wanted them to go, she balked.

Evie was shocked when Brad got annoyed. "You know, when I first met you and saw how much you and your girlfriends were drinking, I just figured you'd be easier than you are."

"Wow, I'm trying to figure out if I should be more pissed off at the fact you make me sound like an alcoholic or a whore. Hold on a sec while I wrestle with that one."

He tried a slightly different approach that turned out to be worse. "Evie, it's just that when you meet someone you like, especially at your age, you should go for it."

"Okay, did you just call me an old, alcoholic whore?"

"Evie," he said, "that's not what I meant, but face it...you're not getting any younger."

"And you, Brad, are not getting any...period."

"Kelly," Evie said, snapping out of that rather painful trip down memory lane, "you do recall that he implied I was an old, alcoholic slut, right?"

"Technically, didn't he say he thought you would be more of a slut?"

"That is true. So I guess what he actually called me was an old, alcoholic prude."

"He didn't call you fat, though. So that's something, right?"

"It is...just not enough for me to ever call him again. New rule," Evie said forcefully. "Just because a guy does not call me fat, does not mean I have to take him to Michael's wedding. Besides, why do I want to bring a date with me anyway? I'm going to be caught up in ton of family stuff, in another country, no less. I will not have time to be playing the role of Julie McCoy at the wedding. I'm going to have a boatload of responsibilities on my plate, frankly."

"I don't know," Kelly said wistfully. "I just thought it might be nice for you to have someone to dance with at the wedding. Stupid, huh?"

Evie smiled at her indulgently. "Nah, you always were the resident romantic of our group. It's just not in the cards for this one."

Kelly suddenly brightened. "You know what? You might be better off if you don't bring anyone. That way, you leave yourself open to the possibility of meeting someone there. Surely Michael will have a ton of single, eligible bachelor type friends, right? "

Evie laughed at her friend, but felt mean begrudging her this tiny morsel of hope. "That's exactly what I was thinking, Kelly. Now let's go meet the other guys for brunch, shall we?"

They hurried down the street, to avoid Maura's wrath at being kept waiting, yet still managed to be the last ones there.

"Oh, look who deigns to meet us for our brunch appointment, and only twenty minutes late this time. Our timeliness is improving."

"I know! You could almost set your watch by us, couldn't you, Maur?"

"A late smartass. I admire your brazenness, so for that I give you a free pass, Evie."

At that moment, Evie's cell phone made a weird noise.

"Shit, I think I just got a text message."

"People may not always be gleeful over the arrival of a text message, but they're not usually overtly angry about it," Amanda said.

"They are if they have no idea how to actually access their text messages. And besides, if I have no idea what my text message address is...how would other people get it?"

Evie was met by three pairs of eyes staring her at disbelief. Kelly spoke first. "Evie, I'm not what one would refer to as completely technically savvy, but, it's uh, called a phone number."

"You've GOT to be kidding me! That's genius. One of you will have to show me how that works."

"Let's concentrate on one thing at a time," Amanda cautioned. "You're so close to mastering the coffee machine timer. I'd hate for you to get sidetracked. Speaking of which, if you can't check your text messages, how did you know that I wanted to go get coffee the other day after work? I had sent you a text asking if you wanted to go and that was practically the first thing out of your mouth when I walked in the door."

"It's eerie phenomena such as that that explains why we are such good friends and work so well as roommates. It's innate, really."

"Give me your phone, Buddha, so I can bring up your message," said Maura. With a few quick punches onto the keypad, Maura passed Evie's phone back to her with a message displayed:

DUDE,
CALL ME WHEN YOU GET THIS.
MICHAEL

"Just Michael. Probably wanting to complain about some new facet of the wedding plans. Last week he called to complain about the fact that he had to look at pictures of flower arrangements for like an hour or so. Who here is surprised at the fact that a lot of flowers are used to decorate the church and reception hall? Granted in the end, Charlotte didn't go with his choice, but really, who here's surprised about that either? Has anyone heard of the groom picking the flowers?"

"Not to change the subject here and embarrass you, Evie, but I've got to ask...how do you get by in this day and age with all sorts of technology just passing you by?" I heard a story about the proficiency of teenagers at texting on their Sidekicks and phones and stuff. They've been banned in a ton of schools because they can text each other without looking at what they're doing and they can do it under their desks, or under their sweatshirts, and the teachers have no idea that the students aren't paying any attention to their lectures. And here you sit, barely able to program in numbers to your address book, completely unable to use your camera phone. It's sad really," Kelly ruminated.

"Things were so much simpler back when we were growing up. Do you remember how you had to pass an

actual paper note to a friend if you wanted to talk to them
during class? Back when the Monchhichi was a marvel of
toy making genius and Donny and Marie dolls were cool?
I thought I had accessorized to the hilt when I wore my
friendship pins on my shoelaces with matching handmade
ribbon barrettes. Seriously, what was I thinking?"

"Uh, Maura, you have an unnatural fascination with
the Monchhichi and it's starting to concern me," Evie
said. "But you're right. They were simpler times. Can you
believe that Michael had a girlfriend, back when he was
in like the fifth or sixth grade, that would use a tape
recorder, not a VCR, because they weren't really around
then, but an actual tape recorder and sit in front of her
television and tape *Dallas*? Her name was Courtney
something. I still remember it."

Maura snorted. "You sound a bit judgmental about
it."

"Let she who does not cast a disparaging shudder
over my collection of Gap tee-shirts throw the first
judgmental stone, my friend."

"Touché. Now let's order. We should probably get
some food with our mimosas, right? And Amanda, we're
going to want to hear the details about last night's date
with Garrett, the lawyer."

"Well, I'm cautiously optimistic about the likelihood
of a date number two. Things actually went really well.
Dinner in a quiet bistro in the Village, a soft and gentle
kiss, without the groping hands that would be considered
inappropriate on a first date. I liked him"

"Just so I can be prepared for life in the
apartment...will you continue to pepper our conversations
with legalese such as 'cautiously optimistic?' I just need
to know if I should be boning up on my legal jargon."

"Well, if you're intimidated by the phrase 'cautiously
optimistic,' I'd say you should be boning up on the

English language in general. Last time I checked, Jack McCoy hadn't called dibs on it."

———————

When Evie got back to her apartment, she found a message on the answering machine from Michael. "Evie, I sent you a text earlier. I don't know if you got it, but when you get in, could you give me a call? I need to talk to you. And don't worry," he added, "I'll call you right back so you don't have to pay for the call. I just need to run something by you."

Again with the mysterious messages, Evie thought irritably to herself. *Why does everything need to be a "Clue" game with him,* she wondered as she started dialing.

"Thanks for calling back, Evie," Michael said when he heard her voice. "Stay put and I'll call you back on my dime." He did just that and then started right in without any preamble. "Listen, I've got what could amount to a big favor I'd like to talk to you about. How would you feel about coming over to London as soon as you could get away and staying here until the wedding?"

"But, Michael," Evie protested, not really sure what he was getting at. "The wedding's three months away. I don't understand. You want me to stay in London for the next two or three months? Doing what?"

"Here's the thing. Charlotte's parents actually want to have a huge engagement party for us in about two week's time. Our Memorial Day weekend. Charlotte and I have been trying to talk them out of it for months, but suddenly it's become very important to her mother and we figured what's the harm really? I was hoping that you, Mom, Dad, Grace, Jack, and the kids would be able to make it over, even though I know it's short notice. Then I got to thinking...how great it would be if you could stay on until the actual wedding. It would give at least someone in my family the opportunity to really get to know Charlotte before we get married. Obviously, Mom and Dad couldn't stay because of work, and Grace couldn't leave the kids for such an extended period of time, but I thought maybe you could manage."

"You know, Michael, even though I'm not married and don't have any children, I do have a life. It's not going to be easy just to pick up and head to London for all that time at the last minute. What about my apartment, my friends, my work?"

"I didn't mean to imply that you don't have a life. I just thought your life might be flexible enough to allow for something like this. And who knows, maybe you'd come up with a couple of different articles for work. Stuff about the differences in weddings between the two countries, fish out of water experiences being a New Yorker transplanted in London...those sorts of things. I thought I could pay the rent on your apartment in New York while you stay with a friend of mine here in London who's got a couple of spare rooms and works a lot. He's got his own coffee house and it's a new business, so he's rarely around. I'd have you stay at our place, except we've already turned the spare room into a nursery. I know you're a skinny girl and all, but I doubt you'd fit in the crib. You could even invite some of your friends over for a long weekend or something while you're here. Will you just think about it? I wouldn't ask if it wasn't important to me."

"Okay," Evie said.

"Great. You'll think about it and get back to me?" Michael asked hopefully.

"No, I mean, okay, I'll do it. I should get to know my future sister-in-law and who knows; maybe it'll even be fun. One question. Will I need to get the part about you paying my rent in writing or is a verbal contract going to be enough between us?"

Five

E vie stared into her closet dismally. "You know what I need?" she asked the room.

Amanda was the first to chime in. "A really great cocktail dress?"

"Nooooo, not what I was thinking."

"Oh, I know," Maura said. "A really great, over-priced pair of jeans that you simply couldn't resist because they make your butt look so good. 'Cause you really don't have one of those, in case you're wondering."

"Still no, but thanks for the super shot of confidence to the ego."

"A pair of cowboy boots. I know that Jessica Simpson has beaten those things like a dead horse, and they're already passé, but I just don't care. I love mine and they go with anything, no matter what anyone says," Amanda threw out.

"Um, yeah, I'm going to stop this conversation before it goes any farther. I really meant that question to be kind of rhetorical and wasn't looking for actual negative commentary on my wardrobe." Evie said. She looked around the room and only when she was certain they weren't going to continue to pepper her with objects she should own, but didn't, continued. "I really need a gay, male friend. Especially if I'm heading to London. Have you noticed that all of the characters in those Brit chick lit books, without fail, have a gay friend, who stands by them through one mad cap adventure after another? Hijinx ensue, witty banter is exchanged in the midst of smoky wine bars and pubs, and love is found. I think it would be kind of like having a good luck charm."

"Evie, I don't think it's favorable to liken a gay person to a rabbit's foot," Maura said.

"So not what I meant, Maur, and you know it. I just think it would be nice to have one person in this room that could look into my closet and maybe come up with some better suggestions of things for me to pack. Things that are actually *in* my closet and not in the minds of my friends."

Amanda turned and looked thoughtfully at Evie. "Are you nervous about your extended vacation? I mean, it'd be perfectly natural if you were. I would probably be."

"Yeah, I think a little," Evie admitted. "But at least I'll have Michael there to show me around and it's really just the perfect chance to get to know Charlotte a little bit more. That opportunity hasn't presented itself before. Add that to the fact that Michael will pay my rent, and I just couldn't say no. I am really going to miss you guys, though. Even my tiny little room."

"Well, remember we are all planning to visit for a long weekend," Maura reminded her.

"And just so you know, Garrett said he'd make sure to keep an eye on things around here." Amanda added shyly.

"That's really big of him," Evie said sarcastically. "But who's going to be keeping an eye on him? Amanda had the good grace to blush. "Enough of this, though...I've got to finish packing."

Maura jumped off Evie's bed and threw a bag at her. "Listen, I've got to head down to the hotel, but I figured you could use these. Now you really do have a really great, overpriced pair of jeans that make your butt look good."

Evie looked in the bag and saw a gorgeous, brand new pair of Seven jeans. "Oh, Maura, I can't take these. They cost a fortune." She started to hand the bag back, but Maura was waving her off.

"Let's just consider them more of a gift to the fellow passengers on your flight. This way maybe you can table the sweatpants with paint down the legs and holes on the knees and travel looking like someone who gives a rat's ass about her appearance. I know I'll sleep easier."

Evie ran across the room and gave Maura a huge hug. "Deep down you're an old softie and you know it," she whispered in her ear. "And I promise to wear them with pride on the plane."

"Make that pride and your red sweater, then," Maura answered cheerfully. "Because if you team them up with your old NYU sweatshirt, I will find out, and I will kill you. Have a safe trip, sweetie, and we'll see you in a couple of weeks. And don't forget to pack your ivory dress, whatever you do."

Six

E vie handed her ticket to the agent at the counter and anxiously looked around for the rest of her family. They would all be traveling to London together for the engagement party. This was fine by Evie since she was a nervous flyer to begin with. She hoped she'd have time to down a couple of beers in the airport lounge and then watch the Annie and Archie show and hope something good was on that channel. Something to distract her from the fact they were hurtling in the sky at crazy speeds, across large bodies of water.

She heard the chaos behind her and without turning around, realized her family had arrived. Four adult voices, all talking at once, all asking variations of the same question. "Where are the tickets? Are they in your coat pocket, hon? Did I grab them off the counter? Are they in your pocketbook?" Also adding to the cacophony were two small voices asking the questions they deemed pertinent. "Mom, do you have my Gameboy? Do you have my crayons? I don't see them in my backpack. Oh no, I can't find my jelly beans."

Evie got her seat assignment and stepped out of line. She actually debated whether or not to carry on to the security line and just pretend she hadn't caught sight of the Dunleavy clan, but figured it was only a matter of time before they were all united anyway. *Might as well get this over with* she thought to herself.

"Hey guys," she chirped. "I forgot we're the poster family for organization and efficiency. I can't believe I had actually blocked out what a family vacation actually entails until just this moment"

"Not me," said Grace. "I knew from the get go we were going to revive the 'Ugly American Abroad' stereotype. And we haven't even hit the 'Abroad' portion of the trip. This has disaster written all over it. We all should've booked separate flights," she muttered miserably. "Even the kids."

"Especially the kids," chimed in Jack.

"I don't want to go on the plane by myself," Archie said, suddenly looking very nervous.

"Oh sweetie, Mommy and Daddy are just kidding. We're just stressing a bit because we can't seem to find the tickets. Oh, scratch that...here they are. In my pocketbook." Grace held up the tickets triumphantly, waving them around in her hand. She suddenly took stock of Evie and her traveling garb and nodded appreciatively in her direction. "You are looking very put together for the upcoming flight. That's quite unusual for you, if you don't mind my saying."

"I could pretend to be indignant, but I do have some sense of reality," Evie laughed. She pushed a lock of her pin straight brown hair behind her ear before continuing. "Maura gave me these jeans as sort of a parting gift, if you will. How great are they?"

"Totally fab. They make your ass look great, also." Grace added.

"The only part of that conversation that I could understand was the part about the ass," Jack said, jumping into the conversation. He looked down. "And it's not looking too shabby." He suddenly looked worried. "Can I say that to my sister-in-law or is that inappropriate?"

Grace laughed. "That one's a freebie, but no more!" She then turned to Evie and said, "I'm totally borrowing those jeans, just so you know."

Evie's family actually sailed through security with no real mishap, unless you count the near stripping of Archie by Archie to go through the metal detector. He quickly obliged his Mom when she told him to take his coat and shoes off so they could walk through, and no one was paying too much attention to him until one of the security guards started to laugh. "Excuse me, but could someone please tell the little guy he's taken off plenty for us?" Everyone turned around to find Archie had taken off his shirt and was going for his jeans as well. His Dad quickly stopped him with a "Whoa, Little Man. No need to give all our fellow passengers a show. Just the shoes and jacket should be enough."

Once they had settled down at the gate they breathed a collective sigh of relief. Silly family. One lost Buzz Lightyear backpack later, which turned into a slight, as Evie would later describe it to her brother, bomb threat, and they breathed another sigh. The Dunleavy's were really excited when it was finally time to board the plane. The police and ground crew at JFK were equally pleased to see them off. They hated the finding of unattended bags. It really put extra stress on the day.

Evie had suggested that she sit with Annie and Archie. That way Grace and Jack could have at least one half of the roundtrip flight be somewhat relaxing. This meant that they would have one stranger sitting next to them in their row. Of course, the moment Evie saw the man with the bad comb over and perma-frown coming down the aisle, she was pretty sure this was their extra seatmate. When she realized his carry on was actually a couple of pints of Chinese food, she was positive. He was.

"Aunt Evie, what stinks so bad?" was the first thing to pop out of Archie's mouth as the man sat down. Annie quickly answered before Evie even had a chance. "Archie." she reprimanded in what she obviously thought was a discreet whisper, but was closer in volume to the guy that screams, "GOOOAAALLL" for all the soccer games, "Don't be rude. It's the man sitting next to Aunt Evie."

Evelyn turned and flashed the man an embarrassed smile.

He coldly said, "Some people should really teach their children some manners, and a little bit about different cultures."

She wanted to snip back, "And some people should really reconsider their carry on choices. Most people just stick with gum." Instead she just gave him a good old 'fuck you' smile and hoped that would be all the exchange needed for the next six hours on the flight.

Luckily, it was. But nothing could prepare her for the exchange she had with her parents about two hours into the flight. Her parents were "doing a lap" as they called it and stopped by to chat with Evie and the kids, and Grace and Jack, who were a couple of rows ahead.

"Did Michael ever mention to any of you the details for their engagement party?" Rebecca asked.

"Just that Charlotte's parents were having it at their home," Jack informed her.

"That's all he said?" wondered Thomas.

"Pretty much," said Evie.

"I think it sounds nice. Much more intimate than having it at some big, stuffy country club where you can't get to talk to anyone," was Grace's take on the event.

Thomas and Rebecca looked at each other and started to laugh. "I hate to break it to you honey, but it might be closer to Door Number Two than you were thinking," Rebecca warned her daughter. "Charlotte's parents are having it at their summer Manor. They're actually titled. Lord and Lady Futterly."

"Shut up!" was all Evie was able to get out.

"Aunt Evie, we're not allowed to say shut up!"

———————

"Mandy?" Evie asked when her cell phone was answered. "Did I wake you? Sorry if I did, but I had to call you the minute we got to the hotel. You are not going to believe this story. Quick, tell me our favorite moment from *The Office* with Angela?"

Without the slightest bit of hesitation Amanda threw out, "The 'Benihana Christmas" episode when one of the Asian waitresses, who went to the office Christmas party with Michael, takes one of Angela's brownies. Angela gets mad and says, 'I don't come to your house and take your Hello Kitty backpack, do I?'"

"And I just figured out on my flight over to London why this is so funny. I am on a 747 to Heathrow, with a couple hundred passengers, and there are two, count 'em two, Hello Kitty backpacks in overhead compartments that I happened to notice while walking down the aisle. Who picks them up, you ask? Only the two Asian groups traveling on that plane. Are there children traveling with these groups you ask? No, Amanda, there are not. Two Asian, adult women walked off that plane with Hello Kitty backpacks slung proudly over their arms. It's funny because it's true. It's more than just a stereotype. There's much truth to be gleaned from the writers on that show."

Amanda laughed and said, "Well, I'm just glad you didn't have a cute anecdote about my second favorite line of hers: 'Poop is raining from the ceilings. Poop.' Remember that episode where there was a bat in the office ceiling and she's got a rain cap on her head while she's uttering the poop line, looking like Polly Puritan? Those writers are pure genius,' I tell you. Although

Garrett keeps telling me he just doesn't get what's so funny about the show."

"And you're seriously still dating him?" Evie inquired.

"Well, I knew there had to be something wrong with him. But he does like *Desperate Housewives*."

"Do we like guys who watch *Desperate Housewives*? What's the call on that?"

"Maura and Kelly said they'll get back to me with a ruling once they meet him. Kelly called it reserving judgment."

"I thought you guys were all going out last night. What happened?"

"Oh, Garrett got called into the office last minute to go over some legal briefs with his boss that he had prepared for an upcoming trial. We postponed until next week sometime."

"Well, keep me in the loop," was all Evie added.

"So tell me...how was traveling with the A-Team?" Amanda asked, using her nickname for Annie and Archie.

"Actually, it all went relatively smoothly by Dunleavy standards." Evie gave her the update on the bomb scare, the Chinese food guy, and Archie doing his male stripper impersonation and then had to end the call. "I've got to run now, Mandy. I've been told I can take a one hour nap before we have to leave for the countryside for the engagement party tomorrow night. Apparently it's more of a posh affair than I was anticipating. It's being held at Charlotte's parents' Manor. Did I tell you they have their very own Manor that they use in the summertime? It's called Country Meadow Manor. I imagine it's in the midst of a country meadow, in case you were having problems with that concept. Did I tell you her parents are a Lord and Lady? Of course I didn't, because I just found out."

"What the hell are you talking about and why did the Hello Kitty backpack story come first?" Amanda demanded.

"I really wanted to tell you about Hello Kitty and I just felt it would get lost in the shuffle of Michael marrying into, for all practical purposes, and what I'll be telling everyone, royalty. My parents forgot to mention it until we were en route. They casually brought it up, almost like an afterthought. They were under the assumption that Michael had brought it up at some point. Which he obviously had not."

"Well, why would he? In this day and age most people's in-laws are one step away from royalty, right?" Amanda asked. "Man, sometimes your brother really misses the boat. I would imagine most people might have managed to bring that up in conversation before the whole family descends upon London." Amanda waited a beat and then asked a question Evie had not thought of. "Do you guys have to curtsy?"

"Christ, I hope not. You know I'm not graceful."

"I'm not saying you have to, but it's a curtsy, not a pirouette. You'll be fine. Just make sure you're not the first one to walk into the party. That way you can watch what other people are doing. Because I've got to think it would be more embarrassing to give an unnecessary curtsy than an ungraceful one."

"All I wanted to do is tell you my Hello Kitty backpack story and now I'm a nervous wreck. I'm going to try to sleep for a little bit."

Seven

The Dunleavy's were all to meet up in the lobby of their London hotel promptly at five o'clock that evening. That meant they all staggered down from times ranging between five-fifteen and five-forty-five. This was not unexpected because no one in their family ever arrived on time. They had even long since stopped playing the "give family members an earlier time than needed so no one's late" game because once an entire branch of a genealogical tree catches on, no one has any idea what time they should really be there, and you don't have a shot in hell of getting to your destination even remotely close to the time you should.

Evie and her parents staggered their arrivals by only five minutes of each other, which was practically unheard of by their standards. Michael was already waiting for them at the hotel bar, where he had a clear view of the elevator bank. It had been decided that he would drive them all down in the van his family had rented for their stay, and Charlotte would drive their car down to her parents' estate. It was the first time he was seeing anyone from his family since their arrival in Heathrow that day and he was noticeably anxious. After the happy hugs and congratulatory kisses were doled out, he started quizzing his sister and parents. "How much longer do you think it'll take before everyone else gets down here? We should really get on the road right away. Traffic out of the city can be a nightmare on a Friday evening."

"Michael, please settle down. You're making me nervous," Rebecca reprimanded her son. "They'll be down any minute. Should we order a drink while we wait?" she wondered, almost as an afterthought.

"Ordering drinks doesn't make it sound like you have much confidence that they'll really be here at any moment, but I'll take a Pinot Grigio to kill some time and whet my whistle," Evie said.

Thomas went up to the bar and ordered wine for his wife and daughter, and a beer for himself. Michael refused anything. Evie joked his principle was going to make him very thirsty. They were on their second round when Grace, Jack, and the kids finally arrived downstairs. As there were four of them they were usually given a bit of leeway. Usually.

"Well, nice of you all to be so on top of the time," was what Michael used as a greeting when they finally stepped off the elevator, overnight bags in hand.

"And thanks for making the first of two halfway around the world trips with two small children in tow to be with me on these really important occasions in my life," was what Grace countered with. Even mild mannered Jack felt the need to follow up with, "It's so important to have family around you at times like these."

Michael realized his mistake and started apologizing. "I'm really sorry, guys. I'm just really nervous about this whole engagement party thing, and I want everyone to get along with Charlotte's parents, and all of the wedding and baby stuff combined are really starting to stress me out. I really don't mean to be a jerkoff."

Rebecca raised her eyes and nodded in the direction of Annie and Archie. "First rule of parenting: Don't swear in front of your children. You look like a prat if you do."

Everyone seemed to settle down as they drove out of London and toward the countryside. Michael kept them entertained with stories about work, and Charlotte's newest cravings—most of which were, oddly enough to Evie, even having never gone through a pregnancy—not of the chocolate variety but the unusual fruit variety. *A craving for cumquats*, she thought incredulously to herself. *And prickly pears? That's certainly odd.* She had assumed that once the stick changed colors, everything you ate started with the phrase "chocolate covered". All you had to do was fill in the blank in terms of what you were covering in chocolate.

"So, Mike," Jack threw out as Michael was navigating the roundabouts and roads leading out of London, "rumor has it that Charlotte's parents are titled? You're not about to become a viscount or anything along those lines are you?"

"Is that like a vampire?" Annie whispered to her mother.

"No, sweetie. We're just trying to figure out if we have to bow down to Uncle Michael or if we can still swat him in the back of the head when we pass him in a hallway."

"Didn't I tell you guys all this before? I could've sworn I had."

"No, because that's the kind of thing at least one of us would have remembered. It's kind of a big deal," Evie ended with.

"Yeah, I guess. Charlotte's just never really talked about it all that much, so it kind of seemed unimportant."

"Next time maybe we should be the judge of determining the worthiness of facts. From now on, disclose everything and let us sift through the excess. That way, I'm not on a transatlantic phone call with Amanda trying to figure out if I have to curtsy to Charlotte's parents or not. It's a bit of a conundrum really."

"Don't curtsy. Conundrum solved," was Michael's succinct answer.

Three hours, four rest stop excursions (only one of which was spearheaded by the children), and seventeen games of I Spy later, they pulled off the highway and onto a quiet, rural street. They drove through a bucolic, sleepy town called Chesterfield, and Michael announced that they were getting close to their destination. They were all staying at Country Meadow Manor for the next two nights, as Lord and Lady Futterly had insisted that Michael bring his whole family out the night before the engagement party. They wanted to have a chance to meet each other before the crowds descended upon the estate for the Saturday night engagement party.

Michael made a sudden left turn off the road and the weathered sign, reading "Country Meadow Manor" let the rest of his family know they were about to arrive at their destination. First, though, they drove on a dusty road, through fields of tall grass and wildflowers of every color imaginable. The natural beauty of the environment stilled even the children into a quiet calm and they all gazed out the window, without a word being uttered. Rebecca was the first to break the silence and comment on the gorgeous surroundings. She just turned to her husband and whispered, "Thomas, we have to come back and take pictures for the garden club. We'd never be able to describe the beauty without photos." He nodded silently, his eyes never leaving the fields.

The change of the landscape alerted the Dunleavy's that they must be getting closer to the Manor. The flowers were no longer running wild and the terrain lost much of its rugged beauty. The road became paved and the car drove smoothly next to huge topiaries that Evie had to look closer at to believe what she was seeing.

"Can someone reassure me that I'm not losing my mind, and tell me that those hedges are really shaped to look like what appear to be circus animals? I could've sworn I just saw a seal balancing a ball on his nose."

"You're right, Aunt Evie. Look, there's an elephant over there," Archie told her.

She ruffled his hair and said to him, "Well, I think this is going to be quite the affair we're going to...I hope you brought your fancy pants, sir."

"I don't know if Mom packed them," Archie answered nervously. "I think I just have my brown ones. But I know she packed my dancing shoes," he said proudly. "I told her not to forget those."

———————

Charlotte and her parents were at the door waiting to greet them all as they piled out of the van. "We look like such a clown car," Jack muttered to his fellow passengers. "Well, that just means we match the shrubs, so we'll fit in," was his wife's response.

Michael ignored their comments as he ran over to give his fiancé a kiss and began the introductions as soon as everyone was within earshot. He gravely introduced the two sets of parents first, and this gave Evie a moment to size up the Futterly's.

Lady Futterly looked exactly as Evelyn would have expected, right down to the three strand pearl necklace adorning her neck. Obviously real. Her super slender frame was dressed casually, yet elegantly. She had on white linen pants with a navy and white stripe boat neck sweater. Navy driving moccasins completed her tailored look. Or maybe it was the ginormous diamond rings she wore on each hand that completed the look, Evie thought when she caught sight of them, as Lady Futterly shook hands with Thomas and Rebecca.

Charlotte's Dad didn't quite fit the Lord of the Manor ideal Evelyn had in mind. The man was actually wearing a track suit. A track suit! Evie immediately felt slightly more at ease watching him greet her parents. Instead of the stiff handshake his wife had offered, he enveloped Rebecca in a bear hug and warmly slapped Thomas on the back. "Can you believe these two kids are actually going to be giving us a grandchild in a few short months? How grand is that?" he boomed. "Ahhhh, but it seems you already have been blessed with grandchildren," he said, spying Annie and Archie, standing quietly next to their parents. Quite atypically. "And, if they're anything like my girls were when they were growing up, I'd say they're probably very fond of the sweets. If it's okay with your parents, would you like to head to the kitchen to see what kind of treats Cook has been working all day to prepare?" He looked questioningly at Grace and Jack, and when they nodded their approval, yelled into the foyer, "Gerard, could you please come out here?" A gentleman in his early fifties suddenly appeared beside the huge mahogany doors.

"Yes, sir, may I help you?"

"Gerard, would you mind terribly showing these two children to the kitchen and tell Cook to let them sample her handiwork in the dessert department? They can't go to bed on an empty stomach," he laughed.

"Why don't we all go inside for the rest of the introductions? Gerard has set up a tray of tea for us in the living room," Lady Futterly suggested. "You can leave your bags in the car and Gerard will attend to them after he gets the children settled in the kitchen."

Evie tried not to stare too obviously as they walked through the grand foyer, but it was unbelievably intimidating. It had to have been at least three stories high and a huge chandelier with glass teardrops adorning it hung from high above. *How did they change the light bulbs*, she wondered?

The hallway was littered with oil paintings of what she could only assume were deceased relatives. She almost started to giggle to herself as she pictured the eyeballs starting to move and follow their procession down the hallway, like at Disney World's Haunted Mansion. Michael seemed to sense her imminent giggle fest and turned a stern eye in her direction. It reminded Evelyn of being in church when unaccounted laughter would bubble up from one of the three Dunleavy children and her parents would shoot them all the warning look. The one that promised they wouldn't stop at the bakery on the way home, like was their tradition. Sometimes it worked, and sometimes there would be no canolli or cookie after mass. Evie figured it was the nervous way Michael kept running his fingers through his hair that eventually stifled her nervous laughter before it started. She truly had never seen him like this, and it freaked her out a bit. He seemed so intent on everyone getting along. She wanted to ask this formal stranger where her easy going brother had gone off to, but figured that wasn't going to help matters any. She simply followed everyone else along the corridor until they got to the living room.

Lord Futterly paused in front of the door and motioned for everyone to go inside. "Right this way," he instructed them all. "I'm sure you're all tired from the extensive bit of traveling you've done already, but hopefully you can stand us for a little while longer so we can all get acquainted. I promise we won't keep you up too late."

When they were all inside Michael picked up with the introductions where he had left off. "These are my two younger sisters, Grace and Evelyn," he said. "And this is Grace's husband, Jack. A decent enough guy to have as a brother-in-law I'd have to say," he added with a laugh.

Jack turned to Michael and quickly answered with the obvious ease of a close relationship, "I don't know if I'd say the same about you, though. I'll keep you posted."

"So, Evelyn, are you married?" Lady Futterly asked.

This is what she leads with, Evie thought to herself in wonder. She gave herself a quick pep talk. *Don't say anything sarcastic; Michael will kick your ass. This is his moment. It's not his fault. I'll take one for the team.*

"Please, call me Evie. And no, I'm not married. I guess I'm about to become the lone holdout in the Dunleavy family. Never thought Michael would throw in the towel before me, though," she added with a laugh.

"Oh?" Lady Futterly said archly. There was quite a bit of underlying meaning in that one word question, and it hung uncomfortably over all of them for a moment. Until Charlotte diffused it with a short laugh. "Oh mother, please. Your tone is going to send the Dunleavy's into an emergency family meeting. I know I've shocked half of London by the fact that I actually got Michael to propose." She laughed again and added, "Of course they probably all think I got pregnant on purpose to arrive at such a result, but who cares what they think? We both know we're perfect for each other and that's what counts, right, sweetie?" she asked Michael, turning toward him.

He looked at her adoringly and said, "Absolutely, Char Char. And I think people were more surprised at the fact that you said yes to my proposal, than anything else. God knows all the men in your PR firm are wearing black arm bands of bereavement, now that you're officially off the market."

Evie and Grace looked sideways at each other, trying to gauge each other's reaction to this completely atypical conversation they were privy to. They were not brave enough to turn and face each other head on, though. They were on the brink of that church laughter again, and the harder they tried to stifle it, the harder it was to control it.

Luckily, their father seemed to realize what was about to happen and steered the conversation to a less giddy topic. One that didn't include the use of a ridiculous nickname like Char Char. "So, tell me...we're all a bit baffled as to how you should be addressed. Do we use your title or do you prefer something else? This is not something that you normally encounter when you're meeting future in-laws over in America, that's for sure."

Charlotte's father immediately told them he would prefer that they call them Peter and Liza. "I really only use it to get us a good table at Nobu, to be quite honest with you. It's quite possible the maitre d' over there is the only one who would know me as Lord Futterly," he laughed. It looked to Evie like Liza would've gone with an entirely different answer, as was evidenced by the quick, disapproving glance she cast at her husband, but her features quickly regained their composure and she repeated what her husband just said. "Yes, there's no need to be so formal with family." And then she took a sip of her tea with her pinky extended. *Way to drive that informal point home*, Evie thought to herself.

Rebecca continued to carry on the conversation. "Liza, I can't believe how gorgeous this estate is. Blimey, it must take quite a bit of maintenance on your part, I imagine." Everyone else nodded in assent, although Evie, Grace and Michael first shot each other a questioning look over their Mom's use of the word, "blimey." But Evie had to agree with the content of her Mom's sentence. She couldn't imagine the number of people needed just to dust the creepy family portraits running down the hallway.

"Yes, but we obviously have quite a bit of help so everything runs smoothly. We have in our employ a team of fifteen, including Gerard, who oversees everything, from Cook to the gardeners. Of course, we've hired extra help for the weekend, so everything is just perfect for the engagement party. Peter and I were so pleased that Charlotte and Michael finally agreed to let us throw one for them. And of course, we're just delighted you were all able to make it over for the event. Family is so important at a time like this."

Jack whispered into Grace's ear, "She almost makes it sound like a funeral, not a wedding." They carried on with some more small talk for a little bit longer until Charlotte made her way over to the antique chair that Evie was sitting on. "Looks like you drew the short straw on seating," she laughed. "That is, without a doubt, one of the most uncomfortable pieces of furniture ever to be made. Truth is, I would have called this more of an instrument of torture during the Inquisition than a settee of the French Monarchy." Evie looked down at the red and gold of the tapestry covering the frame of the chair. "Do you think Marie Antoinette ever sat on it?" she asked in awe.

"Probably not," Charlotte answered reasonably. She turned to Grace, who was sitting with Jack on the couch next to Evie. "I'd like to ask you both a question, now that you've arrived." After a quick breath on her part, she continued. "I hope both of you would consider being attendants at our wedding. I had thought of asking you earlier, on the phone, but I really wanted to do it face to face. It just felt more personal that way."

"Thank you so much, Charlotte," Evie was the first to answer. "I'd be honored."

Grace quickly agreed. "It's so nice of you to think of us and include us like that." She laughed quickly and said, "I hope Michael didn't put too much pressure on you to have us as bridesmaids."

"None at all," Charlotte revealed. "I know we haven't really had too much time to spend with each other, but we're going to become a big part of each other's lives and I'd like you both to know how seriously I take that. I figured nothing like the high stress time of a wedding and birth to break each other in as family, right?"

Evie asked Charlotte who else was in her wedding party and was told her sister was the Maid of Honor, and two other childhood friends, Constance and Jacquelyn, completed the list.

"You'll meet Emily, my sister, tomorrow. She couldn't make it tonight because she had a work function she had to attend in the city, but she said she'd try to make it out a couple of hours before the party begins to say hello. Unfortunately, Constance and Jackie won't be here tomorrow at all, so you won't have a chance to meet them this weekend. They had already planned a short getaway to Greece before we had set the date for the engagement party. I know you'll really like them, though. They're a lot of fun. And when you do meet them, Lord knows they should have some great tales to share with us about their weekend."

By then Michael had ambled over to their corner of the room and asked why everyone looked so happy.

"Our soon to be sister-in-law just asked us to be in your wedding party. Obviously, Grace and I have agreed."

"Well, now would be as good a time as any to ask Jack if he would also do me the honor of being a bridesmaid...I mean a groomsman," Michael joked.

"I'm in...as long as there is no taffeta involved."

"I would've asked you earlier, man, but Charlotte wanted to ask Grace and Evie in person, and it probably wouldn't have gone over so well if you were the first one to get asked."

"You make us sound like a couple of petty thirteen year olds," was Evie's response.

"Was I wrong?" Michael countered.

"Probably not," was Grace's sheepish reply.

It was at that time that Annie and Archie were brought in by Gerard, their faces covered in chocolate. "You are not going to believe what we're going to get to eat for dessert tomorrow night," was all Annie had to say. Her smile said the rest.

Her grandmother smiled indulgently at her. "I'm going to go with something chocolaty."

At this point, Archie, regardless of the fact he had just eaten his body weight in sugar, could barely keep his eyes open. Jack scooped him up in his arms and Grace put her arms around Annie. "I hate to cut the party short," Jack said, "but I think these young 'uns have to get to bed...and Annie and Archie are looking pretty beat, also."

Evie shook her head and just said, "Oh no you didn't."

"Couldn't resist," was all he had by way of defense.

The rest of the travelers had to agree that bed did sound delicious and Gerard was asked to show the Dunleavy's to their sleeping quarters. Evie and Grace trailed behind everyone else and just looked at each other, as they mounted the spiraling staircase. "Do you feel like as big a bitch as I do?" was what Evie whispered to her sister.

"Of course. We spent quite a bit of time these past few months being pissed off we hadn't been asked to be bridesmaids."

———

Evie walked into her assigned room and just smiled with glee. The room just screamed comfort. The dusty blue of the walls was so soothing and the white sailcloth curtains were actually billowing in the slight breeze created by the open windows. On the nightstand next to the bed was a white basin and pitcher that had scattered chips running down the sides. Evie figured it would have felt in place in a Jane Austen novel. Next to that stood a huge vase filled with blue, white and yellow hydrangeas. A scattering of their tiny petals had fallen off the stems in a haphazard pattern along the piece of furniture. But instead of looking sloppy, it somehow had the appearance of an expert floral arrangement. She collapsed onto the bed and closed her eyes in satisfaction. A feather bed...heavenly. It took an almost Herculean effort to rise out of the bed in order to start her usual nighttime ritual. Luckily, Gerard had already laid out her pajamas on the blue plaid sitting chair by the vanity where her toiletry bag had been set. She did a quick mental calculation of the clothes she had brought with her for the weekend. If some strange man was rummaging through her luggage she wanted to make sure she wasn't going to be embarrassed by the underwear she had brought. *Damn, it was all thongs. That's unfortunate. How am I going to be able to look him in the eye?* She tried to console herself with the thought that maybe Grace would've gone with some of the same. Or, if she was really lucky, that Jack had packed his shiny, red Christmas underwear the kids gave him as what they considered to be the "best Christmas present ever". Those are the kind of underwear that can burn a hole in your retina, so she could always hope he got to those first and thongs automatically become a non-event.

Well, slightly slutty wares or not, I've got to get to bed, she thought to herself. She performed the most cursory of all teeth brushing and she couldn't even be sure her entire face actually got wet when she went to wash it. *It's just going to have to do. I don't think I can physically stand anymore,* was how she rationalized her half-assed attempt at hygiene.

The last thing she remembered thinking as she drifted off to sleep was that her pillow must be made out of down. That or a cloud plucked from heaven.

Eight

E velyn awoke with a start, feeling like something was not quite right, but unable to pinpoint exactly what caused her such a sudden jolt. She realized where she was, so the problem was not waking up in a strange bed. No one was peering into her room in a creepy manner. No loud noise from the street below or apartments around her had done it. What the hell was so out of place? And then she took in the quiet and came to the realization that it was possible to be woken up from a deep sleep by utter silence. *No doubt if I was outside in those fields I would be able to hear a butterfly flapping its delicate wings* she told herself. That thought was followed by a quick eye roll at herself for her dramatic flight of fancy. *No doubt I'm suffering from jet lag because that might be the most ridiculous thought ever to land in my head.* She then decided not to be so hard on herself, as at that moment she instinctively turned her head toward her water basin when she was alerted to a lost ladybug flying in her room by the sound of its soft shell landing on the pottery. *That is so cool! I sometimes am unable to distinctly hear the sound of two cabbies arguing and I just heard a ladybug land on that jar.* She looked around in wonder and thought this extended trip might be the perfect way to find a little balance to her life. Or at the very least maybe learn to sleep with the absence of noise.

Evie wandered downstairs a little after nine that morning. She found Charlotte sitting alone at the breakfast nook having a slice of toast with marmalade and tea. "I guess I'll have to get used to everyone drinking tea while I'm here. Back home we like to say, 'It's coffee or it's crap'."

"I miss my coffee almost as much as I miss my alcohol. The good news for you is you'll be staying at the home of a coffee connoisseur, so I think it should be fairly easy for you to get your fix on a regular basis."

"It was actually quite a selling point for me, you know. Living in the home of someone who owns his own coffeehouse? Perfection. Michael always did have the most useful friends. Looking back, I no longer believe it was a coincidence that in high school he had a friend in every deli, ice cream parlor, and beer distributor within a five mile radius from our home. Who's that lucky?"

Charlotte laughed. "That does sound like your brother. Care for some breakfast?"

"Just point me in the direction of the toaster and I'll be fine."

Charlotte pushed her chair out from the table, allowing a fleeting glimpse of the tiny bulge where her impossibly flat stomach used to be, before standing up and straightening out her tunic. "Let me help you get it." She briskly got the homemade bread out of a box on the marble countertop as Evie stared.

"I've never seen an actual breadbox before," she said.

"Cook insists. And we're all so scared of her, she does whatever she wants. The stereotype of the cook who runs the household with an iron fist is very much alive in our home here. We dare not object to anything she says." Charlotte lowered her voice to a whisper. "We even eat venison when she decides to prepare it. And my whole family despises venison. However, we love her to bits and her homemade jams and jellies certainly sweeten the pot, so to speak. You must sample some with the bread." She opened a cupboard that displayed a row of every flavor jam imaginable.

"It's like being in a Smuckers factory."

"Except Cook would probably boil you alive if she heard you compare her homemade jam to Smuckers."

"Are you trying to completely terrify me before I've even had the chance to meet your Cook?" Evie joked. Then she stopped short. "Oh my God. Raspberry rhubarb jam? This woman is obviously a genius and I will revere her always. And I will eat her venison. As long as I can cover it in her jam."

"Everyone else headed down to the gardens to see the rest of the estate. I was actually going to go out for a short horse ride. Do you care to join me?" Charlotte asked.

"The closest I've ever been to actually riding a horse was a carriage ride in Central Park on a surprisingly romantic date."

"Did you enjoy it?"

"The carriage ride or the date?"

"Either, I guess."

"Well, the carriage ride was actually a lovely date, so I guess yes to both. But I can't say I'm ready to get any closer to a horse. Having the driver in between us and him was about as close as I cared to get. They're really big animals. I'm assuming you're aware of that, as you apparently ride them." Evie stopped talking suddenly and looked at Charlotte quizzically. "Can you ride them still? I mean, now that you're almost six months pregnant? Well, obviously you can," she interrupted her own train of thought. "You just said you were going riding."

"Well, I won't be going off at a gallop, obviously," Charlotte answered, a bit defensively. "Just a little walk about, really."

"Well, thank you for the offer, but I think I'll pass. I might just take a stroll outside, though, if that's okay."

"That's fine. If you want me to point you in the direction the others went towards, I'd be happy to do so," Charlotte answered.

It wasn't hard to catch up with the rest of her family, as the sound of the children laughing was practically a directional arrow in the air that helped her to find them. She plodded through the first open meadow she came to and laughed at how the person who named the Manor was really a fan of the obvious. No hidden agendas for that one.

She waved back to Annie and Archie who were running towards her at full speed and braced herself for that inevitable moment when the two of them would hurl themselves through the air and into her arms.

"You two do realize that at some point you guys are going to be too big and I'm going to be too old for you to be throwing your bodies at me like trapeze artists, right?"

"Oh, Aunt Evie, you'll never be too old to catch us," Annie said. "At least I hope not," she added, "because that is a ton of fun to do to you."

"I like the fact that you give me more credit than I deserve. I will do my best not to drop you on your bums."

Rebecca and Tom smiled a hello to their youngest daughter and she stepped in beside them to walk through the wild lilacs, growing all around them.

"Talk about heavenly, huh, Evie?" her Dad asked. "Just look at this place. It's so peaceful."

"It really is," she agreed. "Maybe Michael can find out about having the bi-annual Dunleavy Family Reunion here next time, instead of Robert Moses State Park. It takes a little longer to get to, but it's certainly worth the trip."

"And the food is probably better than anything you and your brothers can grill on those hibachis, Tom. And even I'm a big enough person to admit I don't think the Shop Rite potato salad I bring in my own Tupperware container, in the hopes of convincing even one cousin that I made it from scratch, is going to come even remotely close to anything that their cook makes," Rebecca threw in. She whispered reverently to her husband and daughter, "Cook showed me her pantry this morning and there were three types of homegrown potatoes in there. Three. I don't think I've noticed three types of potatoes piled up in their bins at the supermarket, let alone contemplate growing them for myself."

"Mom," Grace called from the other side of the meadow, "what are you whispering about over there?"

"Why would you say I was whispering?"

"Because your hand is covering your mouth like you're a second grader about to tell a secret and that gives off a tell tale vibe."

"I was just mentioning the array of different potatoes in the Futterly's pantry."

Jack just laughed. "Ahhhh, I can see the obvious necessity for keeping your voice low for that. We wouldn't want that knowledge to seep out to just anyone."

"I am a bit mad, aren't I?" Rebecca acknowledged.

"It's only obvious to those of us who know you best," Tom tenderly replied.

The rest of the morning passed quickly, and they were surprised when Michael came out to look for them and advise them that lunch was almost ready and that

Charlotte's sister, Emily, had arrived and was looking forward to meeting them all.

"And when I say 'looking forward to meeting you all'," he whispered to Evie, "what I really mean is, not at all."

"Not a big fan then?" Evie asked.

"Kind of hard to be. You know what she said to Charlotte when she found out we were getting married?" Michael didn't wait for a reply, but changed his voice to a high, shrilly, English accented one. "Really? How quaint. A shotgun wedding. To an American, no less."

"She. Did. Not," Evie said in a staccato voice.

"Yes. She. Did," Michael answered back in the exact same tone.

"So much for not poisoning the well of unbiased introductions," Evie said.

"What?" Michael smiled mischievously. "Should I not have said anything?"

With that, the Dunleavy's went to meet Emily.

Nine

T he Dunleavy family traipsed in one of the side doors to take off the boots that Charlotte's Dad had given them before their walk.

Rebecca told everyone to pass her the wellies and asked her family if anyone had seen her trainers.

"What's a wellie? And a trainer, Grandma?" Annie asked.

"They're other words for boots and sneakers, sweetie," she responded.

"Why wouldn't you just say that, then?" she asked, perplexed by the change of vocabulary. Everyone waited for her response.

"Well, I think it's important to broaden your horizons and learn new words. Can't always get by strictly on what you're familiar with, right?"

"But that's the only way I know what you're talking about," muttered Archie, as all the adults headed out of the mud room.

"I'm with you guys," Evie whispered to the kids, hanging behind with them, "but why don't we try to humor Grandma and see if we can make a game out of it. The first one to figure out what she's talking about wins a quarter from now on."

"But what will you win, Aunt Evie? To be honest, I don't want to give you all my quarters. I'm saving up for

some clothes for my American Girl doll, Samantha."
Annie had the nervous look of a child who didn't think
the game was going to go her way and wanted to hedge
her bets for the least disastrous outcome possible. One
that didn't involve losing her precious quarters.

"I think I would be just as happy to collect those
monster hugs you guys dole out instead of quarters, so
that will be my prize, okay?" With that, Evie bundled the
two children as close to her as she could while they
giggled and tried to squirm away, protesting the whole
time.

"Aunt Evie, fine, just let us go. You didn't win one
yet," Archie laughed.

"I see the children have lagged a bit behind their
elders," a cold voice intoned from the doorway behind
them. Evie looked up to see a blond goddess turning her
nose down at herself and the children. Even with the huge
black sunglasses covering most of her face, Evie sensed
the distaste that would've been visible without the veil
they provided. Her mouth, perfectly outlined in a bright
red lipstick, was pinched with displeasure, while her hair
was perfectly curled around the frown lines on her
forehead.

"You must be Charlotte's sister, Emily," Evie blurted
out. *Holy shit*, she thought. *Michael had this one pegged
to perfection.* She had on a flowing yellow tunic with the
tiniest bit of lace around the mandarin collar and a pair of
denim walking shorts that looked like—could it really be?
—she had ironed them. Her look was completed with the
wedge heels she wore with gold straps that wrapped
around her ankles. Evie instinctively looked down at her
baggy, brown capri sweatpants, and oversized long
sleeved tee that read, NYU Crew XXL in bold, red letters.
She hastily tucked an errant strand of hair that had
escaped her ponytail, feeling like she was being
reprimanded by the headmaster at a girl's boarding

school. As Emily peeled the sunglasses off her face, Evie could see the dismay she was feeling, mirrored in Emily's eyes.

Emily gave a short laugh that never traveled as far as her eyes and said, "You do have another outfit for the engagement party this evening, I presume?"

"I'm Michael's sister, Evelyn," Evie said with as much dignity as she could muster, considering she had obviously failed some kind of test she never knew she was in for. "I don't believe we've had the pleasure." She let the last word dangle a little and hoped she was able to make it sound as condescending as all of Emily's so far.

"Yes, pleasure," was Emily's short response.

Crap, Evie thought. *Her bitch tone is so much better than mine. I lose that round as well, I suppose.* Because she really couldn't think of anything better to say, and knowing full well she wanted to be as far away as possible from Charlotte's sister, she simply claimed she had to find Annie and Archie's parents. "Well, I should deliver these two back to my sister and her husband. I'm looking forward to speaking with you more at lunch." *What a load of bullshit*, she thought to herself. *I'd rather dip my feet in a pool of piranha.*

"Aunt Evie? Was it me, or did that woman seem kind of mean?" Annie asked as they hurried down the corridor to find the rest of their family.

Evie decided to take the high road and not start a generational war. Knowing these two, she figured anything in their arsenal would be fair game in their minds, and they had watched *Cheaper by the Dozen* and its sequel. She didn't think Michael would be able to handle watching his soon to be sister-in-law get manhandled by all the hunting dogs that were most likely roaming the property after her pants had been sloshed around in buckets of meat. As funny as that would be, it would probably not be considered appropriate in most circles, she sternly reminded herself.

"I think she was probably just tired, Annie. I think she had a long drive out here and wasn't expecting the three of us doing our version of sumo wrestling in her hallway is all."

"Hmmm," Archie said, scratching his auburn hair thoughtfully. "I guess Mom is right. You can tell when someone needs a nap by how cranky they are. I never really believed her before this."

Ten

"There are worse ways to pass an afternoon than enjoying cocktails on a garden terrace at an English Manor, I suppose," Jack said to the crew that had assembled. The Futterly family laughed like those who don't quite know if a joke was being had on them and the Dunleavy's laughed like those who knew it was true.

"Jack's right," Tom threw out. "Thank you so much for the truly kind welcome you've given all of us."

"Dad obviously hasn't been introduced to Emily yet, I suppose," Evie whispered to her sister.

"Oh, come on," Grace replied. "Surely she can't be that bad."

"Don't call me Shirley, and yes she can."

"At what point will you finally get tired of that quote?"

"At what point will you stop loving your children?"

"So what you're saying is that the only hope I have is to actually stop using the word surely?"

Michael walked up behind his two sisters. "Don't call her Shirley."

Grace rolled her eyes and walked over to where her husband stood.

"Never gets old, does it?" Michael asked Evie.

"No, it really doesn't. So, I already had a chance encounter with Emily while I was in the mudroom fooling around with Annie and Archie. You're adding a real peach to your family tree. And that's a deduction I would've come up with even if you hadn't shared your cute anecdote."

"Hopefully she can keep her claws under wraps while Mom and Dad are around. I really don't want her ruining this weekend." Michael was nervously biting one of his fingernails, a habit he had broken years ago.

Evie swatted his finger out of his mouth and told him to relax. "People always act better in front of their elders. Mom still dresses up and uses her "big girl manners" for Grandma and she's closing in on eighty-five and hasn't had a coherent thought in five years now. Everything will be fine. See, it looks like things are going smoothly," she added, pointing in the direction of their parents. Emily and Charlotte stood laughing with Tom and Rebecca, all of them holding their drinks, as a bee lazily circled the terra cotta flower pots filled with geraniums that they stood around. "Christ, they look like a Zinfandel commercial." Michael started to laugh a little at Evie's spot on observation and she could sense he was starting to relax a bit.

Liza asked for the small group's attention and said that they would head around the house to another outside seating area for lunch.

"My goodness, Liza," Rebecca trilled, following Liza around the maze of cobblestones leading to the lunch area, "How many outside nooks and crannies do you have here?"

Evie caught up with Annie and Archie before they could say anything. "The judge rules that one is not British enough for a quarter contest. Even though it does describe the attributes of an English muffin, it does not meet the criteria of words or phrases Grandma hasn't uttered before touching down in England." The two kids looked disappointed until Evie pointed out that their grandmother was uttering new words all the time and it probably wouldn't be long before she pulled another one out.

Liza had been explaining to the group that there were three different outside terraces scattered throughout the property they used for entertainment purposes. "Obviously, the one leading out to the proper backyard will be employed tonight for the engagement party, so we won't use that one right now. Don't want to get in the way of the caterers and the rest of the staff while they're preparing for the soiree."

"I could never use the word 'soiree' without someone making fun of me," Jack groused to the three Dunleavy siblings.

"Why do you talk sometimes?" Michael asked his brother-in-law, smiling.

Charlotte came over to Michael as they approached the perfectly set table in another picturesque courtyard. Half walls were built around three quarters of the area, providing a cozy circle for the group to gather in. If Evie had to guess she would say the stones weren't the typical EP Henry wares that the people in Connecticut, her parents included, used for their patio needs. They were most likely stones cut from local castles, fallen unto hard times during the medieval period, or something completely romantic like that, she mused.

She glanced at the table and marveled at how beautiful, yet rustic everything looked. The green earthenware was slightly chipped but looked perfect in the outdoor setting. Each place had its own individual vase filled with pink and white peonies and green leafy foliage. A green and pink striped table runner brought the colors of the flowers and pottery together. On each plate lay a white card that had everyone's name done in calligraphy, showing everyone where to sit.

"Will you help me with the drinks trolley, Michael?" Charlotte asked her fiancé.

"Of course, lead the way, hot stuff."

"If you pinch my bum on the way out, you're in a lot of trouble, mister," she laughed.

Evie started to look at the placards and was happy to see that she was on the other side of the table from Emily. *Small wonders and all that* she happily thought.

She had Archie sitting directly to her left, and Annie was on his left. Michael was on her right. Immediately across from her was her Mom, so she figured Annie and Archie would be paying particularly close attention to what their grandmother was saying, in hopes of lightening her stash of quarters. *I'm certainly going to need to be on my toes.*

As everyone was ohh'ing and ahh'ing over the beauty of the table and finding their places for lunch, Michael rolled out a cart that had already been laden down with a huge assortment of drinks for the group. Charlotte followed behind him, carrying an ice bucket.

"I guess I'll stand in as the bartender of the moment...really give me a chance to show off the skills that helped put me through college," Michael bragged.

"I've got a couple of bank statements that would challenge you on the fact it was just bartending that helped put you through college, son," Tom replied.

"Well, it at least kept me in beer through my college years. Step on up and just try to stump me." Michael executed a pitiful attempt at throwing a cocktail shaker in the air.

"Oh God help us," Grace proclaimed loudly enough for all to hear her from the sidelines. "He's busting out his Tom Cruise in *Cocktail* moves. It's like a train wreck...I want to look away, but I just can't." She continued to tease her brother and started to yell out, "Oh, my eyes...my eyes are burning," as she pretended to shield her eyes from the spectacle.

"Just for that, you can place your drink order last. And you can't make it fancy."

Archie decided to make his way to the front of the line, since he was a little parched. "Can you make me a Coke?" he asked his uncle.

"That's it? That's all you got?"

Archie looked confused. "With ice?"

"Can do, little man." Michael added a maraschino cherry for garnish and handed it over to his nephew with a flourish.

Archie broke away from the crowd, shaking his head slightly. He looked over to his Dad and whispered, "Who asked for this?" pointing at the cherry. "You want it, Dad?"

Everyone else grabbed drinks as Michael poured good-naturedly. Evie and Grace opted for simple glasses of white wine, while their Dad ordered a white wine spritzer, much to their amusement.

"Look at him," Evie laughed with Grace. "The drinks keep getting girlier and girlier all the time. The man is six feet two inches tall, two hundred and twenty pounds and he's sipping a cocktail that wouldn't put a dent in a high school girl who isn't legal yet."

"Well," Jack said, walking up to his wife and sister-in-law and catching the tail end of their conversation, "at least your Mom is manning up and drinking a beer."

"Yeah, but is that really any better?" Grace asked.

It was at this time Gerard stepped out of the door onto the terrace and told everyone if they could find their seats, he would start serving lunch. It was all handled quite elegantly by himself and two young girls, wearing maid's uniforms. They somberly laid down the first course, which turned out to be a light and summery spinach salad covered with strawberries and walnuts and goat cheese with little toast points on the side.

From there, things only got better. They were served pan seared tilapia with a tomato chutney on the side, and a robust helping of grilled vegetables. Also on each oversized plate was a generous portion of homemade french fries made from sweet potatoes and covered in what looked like Old Bay seasoning, but you just knew was some secret concoction of Cook's from her herb garden. Of course, the kids ate well, also, just differently. They each had a grilled peanut butter and jelly panini. It took some prodding on their parent's part to get them to taste it. ("But it has black lines all over it," Annie complained quietly to her Mom, who was sitting across from her.) However, once the first bite was in, they couldn't stop gorging themselves on it. They barely touched their own homemade fries—of the normal variety, no seasoning—and that was quite unlike them.

The conversation was flowing quite nicely among the two families at this point. They were between too little and copious amounts of alcohol, which always seem to be the best for conversation starters. There was the requisite sharing of silly family stories regarding the bride and groom. ("Do you remember when Michael went on his rock eating rampage. He wanted to see how many pebbles off the driveway he could eat in a half hour time allotment," to "How about the time Charlotte wanted to run away and join the circus and actually walked about two miles into town, with Gerard following a safe distance behind in the car, before she changed her mind? It was about that time we started having to ask the gardener to design the shrubs into the circus themed topiaries that you saw driving up. We just keep doing it for sentimental reasons at this point.")

Dessert was produced and miraculously inhaled even though everyone claimed to be stuffed from the magnificent meal they had just eaten. How could they not? It was a pile of homemade brownies, apparently Cook's specialty, covered in caramel sauce and homemade, of course, whipped cream.

"So, Peter and Liza, I imagine you use up quite a bit of petrol with all the farm equipment we saw while exploring the estate today," Rebecca commented.

Annie and Archie looked over at Evie and she gave them a nod of encouragement. Game time.

"I know this one," Annie said proudly. "It means gas."

"By George, she's got it," Evie told her. "I officially owe you the first quarter of our new game: What in The World is Grandma Talking About."

The conversation had now turned to that evening's festivities. It turns out that Charlotte's parents had invited about two hundred of their nearest and dearest friends to the "little" engagement party and they would all soon be arriving at the Manor. Emily couldn't wait to tell everyone what she was wearing that evening.

"Charlotte, you are not going to believe the dress I just got for tonight. It's a Stella and it's gorgeous."

Grace, seeing Evie's confusion, mouthed in her direction, "McCartney." Evie stared at her blankly, waiting for her to say more. "Oh, for God's sake," Grace hissed. "Paul McCartney's daughter? Big designer? Loved by all, especially Americans who pretend to be British, like Madonna and Gwyneth Paltrow? Ringing *ANY* bells?" Evie just pursed her lips and shrugged.

"You're getting a subscription to *US Weekly* and *EW* for your birthday and that's final." Watching Evie start to protest, Grace just shook her off with a calm, superior tone. "I don't care if you like to be surprised; you can no longer live in such a pop culture vacuum. You've got no litmus test for current events."

"Would you care to discuss the last State of the Union Address that was made to our country?"

"Interesting current events."

Seeing the conversation between the two Dunleavy sisters, Liza Futterly asked, "Oh, do you girls like Stella's work as well?"

"She's fabulous," Grace said, enthusiastically. I've got a gorgeous red jersey halter dress of hers that I absolutely love."

Emily arched an eyebrow in Evie's direction. "And you, Evelyn?"

Evie fought the urge to lie and pretend she knew what everyone was talking about by convincing herself in that hairsbreadth of time that it would be petty and shallow to do so. That and she knew she'd never be able to even remotely fake her way through a conversation about fashionable designers. "Sorry. I can't say I'm very familiar with too many designers. I'm not a big shopper, really."

"You don't say," Emily drawled. Although Evie thought the outfit Emily had been wearing would've been perfect for lunch, Emily had changed before they had met up on the terrace for drinks. She casually picked a piece of lint off of her lemon colored linen shift dress that she was now wearing. Which she had miraculously been able to keep wrinkle free, somehow, even though they had been sitting at the table for well over an hour at this point. *It's like she made a deal with the devil*, Evie reflected. She took in Emily's yellow peep toe spectator pumps, and the yellow eyelet headband that managed to contain her long, wavy hair in a neat cascade. *Very polished*, Evie had to admit to herself.

She was feeling less so, by comparison, even though she thought she had looked good when she came down for lunch earlier. She had even gotten a few compliments on her Ann Taylor brown and cream batik print skirt that she had paired with a cream colored shirt that was pin tucked in the front around the collar. She put it all together with a pair of dark brown wedge heels that she had borrowed from Grace and had even taken the time to blow out her hair, so her layers looked sharp and crisp. She double checked that her outfit hadn't magically transformed into sackcloth, because that's certainly the vibe that Emily was giving off.

Michael and Evie exchanged a quick look, and Evie knew that she wasn't being super sensitive or imagining Emily's disdain. She quickly decided she really didn't care what Emily thought of her. Michael wasn't marrying her, he was marrying her sister. "Yes, well, I find the *Wall Street Journal* doesn't do too much coverage on the fashion world, except when Fashion Week hits New York, so that's the payoff, I guess. I live my life in a bit of a fashion rut."

Eleven

E vie opened the closet door to see the end result of all the primping done to her for the past hour by way of the mirror hanging on the inside. She was actually pretty surprised by Grace's handiwork. Her brown hair, usually so thick and straight, had the tousled waves she only assumed those working in Hollywood with a hairdresser in their entourage would be able to manage. And Grace had used her deft hand with the makeup brushes to her advantage as well. Her skin looked like porcelain, her blue eyes bright and shiny, and the nude lipstick was artfully, but discretely applied.

All Evie could blurt out was, "Holy crap, I'm gorgeous. And you're an absolute genius. You have a serious calling. I think now is when you have to promise to use your powers only for good, and never for evil. It's a superhero thing."

Grace laughed at her younger sister good-naturedly. "It's true. I was up late last night battling zombies armed only with my good blusher and an eyelash curler." She laughed again as Evie spun around to admire herself once more. "What can I say? It's a gift. It also helps that my canvas," she said with a touch of the dramatic and air quotes, "was so beautiful to begin with."

"Seriously, thanks again, Grace. I don't know why I feel the need to look so posh tonight. I expect it has something to do with the way Charlotte's sister, Emily, gave me the once over and I felt I had been found wanting. Kind of felt like the ugly stepsister all day."

"Please, Evie. She was probably threatened by how gorgeous you are even in your most natural of states."

"That's the kindest attempt at saying I don't put much effort into my appearance that anyone has ever tried out on me. And I love you desperately for it."

"Well," Grace continued on with. "She'll certainly see a different side of you with that number you've got on. I can't believe Maura had the good sense to talk you into it before you left for London. Once again, you're on notice that I will be calling on you to wear that at some point. Once I can convince my husband to take me somewhere that doesn't have chicken nuggets on the menu."

Evie looked down at her dress and silently thanked Maura for her power of persuasion. She had convinced Evie to buy the dress months ago, for absolutely no reason whatsoever, when they had walked past this trendy little boutique in Soho. Evie, who never gave too much thought to her clothes, had literally stopped dead in her tracks at the window as soon as she caught a glimpse of the ivory concoction she was wearing now. The empire shape of the dress and the chiffon fabric floated delicately around Evie's small frame perfectly. There was exquisite black beading on both the hem, that just caught her knee, so it was short without being the least bit trampy, and the halter top that snaked around her neck. It really was gorgeous. And more importantly, she felt gorgeous in it. For a woman, that was half the battle.

"Maybe Michael will have invited some cute friends to this engagement party," said Evie. "Then all of your hard work will not have gone to waste."

"Hey, who says you need a man to notice you or you've wasted your time? Did you just transport yourself back to the fifties? You're not going to throw an apron on over your dress, are you?"

"Nah...I'm just saying it's been a while since I've made an effort and it wouldn't feel so bad if I got some positive feedback is all."

"Well, I don't think you're going to be disappointed, Evie. You look fabulous. Now I should probably head back to my room and get myself all gussied up, or I'm totally going to look like the tired, harried, mother of two small children that I am." With that, Grace sailed out of Evie's room and headed down the hall to her own. Evie watched as Grace passed by an open bay window, with its chintz curtains blowing about, and how she had suddenly stopped to watch the scene below. She called Evie over to check out the workers scurrying below. The two women stared with wonder as caterers, gardeners, and wait staff ran around at breakneck speed, trying to get ready for the night. The two large tents off the garden terrace had already been assembled and the tiny white lights were strung up through their rafters. They both knew that the effect this evening would be dramatic.

"My God," Grace muttered, taking in the scene before her with something akin to bafflement. "If this is the engagement party, what the hell is the wedding going to be like?"

Evie watched the scene unfolding before her eyes and just laughed. "Thank God we won't have to worry about what to wear that day. Bridesmaid dresses will take that headache away."

"Ahhhh," Grace yelled out. "I seriously have to hurry up or I'll never be down on time." Both girls giggled at that one. It wouldn't matter what time Grace started on herself. She wouldn't be down on time, regardless.

"Try not to be more than a half hour behind me, Grace, or I'm going to be seriously annoyed at you guys."

Grace merely glanced back with a benign smile on her face.

"I mean it, Gracie." Evie lowered her voice to a stage whisper. "If you force me into small talk with Emily you will be sorry."

With a "go practice your curtsey, Evie," Grace departed behind her door.

Twelve

E vie went down at exactly seven-thirty; the time the
cocktail hour would be starting up. She figured at
least one member of their family should make an effort
and be on time. She was greeted by a smiling Michael. "It
looks like I've managed to put the fear of God into all of
you guys," he laughed. "Mom and Dad are already in the
backyard, meeting some friends of Charlotte's parents."

"I should probably go back upstairs, then, so you
don't get spoiled by too much promptness on our part.
You don't want to get used to it, because when it
disappears, and you know it will, it'll be that much harder
to deal with the tardiness."

Michael gave her a gentle shove. "I'll take what I can
get when I can get it...now why don't you head out with
Mom and Dad and I'll be out shortly to introduce you to
some of our friends. I've got to run upstairs and get Char
Char first. She wanted me to see her dress before she
comes down." And then he was off before Evelyn could
even form the words that were swirling in her head about
the nickname her brother had for his fiancé. *That will
definitely need to be addressed at a time still to be
determined*, she mused to herself with an indulgent head
shake, as she watched his form retreat up the staircase.

For the next half hour she was introduced to several
friends of Lord and Lady Futterly, and the names were

beginning to swirl together. She was relieved to sense a bit of a whirlwind behind her, and figured, correctly, that Grace, Jack and the kids had arrived. Noise levels always seemed to ratchet up on their arrival.

Annie and Archie were soon ensconced with about twenty or so other children of various ages, playing games set up under lights on the far side of the backyard with the three babysitters that were so ingeniously supplied for the party.

"This is just heaven," Grace sighed to Evie, while sipping a flute of champagne. She had on a navy blue silk shift dress, with navy patent leather heels. A long strand of different colored stones of various sizes made it modern. Her dark eyes were done up in the 'smoky' eye look that looked amazing with her dark eyes. If Evie had attempted it on her own with her limited make up application skills, she would've ended up looking like the lone Goth attendee at the party. Grace had pulled her long, curly dark hair into an interesting side ponytail that looked extremely sophisticated. She was the picture of poise and class. Basically, she was just masking the party animal side of her personality. "The kids are here, so they don't feel like they're missing anything, and I don't have to cut up any hotdogs or get yogurt all over my dress for that to happen."

"You look great, by the way. So not the harried mother of two young children you were afraid you'd come down as."

"She does look great, doesn't she," Jack agreed, throwing his arms around her and nuzzling her neck. "And I will be keeping an eye out for any sort of leering English gentlemen." He adopted a Cavemanesque grunt. "You my woman."

"Fabulous. First Evelyn turns into June Cleaver after her makeover and now you're doing your best Neanderthal impression."

"You guys are still cute," Evie said with genuine warmth. She was feeling a little vehklempt—to paraphrase Mike Myers, paraphrasing Linda Richards—watching the two of them together. They were a perfect match, even after nine years of marriage. Grace with her dark, striking looks, and Jack with his blond hair and blue eyes, they appeared to be a living version of opposites attracting. But with their shared love of the outdoors, books, and an ever present sarcastic tongue, personality wise they were clones. Evie took another swig of the champagne and tried not to dwell on the question that was taking shape in the back of her mind more and more often...when would it be her turn?

It was at this time that Michael strode over to their little circle with a friend of his in tow.

"Oh, guys, I want you to meet a good friend of mine who will be in the wedding party...Nathanial Alowicious Corgin III," Michael said to his family.

"Isn't that a mouthful," Grace giggled to Evie.

"I hope so," Evie mumbled to herself.

"What did you say?" asked Grace, looking at her sister with wide eyes.

"I'm sorry, Grace. Apparently the change in the time zone, and staring at a gorgeous man, has turned me into a bit of a perv." Michael was staring at his two sisters whispering to each other but Evie didn't care. She was actually transfixed by the man in front of her. She thought he was gorgeous. Tall, dirty blond hair, eyes so green you had to wonder for a second if he was so vain he had colored contacts in. *Please God, don't let them be colored contacts she thought fleetingly to herself. And, oh my God, how cute...is he turning red with embarrassment*, she wondered?

"Nate should suffice," he said. "Your brother has been kind enough to throw in my middle name to anyone within earshot since that tidbit came out after a long night of drinking a while back. You'd think I'd have learned a long time ago how funny that name sounds to a bunch of blokes when they're out drinking. I guess I just had higher hopes for the maturity level of Americans, which have sadly not been upheld by your brother here." Nate was slowly returning to a normal color, so Evie guessed he was feeling slightly better.

"Yes," Evie said, "Michael can be such a cad."

Michael, Grace, and Jack all looked at her like she was nuts. She wanted to look at herself like she was nuts. *A cad? Really? That's the best you could come up with? Who talks like that? Say something else, Evie,* she reprimanded herself. "Oh, is that shrimp? I love shrimp. Nice meeting you, Nate." Evie sprinted off, belittling herself in her mind. *The first guy you're even remotely attracted to in who knows how long and you start speaking like you're a character in a terrible soap opera and then bolt like you're Marion Jones. Way to make an impression, Evie,* she scolded herself.

She tried to glance casually over at where Michael, Grace, Jack and Nate were standing around, still talking. Jack said something that made everyone, including Nate, laugh out loud. For an instant, she was completely and overwhelmingly jealous of her brother-in-law. Then she realized the ridiculousness of her emotions. *Get a grip, Evie,* she thought to herself. *Bury that desire to scratch out your sister's husband's eyes because he made a guy you think is cute, laugh. Because that may be the saddest thing ever!* She scanned the room, hoping for some inspiration on something that could be considered sadder than being jealous of Jack talking to a guy she met minutes ago that she thought was gorgeous. Her eyes fell on Charlotte's mom, Lady Futterly, in her 4 inch stilettos and tightly cinched wrap dress, trying to look like she was in her 30s instead of her 50s. *That would be a sad sight,* Evelyn thought glumly, *except for the fact she looks so damn fabulous it makes me want to become bulimic. Great, now I've got to figure out what's sadder than a woman who thinks turning into a bulimic is a good idea after meeting her brother's soon to be mother-in-law. I should just stop this now, before I end up jumping off London Tower,* Evie thought to herself.

Charlotte interrupted her thoughts as she sided up to Evie, who was going to town on the shrimp tray, almost unconsciously. The waiter started to nervously back away with the silver platter, as if he was afraid Evie was going to take every last one of them before he could officially start to circulate through the party. He was pretty sure Lady Futterly would consider that a party foul and he'd end up bearing the brunt of the blame.

"Hi Evelyn. It certainly looks like we've got at least one fan of the shrimp tonight," she said brightly.

"Oh, hi, Charlotte. I'm sorry. I didn't even realize how many I stuck on my plate here. Care for a shrimp?"

Charlotte looked at her like she had suddenly grown a third eye in her forehead. "No, thank you. You're really not supposed to eat certain fish when you're pregnant."

"Oh. I thought it was just sushi," Evie said. "But then again, what would I know about it, right?"

"No, you're right about the sushi, but there are several things you're supposed to avoid. Obviously ridiculous amounts of alcohol would be the first. Obviously unfortunate. Any kind of soft cheese is one, shell fish is another I think. I really need to sit down with my OB and go over this stuff." Charlotte paused and looked at Evie. "Shrimp are a shell fish, right?"

This gave Evie pause. "Good question. I'm not one hundred percent sure, but this probably falls under one of those situations where you'd rather be safe than sorry. It'd be a shame if the baby ended up being born with gills or something. Although I would imagine he or she would be a shoe-in as a future Olympian in one of the swimming events."

"Good point. Although I think we'd rather go the old fashioned route of pushing a young child to the brink with ungodly early morning workouts with Russian task-masters and berating their horrific times until they cry and promise they'll do better. We're Old School like that."

"Glad to see you guys have thought this through. It's obvious parenting is going to come very naturally to the two of you," Evie laughed.

"I'm really sorry we don't have the room to put you up with us while you stay on here for the next couple of months. I hope you're not offended."

"No, not at all," Evie told her. This will be perfect for while I'm here. Otherwise I imagine Michael and I would end up having a food fight or something equally ridiculous before my time was up. The whole 24/7 thing would probably be the beginning of the end."

"So did Michael have a chance to introduce you to his friend whose flat you'll be staying at?"

"No, I don't believe so. To be honest, I don't even remember if he gave me his name."

"Oh, it's Nate. Nate Corgin."

Evelyn stared at Charlotte for a good minute before being able to speak. *Of course it is*, she thought to herself. Out loud she said, "Well, then he did introduce us, he just didn't tell me that was who I'm bunking with. I only had a chance to talk to him for a moment, though. He seems nice," she added because she didn't know what else to say. She was just proud she didn't use the word dreamy instead.

"And quite the delicious dish, as my sister, Emily, says," Charlotte added. "She's had her eye on him for quite a while, but hasn't made much progress, much to her dismay. Maybe you'll have better luck," she laughed.

"Oh, I don't think so," Evie said, self consciously pushing a strand of her hair behind her ear. To herself she thought if a blond Amazon like Emily couldn't get his attention, what luck would a tiny brunette have?

"Yes, I suppose dating a friend of your brother's might be taboo. At least as far as Michael's concerned. I'm sure he's already promised tons of bodily harm to Nate if he so much as looks at you. Isn't that what big brothers do?"

"Well, at least mine does. Although he's never had a problem dating any of mine or Grace's friends," Evie said and then stopped. "I'm sorry, maybe that wasn't an appropriate joke, considering the fact I'm speaking with his fiancé."

"As long as that's not an ongoing thing, I can handle it. Why don't we head over to where they're talking and I'll give you and your new roommate a proper introduction."

Charlotte and Evelyn headed back to the group she had left a few minutes earlier. When they reached them, Charlotte said, "Nate, I know Evelyn didn't fully realize who you were until I just mentioned it, but she's Michael's sister who'll be sharing your flat while she stays on until the wedding. Apparently Michael decided that information was need to know and has a very strange idea as to whom that would apply to."

Nate smiled at Evie and then looked down at her plate, still laden with the shrimp she had piled on it. "I've got to be honest. I don't think I have enough shrimp in the flat to keep you happy. However, there is always a ton of takeaway curry if that makes things better."

"Curries, huh?" What are you thoughts about pizza?" she countered.

"Not a huge fan, believe it or not," Nate said.

"That's decidedly un-American," Evie laughed.

"We're decidedly not *in* America," said Nate.

"Touché. At least tell me you have beer," Evie begged.

"We have reached a compromise, folks," Nate yelled to no one in particular.

Their little group continued to grow in size as more of Michael and Charlotte's friends came over to introduce themselves to the Dunleavy siblings. It seemed to Evie that the sound of laughter and muffled conversations hung in the air above their heads, but she was feeling too tired to try and partake. She turned to Grace and whispered, "I'm going to go over to the far terrace for a moment and try to clear my head and get a second wind."

Evelyn stood on the porch, a glass of wine in her hand, wondering at the glorious garden. All the flower beds were in neat rows, and the hedges trimmed to perfection. It was obvious that Rebecca and Thomas hadn't been anywhere near these gardens. In a strange way, the absolute sense of order amongst those flowers made Evie a little sad. They reminded her of little soldiers, in their much more colorful uniforms than your standard army green, standing at attention, waiting for their drill sergeant. She realized she favored a little more chaos in a garden. And maybe a weed or two to show that the gardener—because Lord knows the Futterly's weren't puttering around out there—was human.

"You know, I've heard that Charlotte's Mum made the gardener plant the flowers in alphabetical order. Of course, being shit with the names of flowers I can't testify to that as fact." Nate was suddenly standing by her side, slowly sipping a pint of Guinness.

Evie snorted with laughter. *Christ*, she thought, *a snort? God forbid I produce a coy laugh.* "I can't really say that surprises me, seeing as how I saw a whole area of hedges cut to look like circus animals when we drove up here. To be honest, the greenery looked as if they felt a little embarrassed by it."

"But you must give the gardener his due," Nate added. "It can't be easy to cut out a bear on a unicycle with clippers."

"To the gardener." Evie held up her glass of wine in a toast to the garden Picasso.

Nate laughed and hoisted his Guinness high in the air, making Evie realize just how tall he was. All of her friends found it ridiculous that Evie wouldn't even consider a guy if he was under six feet tall. Considering she was barely 5'4" they thought she had a little more room to play with, so to speak. But Evie loved fitting under the crook of someone's arm and that sense of protection that seemed to come with it. This didn't mean she felt like she needed someone to look out for her, she just liked that sense of security on a bad day. She couldn't help but wonder how she would fit under Nate's arm.

Almost on cue, Nate asked her if she was cold. "I know that it's the end of May, but these evenings can be a bit brisk out here in the country. Would you like to throw on my jacket?" he asked.

Evie was surprised to see that she did have goose bumps on her arm. She couldn't say for certain if it was because it had gotten a bit cool without her realizing it, or from the way Nate's hand skimmed her shoulder when she nodded her assent to his offer and he draped his sports coat around her arms. His coat smelled like coffee beans and Ivory soap and Evie thought it was the sexiest scent she had ever breathed in. *No heavy and cloying colognes for this guy*, Evie thought happily to herself.

The smell of the beans on his coat reminded Evie about one of the few facts her brother had mentioned to her about her flat mate, before she found out who he was. "So...Michael said something about you opening up a coffeehouse? How is that going?"

"It's actually quite a bit of hard work. I suppose any new business is like that, though, when you're trying to get it off the ground. I had spent a couple of years working in the City at the bank your brother works at—that's how we met—but I quickly realized that wasn't what I wanted to do. I wanted to be my own boss, make my own hours, that sort of thing."

"I gotta' think your hours aren't so great, though, huh? I mean, you've still got to keep those early morning banker hours so they can get the caffeine they need to get their day started."

"That's true. We open at six o'clock in the morning, so that means someone's got to be there by five a.m. to get the coffee machines started, receive the bakery delivery for the day, that sort of thing. Luckily for me, I found a fabulous woman, Hannah, to be my manager and we alternate days for the early shift." Evie felt her entire core being eaten by jealousy over this 'fabulous woman' Nate spoke so highly about. Could Nate see the color green actually coming off her skin she wondered? He continued on, "Thankfully, her husband gets their kids off to school on the days she's in early, so it's worked out quite nicely." *Husband and kids? That's much better,* Evie thought. *Oh my God,* was her next thought. *What is wrong with me? I've got to get off Planet Crazy if I'm going to live with this guy in his apartment for the next three months. He probably has a girlfriend that I'm going to have to see every day, prancing around the place and I've got to come to grips with that. Actually, that's not a bad idea...I should find out if he has a girl friend, so I can start preparing myself. Let's see...how can I say this nonchalantly?*

"So, Nate, are you seeing anyone?' Subtle, Evie, she chastised herself mentally.

If Nate was surprised by the sudden change in topic, he was gentleman enough not to show it. "Actually, I just got off a relationship a couple of months ago and haven't really had a lot of time for dating, what with the coffee shop and all. How about you? Anyone going to be pining for you in New York, while you're visiting with us these next couple of months?"

"Well, if I answer yes, it'd only be a half truth. But if anyone's pining, it's strictly my friends. Who, I should add, are planning to come out and visit me in a couple of weeks anyway, so they should be able to tough it out. Oh, and they're totally planning on staying at a hotel," she hastily added, in case he thought she was planning to take over his home and use it like a Sheraton.

"Why bother with hotel rooms?" he asked. "You'll see when you get there, but I have two spare rooms, so if people don't mind doubling up, they're more then welcome to stay with us." She couldn't help it, but when he said 'stay with us' in a coupley kind of way, it made her insides go all funny. And Evie was not used to her insides going all funny. She was not that kind of girl. *Please God*, she silently prayed, *don't make my life turn into a Harlequin romance, because that is not who I am.* What she was, though, was cold, and she couldn't help shivering, even with Nate's coat draped on her shoulders.

"We should probably go back in," Nate said. "You're looking pretty chilly and I'm sure Michael has sent out a search party for us by now. Don't want him to get the wrong idea about us...he might not let you stay at my flat if he does." Nate flashed Evie a quick smile and used his arm to guide her back inside to where the rest of the party was still in full swing. Evie was a little disappointed that they were heading back in, but she really was cold, so figured it was for the best. Besides, he couldn't have been any clearer with his 'wrong idea' mood killer statement and she didn't want to look foolish and start fawning all over him. On their way off the patio they practically crashed into Emily, who pretty much glowered at Evie before turning her attention, and killer smile, in Nate's direction. "Nathanial, I've been looking for you all evening. Where have you been hiding yourself?" Evie couldn't believe her ears, but the girl didn't laugh, she actually tinkled. *I so did not think that was an actual sound,* she thought to herself. She prepared herself to leave Nate's company, so he could flirt with this gorgeous creature, and was about to hand him back his jacket, when he surprised her by tightening his hold on her arm and saying, "I've been getting to know my soon to be new flat mate a little bit better. If you'll excuse us, we're heading over to Michael and your sister. Lovely to see you again, Emily." Nate kept his hand firmly on Evie's lower back and steered her away from Emily, who, if Evie was a betting woman, would've placed quite a bit of money on the fact she was boring holes into her back with an angry stare while their figures departed.

Nate surprised her again by saying, "That one is quite sure of herself. If I'm to be quite honest with you, she scares me a little. Thank God you were there to protect me."

"So I guess my sole purpose while I'm in your apartment is to be your buffer? Protect you from the unwanted advances of unbelievably gorgeous blondes, huh?"

Nate stopped and looked at Evie right in the eyes. "She's not my type," he said simply and then continued on down the hall, leaving Evie to hurry and catch up with him and wonder if there was a hidden meaning to what he just said, and the way he looked at her when he said it.

Michael and Charlotte were sitting down talking to Grace and Jack when Evie and Nate found them again. "There you guys are," Michael said. "I was starting to get a little bit worried about you two. Figuring out which shelf in the fridge will be whose once Evie moves in? Because I've got to warn you, Nate. She's going to need at least two of them."

"Something like that," Nate said.

"Well, we were just telling Grace and Jack that we've finally finished with all the arrangements for the band that'll be playing at our wedding. We're so excited...they play all the standards and they sound wonderful," Charlotte said.

"Like *Under The Bridge* by the Chili Peppers?" Grace threw out.

"No, standards mean stuff like Madonna's *Vogue*, Grace," Evelyn said with disdain.

"Hello? That means anything by Abba," was Nate's contribution. When he looked around the circle and saw everyone staring at him in silence, he pinched the bridge of his nose and wondered aloud, "Why do I even talk sometimes?"

"I don't know, buddy, because you do know that now you're going to be introduced as Nathanial Alowicious Corgin III, Abba fan, right?" Michael said.

Jack looked at all of them with disgust. "Um, guys, this is Michael we're talking about. Standards for him would mean the unforgettable works of Van Morrison, except for *Brown Eyed Girl* for the obviously overplayed reason, Bruce Springsteen, U2...do you people even know your own brother at all?" he asked, turning to Grace and Evie.

"No, silly," Charlotte laughed. "Standards like those sung by Frank Sinatra, Smokey Robinson, and Tony Bennett, to name a few. Those artists."

"Clarifying question," Evie threw out. "Do you mean hip, octogenarian Tony Bennett or *I Left My Heart in San Francisco* Tony Bennett? Because the answer's kind of crucial."

Michael frowned at Evelyn, while the others laughed. "We're going for a more traditional sound for our wedding music," was all he said on the matter.

After a period of uncomfortable silence, and a bit of shoe staring, Grace saved the moment by announcing loudly, "I seem to be out of champagne. Anyone else care for a glass?" When everyone voiced their assent, she hurried off to grab the nearest server and ask for five glasses of champagne for their small group. It was the same waiter whose shrimp tray Evie had descended upon like a vulture earlier, and when he saw her, he smiled and left the bottle there as well. "If you like champagne as much as you like shrimp," he whispered, "it'll probably be easier for me to just leave this with you."

She grinned sheepishly and said, "You're probably going to have to pop by shortly with another bottle. I actually like champagne more than I like shrimp. Shocking, but true."

"You know what else is obviously true?" Nate asked softly in her ear.

"What's that?" Evie asked.

"Pretty girls do get better bar service then the rest of us."

And right then Evie just didn't care if she was fooling herself that anything could happen between her and Nate. So she said the first thing that popped into her head. "Well, stick with me and I'll be happy to help you get drunk." And that's basically what they did. The five of them quickly polished off the first bottle of champagne while Charlotte watched jealously with her seltzer water.

"The first thing I'm going to do after I give birth is have an IV drip of champagne set up for me," she said longingly.

Michael put his arm around her and kissed her ear. "I promise to sneak in the biggest bottle of Dom to the hospital room as soon as our baby is born, okay? And one straw if that's what you want. You can go to town on that bad boy all by yourself. Fair is fair, right? You've been my designated driver for the past six months. I'm willing to drive the new and intoxicated mother home from the hospital."

"You might have a problem getting the baby away from social services if Charlotte's rip roaring wasted when you leave the hospital. You should probably at least wait until you get home, to avoid a messy custody battle with the state," Grace laughed.

It was during the consumption of the second bottle of champagne that Jack had the epiphany for his joke. Grace, Jack, Evie, and Nate made their way over to the DJ booth that was set up outside next to the dance floor and asked for a medley of songs, with seemingly no connection whatsoever, to be played. Jack made sure the DJ understood that he had to play all four songs right in a row: "*Under The Bridge* by the Red Hot Chili Peppers, followed up with *Vogue* by Madonna, *Take a Chance on Me* by Abba and *Domino* by Van Morrison," he excitedly told the DJ. "And you can't play anything else in between, or it won't make sense."

The DJ just stared at Jack. "Are you quite sure it makes sense even when played in this exact order, mate?" he asked.

"Oh my God, he really is a like a kid on Christmas," Grace whispered to Evie. "It's part of why I love him."

"This next eclectic group of songs go out to Michael and Charlotte with wishes of love and luck through the years ahead, although, I'm not quite sure how these songs would apply," was all the DJ had to say to get the four of them to start jumping up and down. It never dawned on them that the engaged couple didn't hear the dedication or bothered them that they never found their way out to dance floor that had cleared immediately when their foursome went running towards it at a dizzying speed. What mattered is they thought they were absolutely hilarious and enjoyed every note of their bizarre medley. Other revelers at the party thought they were a bit insane, but that's beside the point.

"You look rather lovely when you dance," Nate told Evie solemnly, as she twirled around the dance floor. She figured it was the booze talking so did what any other self respecting girl in her situation would do. She flagged down a passing waiter and got two more flutes of champagne. *Let's keep that train of thought chugging along*, she told herself as she spun one more time around, and then quickly decided that centrifugal force and large amounts of alcohol were a bad combination. She stopped spinning. At least physically. Only to find Nate staring quite intently at her. She proceeded to do a bit of a stutter step at the sudden halting of her motion that made it obvious to everyone around her that the messages her brain was sending down to her limbs were not being received as quickly as they usually were. She flung her arms out like a gymnast sticking a landing and added a "ta da," for comic relief. "And you're quite funny to boot. You are not your average girl, are you Evelyn Dunleavy? I believe I am in for an interesting couple of months."

It was at that moment the DJ opted for mood killer music. Because it was at that moment *I Will Survive* started to blast from the speakers covered with ivy and white lights that circled the dance floor. Evie had long ago decided, along with her friends, that this was one song they could not conceivably dance to one more time in their life. They figured between the college dive bars, the frat like experiences of the Upper East Side bars, and the weddings that were starting to roll out for friends and family, they had to have danced in circles and screamed these lyrics with all their might hundreds of times. Evie, Maura, Kelly, and Amanda had decreed this song off limits for dancing about a year ago when it came on while they were at the Bubble Lounge in Tribeca. They found themselves watching with something akin to distaste as group after group of girls in their early to mid twenties screamed at their friends and then paraded to the dance floor when the song came on and began this girl bonding ritual.

Amanda was the first to say out loud what they all were thinking. "Anyone really care if we just sit this one out for a change?"

"Oh, thank God," Kelly sighed. "I don't know why, but this song is starting to really piss me off. I wonder if I ever even liked it in the first place."

Evie looked into the crowd that was now predominantly women. "I don't begrudge them this moment, but I agree. I think I'm over it, too."

"How about this then?" Maura asked while holding her champagne flute aloft. "This is a song we leave to the younger generations, who have no real idea just how exhausting it can be to "survive" and from this moment forward, we will no longer join them on the dance floor. And it's not that we don't believe in the solidarity this song creates amongst women...we're just tired of the tune."

"This may be so ballsy of me," Amanda said, looking from one friend to the next nervously, "but as long as we're drawing a line in the sand over one song, I'd like to throw in another for your consideration for a dancing ban." She took a deep breath and dove right in. "I don't think I can pump my fist in the air and yell, "Ba, Ba, and Ba" to *Sweet Caroline* ever again, either."

"I will second that in a heartbeat, roomie."

"This may turn out to be one of the greatest nights out ever, considering the revolutionary ideas that are just pouring out from our group," mused Maura.

"Better then the night you met Ray Newell out at the Hampton's and had what you refer to as the most romantic night and passionate sex ever?" Kelly teased.

"Considering he turned out to be one of those exhausting survivor moments from my life, I'd say yes. However," Maura added with a twinkle in her eye, "maybe the actual night of great sex on the beach might beat out tonight's listing of songs we're blackballing for the dance floor by a smidge."

"I can't believe that someone who would have sex on a public beach uses the word smidge, but that's just me," laughed Evie.

And that was how Evie explained her abrupt departure from the dance floor to Nate, after he found himself standing alone, talking to air, when the first strains of that song wafted over the dance floor.

"I get that after a certain number of years a song would lose its appeal and you'd no longer care to dance to it," he joked with Evie as they stood by the impromptu bar that had been set up close to the dance floor, watching the girls in their mid-twenties grab hold of each other's hands and dance in a circle. "I myself am all for giving the toss to any Kylie Minogue song that gets played, but I don't think she gets the air time needed in America to warrant adding her to your list. I'm just saying that you might want to clue the person next to you in regarding your dance embargo...on the off chance they didn't get the memo. I have a feeling I was looking like a bit of a prat out there on the dance floor. At least that's what I could gather by the way a few of my friends were snickering at me from the sidelines. It might be a useful tool for me to have you jot down anything else along these lines that I might need to know about you before you move in."

"I really love green eyes," Evie blurted out in a semi-drunken manner before realizing she had actually spoken out loud. Her eyes widened in wonder that she had given voice to her thoughts and she mentally berated herself over it. She bit her lower lip and tried to come up with some plausible rationale for that "sneak peek" into her subconscious. "Along with pizza, which you already knew, the color blue in general, my Seven for all Humanity jeans, and all the Harry Potter books. Does that give you enough input about me that you'll let me unpack my stuff?"

"I have a feeling that's only going to be the beginning of what I learn about you."

It was close to two in the morning before the last of the party stragglers finally relinquished the dance floor to the poor souls who were trying to collect it for the party supply company.

Grace and Evelyn had found a quiet corner on the patio and were talking softly, letting the memories from the evening wash over them, and laughed over some shared moments.

"I told you Dad was going to do the Macarena, Evelyn. The man cannot resist that song."

"You were right. I don't know why I bet against you on that. *Every* time he does it. And I think he was the one who requested it."

"I'm not surprised. So," she said, changing course very quickly, "your new roommate seems like he's going to be very nice. Kinda', sorta' somewhat good looking, too. In case you didn't notice."

"It did not escape my attention that he resembles a certain Daniel Craig, only with green eyes. I thought British people were supposed to have bad teeth. All I could see was a dazzling array of pearly whites."

"And his green eyes."

"Oh my God, Grace, I told him I totally love green eyes."

"Christ on the cross, as Grandma used to say, you did not!" Grace exclaimed. "Why?"

"Aside from the obvious answer that I do love green eyes, I did my old party trick of just blurting out whatever comes to the forefront of my mind at the exact moment that I think it. But I totally covered myself by throwing out a couple of other things I love, like pizza and Harry Potter books."

"You do realize that starting with that last sentence you are completely interchangeable with Annie. This could be a conversation I'd have with her any day of the week. It's both disturbing and comforting at the same time."

"I'm just going to blame it on jet lag and too much alcohol. Chances are he won't even remember I said it anyway. It was late, drinks were drunk..." Evie's voice trailed off in contemplation. "Besides, this was a guy who declared his love for Abba way before I mentioned how much I liked green eyes. Seriously, which of the two of us should be more embarrassed?"

"You do have a point there," Grace agreed with half closed eyes. "I never thought I'd make it as long as I did tonight. Not too bad for an old lady, huh?"

"Who are you calling an old lady?" Jack asked, coming up from behind his wife and rubbing her shoulders as he stood in back of her chair.

"Hey, I was just about to look for you. I don't think I could keep my eyes open for another minute so I was just about to head in and check the kids before surrendering to sleep. Are you staying up?"

"Nah, I'm beat, too. I'll go with you to poke our heads into their rooms and go to bed with you. Good night, Evie. See you in the morning."

Evie said goodnight to her sister and brother in law and overheard Jack murmur suggestively into Grace's ear, "Hopefully you can keep your eyes open for possibly just one extra minute," and they both laughed.

Evie watched the men and women from the caterer, party supply, and tent rental companies stacking up tables, linens, chairs, and even the parquet dance floor in what seemed like record time. She must've closed her eyes while watching their dance, because the next thing she knew a young man of about twenty years of age, with shocking red hair, and an Irish brogue, was cautiously tapping her elbow saying, "Excuse me, miss, but we'll be needing the chair you're sitting on. It's one of the ones that we've got to take with us."

"Oh my goodness, I'm so sorry. Let me get up. I obviously should get some sleep now, shouldn't I?"

"I'd imagine it wouldn't be the worst idea you've ever had," he laughed easily with her as she got up and he claimed her seat. "That's grand now, thanks so much," and he continued to stack up the remaining chairs in her vicinity.

She waved goodnight to her parents, who were still up talking to some of the Futterly relatives and headed up to her room, to sleep a dreamless sleep.

Thirteen

S he awoke earlier than she would've personally chosen, to the sound of Annie and Archie running down the hall towards freedom...otherwise known to anyone else as the backyard. She was surprised to find she couldn't fall back asleep, and even more surprised to find her head didn't hurt as much as she was anticipating. She recalled telling Nate how much she loved green eyes and assumed such a statement could only have been uttered under the extreme duress of severe drunkenness. As she felt perfectly fine she decided, a bit ruefully, that either her tolerance was going up, or she couldn't blame her loose lips on too much alcohol. She didn't relish either option and tried not to think about it.

She realized she was quite ravenous and wondered what she could get for breakfast. She tiptoed downstairs towards the kitchen, to be greeted by a woman with the bronzed face of someone who spends much time outdoors and a starched white apron. She turned away from the stove when she heard Evie's footsteps fall in the room.

"Ach, and you must be one of Michael's lovely sisters. So happy t' meet you. Why don't you have a seat and I'll prepare you an omelet. What would you like in it?"

"Um, would you have tomatoes and cheese handy?" Evie asked, not quite prepared to be meeting Cook in the flesh.

"Sure thing, love, just sit down and I'll whip it right up for you."

When Cook brought over her plate with a heaping omelet, home fries, and toast with some homemade jam seeping over the sides, Evie wanted to cry from happiness. "You should know I don't think I'll ever eat as well as I have for the past two days here. Your cooking is beyond description. This is wonderful." Although it came out sounding more like "wonerfl" as her mouth was stuffed with omelet. "Sorry for talking with my mouth full like that, but I couldn't wait another moment to try this," Evie apologized.

"Glad you're enjoying it. It's a treat to cook for someone who isn't watching what they eat all the time. Now eat up and just let me know if you care for anything else, sweetheart."

Evelyn felt genuine affection for Cook as she turned away from her and continued to stir whatever was on the stove. Then she cocked her eyes skyward as she had another thought. Did Cook just call her fat? She realized she didn't care as the gooey cheese and fresh tomatoes mingled in her mouth for a moment until she swallowed.

One by one family members, mostly still in pajamas, came into the kitchen, all bleary eyed, to be greeted by Cook, who began cooking any request that was thrown at her. She was in her glory, obviously.

"I just love cooking for large numbers. It keeps me in grand cooking form," she laughed at everyone sitting at the table.

"Is it possible to kidnap her and stuff her in our luggage," Jack asked Grace, not at all joking.

"How heavenly would that be? I bet she could even get the kids to eat their veggies with some of her magical Nanny McPhee'ishness," Grace agreed.

Right after breakfast, the whole crew lumbered back to their bedrooms to pack up their belongings to begin the trek back to real life; one without a cook and butler at their beck and call. For everyone aside from Evie, that meant onward to Heathrow and back to the States, until they returned for the wedding. It had been decided that Evie would drive back to the city with Charlotte, and Michael would bring the rest of his family to the airport. Then he would take Evie over to Nate's that evening, after he, Charlotte, and Evelyn had had dinner back in London that night.

Tom Dunleavy pulled his youngest daughter aside before jumping in the van, and gave her yet another envelope full of Euros. "Don't say a word; I want you to have this for your time here. It's so nice of you to uproot your life for a couple of months to get to know Charlotte a little better, and spend this time with Michael, as well. I know it means a lot to him, and you should know how delighted your mother and I are that you were willing to do this. You're a great sister and daughter and you make us very proud, sweetie."

Evie was more then just a little surprised to see her Dad's eyes misting a bit as he spoke, and figured a bit of humor wouldn't be remiss, if only so she could see him laugh before he boarded the van. "God, Dad, if I had known you and Mom would've supported me during a European jaunt I would've done this years ago." It did the trick and she watched her Dad start to laugh deeply as he climbed in beside Rebecca. Then everyone was waving goodbye and there were the shouts between the two families of, "See you at the wedding, see you in a couple of months, safe trip," that you'd expect to hear out the lowered windows.

Evie realized she was all alone with the Futterly's then. Peter asked her if she had any idea as to what she'd want to visit while she was in London. She realized she hadn't planned anything too specific. All the guidebooks she had purchased before she left hadn't been opened at all. She admitted this with a slight blush. He laughed and said, "That's what we're here for...you won't need those guidebooks. We can let you know what to hit and what to avoid."

"And Michael and I will take you wherever you have some interest in going to whenever we can. We should probably come up with some sort of list for places you might like."

"Like the Tate Modern and Tate Britain," Liza added. "And of course, Westminster Abbey and Buckingham Palace."

"And Portobello Road Market," was Emily's contribution. "Great shopping," she added unnecessarily. "Along with the Knightsbridge shopping area, where you can go to places like Harrods and Harvey Nichols. The prices might be out of your range, but you could always window shop." Evie wondered why she had to ruin a perfectly good suggestion with a bitchy afterward.

"Of course, there are all those beautiful parks you can wander around in for days," said Peter. "St. James Park, Kew Gardens, Regents Park with the London Zoo."

"It sounds like I won't have too much time to miss my family and friends back home," Evie said. "Let alone get any writing done."

"Well, I promise we won't overwhelm you during your first couple of days. We'll let you get your bearings at Nate's place and let you try to catch up on your sleep. I can't imagine you got very much during your first couple of days here. It's probably going to sneak up on you at once and you'll find you won't want to move off the couch, let alone tour all of London," Charlotte wisely guessed. "Anyway, we should probably load up the car and start to head back to the City, so we have time to rest up a little before heading out to dinner with your brother. We're only going to be going to this quiet little Italian place we frequent by our flat. Think red and white gingham tablecloths and wine bottles with melted hot wax down their sides from the candles that they hold. And then picture Cook, making Italian food in their kitchen and you get a sense of the heaven that awaits us for dinner."

The two women were on the road a short time later. Evie promised Peter she would try to find some time to come back and visit the manor when the hustle and bustle of the city got to be too much for her. She had to bite her tongue not to remind him she lived in New York City, and she had no doubt she could hold her own with whatever kind of chaos London had to offer. She was looking forward to hearing more than one automobile every thirty minutes, frankly.

Fourteen

C harlotte nudged Evie awake as they approached Michael and Charlotte's flat. "We're just about here, Evie," she whispered, hesitant to wake someone up who looked so peaceful. Evie, for her part, wiped the line of drool away that had begun to pool at the corner of her mouth, as she started awake. It's funny how peaceful one can look with their mouth agape and spit drifting out of it.

"I'm so sorry for falling asleep on you like that. Just call me rude, I guess."

"Don't worry about it. For a change I was able to be in full control of the radio station, so I was happy. Your brother has this insatiable need to always find a sports radio station, and I'm always scanning for the likes of Amy Winehouse and Robbie Williams."

"Are they my Britney Spears and Justin Timberlake?"

Charlotte looked a bit shocked at Evie's comment. "Not even close, my dear. At least if you're talking in terms of relationships. Although, personally, Britney and Amy are kind of kindred spirits, now that I think about it. Do you really not know who Amy Winehouse is? She's kind of famous. Even in New York City. Big time tabloid fodder."

Evie just shook her head. "This is something that would embarrass Grace, isn't it? Promise me you won't tell her," she pleaded.

"I'm sorry, but there's no way I can promise that," Charlotte said as she parked in front of a two story building that reminded Evie somewhat of the brownstones she'd seen in Park Slope, Brooklyn, the few times she had visited an old college friend who had moved there. There was even the same kind of black, wrought iron gates separating each home from the next. Charlotte and Michael's place had a tiny strip of green grass that lay next to the concrete path leading to the door. On that door was the biggest claddagh knocker Evelyn had ever seen. If Evie thought the Irish symbol for love, loyalty, and friendship (usually seen on rings like the kind her and Grace always wore), was an odd choice for a door knocker outside of London, she didn't say. Charlotte noticed Evie take the brass knocker in, and shrugged her shoulders. "It truly is the bane of my existence. But your brother insists. I think it makes him feel like a dangerous IRA operative or something. He claims that he's just being proud of his heritage, but I think he really just likes to piss off the Fed Ex guy. The trade off was that I got to decorate our bedroom however I chose, and he now sleeps under a very flowered duvet. I think in the end I got the better deal."

They walked inside and headed straight for the kitchen, where Michael was just getting off the phone with someone. He gave Charlotte a long kiss and ruffled Evie's already disheveled hair. "Good news, guys. Nate's going to join us for dinner over at Flora's tonight. He said he couldn't bear the thought of anything but Italian to try to cure his hangover."

"That's weird," Charlotte whispered to Evie with a wink. "You're not Italian."

Evie cursed herself and wondered at what point during last night's festivities had she let her little crush become evident to Charlotte. Luckily, she thought, Charlotte was the only sober person in attendance, so she was fairly certain no one else was thinking the same thoughts.

"I guess Evie and I should at least wash our faces and change before heading out. Evie, do you need Michael to help you bring in any of your bags from the car? Will you actually be able to find what you need from all the luggage you're traveling with? You know, if it's easier for you, you're welcome to raid my closet and use any of my pre-pregnancy clothes for tonight. Save you the hassle of sifting through all your bags to find one particular shirt."

Evelyn hesitated for a moment trying to decide. Packing was never her strong suit and she knew she had just thrown articles of clothing into bags as she came upon them. She was as likely to find something suitable to wear in the first bag she opened as she was to find a guy with low cholesterol at the Wing Bowl. It just wasn't going to happen.

"If you're sure you're alright with my borrowing something, it would probably end up being quicker in the long run. I'm not too sure what I have in those bags; let alone which bag they'd be in. Do I need to get very dressy or can I wear my jeans with a clean top of yours?"

"Definitely jeans. Come on up with me and you can pick whatever you want. Michael, we'll be down in a couple of minutes."

If Evie thought Charlotte was going to say something else about Nate she was wrong. *I now know that the girl can be discreet, so that's good*, she thought to herself. Charlotte heralded her into a walk-in closet pretty much the size of Evelyn's entire bedroom and pointed to one side. "Grab whatever you like."

Evie gasped at the enormity of that project. "Maybe it would be quicker going through my luggage. I have sensory overload with all these choices." She lowered her voice to a stage whisper. "Are you a shopaholic?" she joked.

"I can't deny it...it's a vice. But right now, it's my only one, so I'm feeling less guilty about it these days. Here, why don't you try this blue shirt on? It'll look great with your eyes."

Evie glanced at the sapphire blue silk tunic with bell sleeves. "This is like having my very own personal shopper. I'm feeling very Cameron Diaz right now. I could get used to this," she giggled.

"See, I was right," Charlotte proudly announced when Evie returned from the bathroom with the shirt on her body and make up freshened up. "It's the perfect color for you. And it fits perfectly. You know, I actually think I had this on the first time we met. At Newark airport? How awful was my eye dilemma that day?"

Evie, having no idea what Charlotte was talking about, just squinted at her in confusion.

Charlotte stared at her for a moment, then closed her eyes and sighed. "Please tell me your brother explained why I had been talking to him and not you when you first approached us!"

"I, I still don't really know what you're talking about," Evie stammered.

"Oh, for crying out loud I'm marrying a moron. I had just had laser eye surgery, literally the day before the flight, and unfortunately I was one of those people who had blurry eyesight for a couple of days after the procedure. The dry cabin air was making things worse, and I had just put eye drops in. Between the drops and the fuzzy eyesight I had never realized you were right there when I started to ask your brother questions about you. And he never clued me in that you had been standing there and heard me until we were on the next leg of our journey. He promised he was going to apologize for me and explain that I wasn't normally that rude."

"I'll be honest, that does explain a lot of unanswered questions I had from that day. I am relieved to hear this had nothing to do with the fact I probably looked like a mad woman, trudging around the airport with multiple bags of Jax."

"Well, since your brother never got around to it, please accept my deepest apologies if I looked like a raging bitch that day."

"You've more than made up for it by letting me go shopping in your closest. Thanks again for letting me borrow this top. I love your outfit, by the way." Charlotte had changed into a cream shirt with a cute black bow that rested where the baby bump would be expected. Charlotte's belly was so small, though, it looked like a normal person's who might have overindulged and ate half a pizza with a gallon of ice cream right afterward. It made Evie grateful that the soft material of her borrowed shirt draped loosely, rather than clung to her middle.

Charlotte called from the top of the steps down to her fiancé. "Michael, we're heading down now...and in record time, I might add."

"I'm impressed," he answered. "I didn't even have time to watch all of *Sports Center*. Your timing has vastly improved."

"So how far is this place?" Evelyn wondered. Do we walk or drive?"

"Oh, definitely walk," was Michael's quick response. It's not that far and this is going to be one of those meals where you'll wish you had worn elastic pants. The walk home helps with the digestion. Nate will drive over here after we all have dinner and we'll switch your bags into his car. You ladies ready?" he asked, holding the door open for Charlotte and Evelyn.

"Michael, your manners have greatly improved since you've become an ex-pat. You know, Charlotte, this is the same guy who would not only *not* hold a door open for you, but relished being able to shut one in your face. You've obviously been working hard over here and you should know it hasn't gone unnoticed."

"It's not like I was some puppy who needed training," Michael sputtered in annoyance.

"Really?" the two women said in unison.

"Putting the two of you together might possibly be one of my worst ideas ever. What the hell was I thinking?"

———

When they walked into Flora's that night, Evie could see immediately why this was one of Michael and Charlotte's favorite haunts. The air was heavy with garlic and spices and she breathed in deeply to savor the delicious smells that tantalized her now growling stomach. When she opened her eyes—they had closed involuntarily when she had inhaled—she saw that Charlotte had been spot on in her earlier description. The red and white gingham tablecloths were littered with raffia covered wine bottles with tapered candles leaving a trail of hot wax down the side. There was a mural on the back wall with a pastoral scene of a place that Evie could only guess was somewhere in Italy, never having been. The wait staff wore simple black trousers and red and white striped boat neck shirts. She looked around, half expecting a canal and a gondola to sprout up and begin snaking around the tables, everything felt so authentic.

"This is so *Lady and the Tramp*. I love it!" she exclaimed joyously.

"Maybe we can share a plate of spaghetti and meatballs," a voice spoke quietly in her ear.

She turned quickly to see that Nate had arrived as well and was standing beside her. "I suppose if you promise not to nudge the last meatball towards me with your nose, I might consider it. It was cute with the dogs, but there might be some hygiene issues with it, among people," she countered.

Michael and Charlotte realized the last person in their party had arrived and let the maitre d' know they were ready to be seated.

They all hungrily turned their attention to the menu, and Charlotte glumly announced that everything looked delicious and she was never going to be able to decide.

"You say that every time we come here," Michael reminded her. "And then you always get the chicken parm with a side salad."

"Maybe tonight is the night I'll throw the world off kilter and order something different."

"What are you going to get, Charlotte?" Michael asked.

"Chicken parm and a side salad," she answered good-naturedly.

They each decided on a different entrée and ordered an antipasto and fried calamari dish as appetizers for the table. Two huge platters of food were placed before them in no time, to go with the bottle of merlot that was already half empty.

"Wow, that's a lot of food," Evie said, a bit in awe of the size of the appetizers.

"That which does not kill us, makes us stronger," Michael duly recited.

"I think you were right about the elastic pants," Evie agreed as she piled a little bit of both dishes onto her plate.

They did good work on both plates, leaving just some stray pieces of salami and cheese on the antipasto platter, and a few neglected rings of calamari on the other.

When their waiter cleared the table and put their entrees down a short time later, Evie could only stare at her plate, in sort of a bewildered state. "I almost forgot we still had our entrees to go," she said, looking at her glazed Chilean sea bass. She took a deep breath, like she was preparing for some kind of unpleasant task. "I'm going to muscle through this, though."

"That's the spirit," Nate said encouragingly, as he began to make short work of his veal chop.

The four of them continued to eat, but their pace had slowed down dramatically from the onset of their starter course. The wine had been polished off and they had all switched over to Cokes and bottled waters. The conversation never lulled and Evie was surprised to realize she had finished her dinner, the plates had been taken out from under her, and dessert menus were being handed out. No one felt like dessert after all the food they had just consumed, but all opted for some coffee.

"So, Nate, when you go out and order a coffee, are you a big critic?" Evie wondered. "I imagine you've got some experience in the field, as owner of your own coffee shop."

"Nah, I just enjoy it. Especially if the company is as stellar as it is tonight," he added as he looked around, but his eyes lingered on Evie's longer than anyone else's. Or so she thought.

She felt slightly giddy and tried to reign in what she could only imagine was her goofy grin, but her lips had obviously decided not to pay any attention to what her mind was saying. They kept going and going, curving upwards the whole time. What she had no way of knowing was that as goofy as she imagined she looked, Nate found himself unable to take his eyes off her smile and thought she was positively radiant. And what neither of them realized was that Charlotte was watching both of them with a small smile playing around on her own face. Michael just asked his sister to pass the milk and sugar.

Fifteen

E vie had some serious problems staying awake for the fifteen minute car ride from her brother's place to her new, temporary housing at Nate's.

"I am so sorry," she said, as her head gave one of those embarrassing, jerky starts that tend to happen as you doze off. "If it makes you feel any better, you are not the first person who I fell asleep on today. Poor Charlotte had to spend most of the ride back from her parents' place with, what I can only assume was a snoring sidekick riding shotgun."

"No worries," Nate responded easily. "It was bound to happen sooner or later. You guys had pretty much been going non-stop all weekend. Jet lag eventually gets you. But look...we're pulling up to my place now. Your bed is just a moment away."

The two of them walked up to Nate's apartment, each laden down with Evie's luggage.

"I'll give you the grand tour tomorrow, all five minutes of it, when you've had a chance to get some sleep. Right now I'll show you to your room and let you have at it."

"You have no idea how fabulous that sounds to me right now. Thank you so much. And thanks again for letting me stay with you. I hope you don't regret your hospitality. I promise to be the perfect houseguest. Or at least try to be. I probably shouldn't set the bar too high in the beginning with extreme qualifiers like 'the perfect houseguest.' That's just a set-up for failure."

Nate laughed at Evie's endearing babbling. "I don't expect perfection. What if we just aimed for engaging conversation every once in a while? Is the bar low enough with that?"

"I think that places things at a manageable level of expectation."

"Alright, then, if you just follow me, I'll show you where your room is." The two of them headed up the stairs and Nate pointed at the room closest to the staircase. That's the other spare bedroom that you can offer your friends when they visit. Down the hall a little is the room I've got you set up in. I hope it's okay. The bathroom's across the hall." He gave a quick point with his elbow, since both his hands were still full with Evie's luggage. He set her bags down next to a walk-in closet. It was no where near the size of the one in the master bedroom at Michael and Charlotte's place, but still had more storage space than Evie had ever had in Manhattan. She smiled. He smiled back and said, "Good night, Evie. I'll be gone early tomorrow morning, but feel free to laze around all day and try to catch up on your sleep. Were you planning on doing anything special tomorrow that you need any information about, or were you just going to take it easy?"

"Definitely plan B. I hope that doesn't stick me with a lazy label, but it's going to feel heavenly not to have anything to do or get ready for. I'm going to enjoy it."

"Alright, then. I should be home by around three o'clock or so, so if you manage to get up by then, I can give you a walking tour of the neighborhood, so you can get your bearings. Help yourself to anything in the fridge, also. See you tomorrow."

"Thanks. See you tomorrow," said Evie who was already looking in her bags for a pair of pajamas to jump into.

She barely managed to get into them before jumping into bed and falling instantaneously to sleep.

Sixteen

E vie's eyes fluttered awake and she looked in wonder at the clock hanging on the wall opposite the bed in wonder. Could it really be twelve-thirty in the afternoon? She couldn't believe it, but she was still kind of lethargic and just stayed in bed, cataloging her surroundings, instead of jumping right up. *I'm not lazy* she thought to herself, *I'm just getting a lay of the land.* And the lay of the land was as follows: one dresser and one nightstand next to the bed. Both in the same rich mahogany color the bed was made of, and one red tartan comforter covering the queen size bed with a matching valance on the window. There was a red throw rug next to the bed and even a faded red bookcase, completely full with books and magazines, their spines sticking out towards her. It was cozy, yet still masculine. And most importantly, clean. Really, quite a bit more than she was expecting for the guestroom of a bachelor.

It was after one o'clock before she wandered downstairs in the direction that she hoped the kitchen was in. She probably could've remained in bed even longer, except for the fact her stomach was protesting her slovenly ways and was now demanding to be fed. She scolded her stomach severely. After everything you were given last night, you are really greedy.

The kitchen was very modern, with black granite counter tops that gleamed, and stainless steel appliances littering the space. A very fancy looking (read: difficult looking) coffeemaker was one of the lone items on the counter. A green ceramic bowl that was filled with apples and oranges was another. Lastly, there was a note with Evie's name that caught her attention:

Evie,
Coffee machine is all set. Just hit the on button and it will start up for you. (Fair warning, I can't help it, I make my coffee strong. Sorry if it's not to your taste.) Some cereal in the cabinets, although lunch meat is in the fridge if it's closer to your midday meal when you get out of bed. See you this afternoon.
Cheers,
Nate

She hit the on button for the coffeemaker as instructed and opened the refrigerator to get to work making herself a turkey sandwich. She set her plate on the granite island and grabbed a coffee mug to pour herself a cup. After adding milk and sugar, she sat down with her sandwich and dug in. She took a sip of coffee and sputtered a bit, spraying a small amount of the beverage on her sandwich plate.

Holy crap, she thought, *he wasn't kidding about the strong coffee.* She poured more milk in to try to dilute it. *This can't be good for business if this is how he makes his coffee there,* was her next thought. Another sip and she just changed her mind completely and poured herself a glass of milk instead.

After she ate she looked around the other rooms downstairs. In addition to the kitchen, there was a small bathroom on this floor and a den. The den was outfitted in a brown leather sofa and matching oversized chair and ottoman, with the expected flat screen television, natch. Without actually taking out a ruler, Evie guessed it had to be at least forty-eight inches. She was also fairly sure that it would be plasma or high def or both. *Could it be both?* she wondered. She herself had no idea what any of that meant. They were just terms that her Dad and brother both got very excited about and she figured it was a typical status symbol for the male species. The way some girls, like her sister, Grace, might get excited about a Prada bag or a pair of Manolo's. Again, things she didn't know much about herself.

Seventeen

E vie had been staying at Nate's place for a week when he finally asked her the big question. Well, not *the* big question, but *a* big question. "So. Do you want to head over to the coffee shop tomorrow and see where all the magic happens?" It would mean you'd have to get up ridiculously early, but you'd get a chance to see London as it mostly sleeps. That's kind of nice. Or I could give you directions to the Tube and you could meet me there when you woke up. Your choice," he said casually.

"So I'm finally invited into the inner sanctum? This is big. I think I'll go with you in the morning if you don't mind the company. Although, company might be over-stating it somewhat. I can't imagine I'll be my usual witty self at four a.m."

"Are you witty at seven p.m.? I hadn't noticed." Nate did notice one of his large, green throw pillows being hurled at him, and managed to duck in the nick of time.

"What time should I be ready to go?" Evie asked Nate.

"I'm out of here by four-thirty at the latest," was his scary reply.

Evie glanced at the digital clock and read the time. 8:16 p.m. blinked back at her in those red Morse code dashes. "Time for bed," she declared and went upstairs to get her nighttime routine started. A quick brushing of her teeth and washing of her face that was more for show than anything else and she was off to bed.

Evie had been surprised to realize she had fallen asleep almost immediately the previous night, and less surprised to realize that rising at three forty-five is no more bearable after seven hours of sleep than it is after four. *Early is frickin' early*, she complained to herself. Her immediate thought was no shower, wear sweats. Her compromise was shower, wear sweats. And really, the only way she got to that conclusion was that Nate yelled in the general direction of her room, "Shower's open," when he left the bathroom. She had felt kind of backed into a clean corner, but realized it was just the thing to make her a little less bleary eyed as she got ready.

Nate greeted her by the front door with an affectionate smile. "You know what I could go for right now?"

"If you say, 'a big cup of coffee' I'll have to punch you in the face," was Evie's grumpy reply.

"See, you just get me."

Evie started to smile. "If you follow that up with 'You had me at hello' I'll also have to punch you in the face."

"It's like you can read my mind. Amazing." Nate jiggled his car keys and asked if she needed anything else before they headed out. Evie grabbed her tote bag that had her computer, some books, and her wallet and held it aloft.

"Take me, I'm yours."

"Now that is more like it," Nate responded with a wicked gleam in his eye, and they headed to the car.

Evie loved the fact Nate drove a Volvo. She always thought it was such a great family car and blushed at the implication that this could involve her in any way. What he drove was really none of her business. *Note to self*, she thought: *Never blurt out that she loves the fact he drives a family car!*

The drive to the City didn't take as long as Evie's previous trips. When she mentioned that to Nate, he was matter of fact. "Well, we are on the early side of even the earliest commuters. That shaves at least fifteen minutes of drive time, easily."

Evie watched the buildings go by in a blur, her window down, the darkness broken up by the building and street lights. "You know, it doesn't matter where the city is, there's just something about being a witness to this time, before all the hustle and bustle brings it alive, that I love. Lights twinkling, dew glistening, walks of shame occurring." That one was added as Evie watched a girl in a halter top, jeans, and high heels try to maneuver her way over a set of cobblestones. "Probably has something to do with the fact that it's not something I'm used to, since I am rarely out at this time of the morning. It has an aura of mystique for me."

"I don't know about that. I don't know if you ever get used to seeing a city that's usually so alive, so, I don't know...peaceful, I guess I'd say," Nate answered. "I love it every time. It never loses its power for me. It's a time of great potential, I think. Anything could happen today."

Evie realized he was being quite serious, so in her most un-flippant tone told him, "You are an extreme optimist. What a lovely way to live your life." He looked at her strangely after she had said it, but didn't respond.

"Well, here we are," Nate exclaimed robustly, and swung his arms out for effect.

"Could you hold off on the grand arm gestures until the car is in park, perhaps?"

Nate threw the car in park and swung his arms around once again. "Well, here we are."

"Much better, thanks."

Evie stood up after unfolding herself from the car and glanced at the storefront. The lettering on the window was done in black and green, and read, "The Olde Grind" and had a green circle with a coffee bean inside it directly under the writing.

"Hey, I like the name of your store. I hadn't thought to ask before. Cute." Evie called over to Nate, who was using a vast number of keys to open what was obviously a vast number of locks.

"Oh, thanks. I was going to call it "Ye Olde Grind" but changed it at the last minute."

Evie pondered that for a moment, with her head tilted to the side. "You made the right call. I think the combination of the word "ye" with old spelt with an e at the end would make it too "town crier-y." This name speaks of charm and class. The other one says crazy guy who likes Renaissance Fairs too much."

"So now you're anti-Turkey leg? Who are you?"

"You know what I mean," Evie said rolling her eyes.

Nate finished unlocking his very own Fort Knox and ushered her inside. Evie was truly impressed.

"Nate, this is gorgeous. It's so homey and comfortable. Yet you look at those huge machines behind the counter and think clean and modern. You've managed to combine the best of both worlds," she said in awe as she took in her surroundings.

All fifteen or so tables were the same honey colored wood, but each table was different. Different sizes, different nicks on them, different chairs surrounded them, but they all went together somehow. A huge, distressed hutch in a sage green color held all sorts of crockery, just not entire matched sets. An old chandelier glowed brightly when Nate pulled a switch and lent the room an ethereal quality. The till, which was made of polished copper, had an air of old time charm, but quickly whirred to life when Nate touched a button on the side. Then there were the machines! Evie stared with delight at the five huge machines set up along a marble counter at varying heights, in the same polished copper of the cash register. Nate set about turning everything on, prepping the milk, grabbing all sorts of bowls containing spices like cinnamon and nutmeg and setting up the flavored syrups so they could be on display for all to see.

"No wonder you get up early," she said seriously. "It's truly fabulous."

"Thanks," Nate said sincerely. "Now why don't you pick out a table and get yourself set up for some interesting people watching. You may even come up with some possible characters for a novel if you pay close attention. What do you want by the way? It's all on the house."

"I don't want to put you to any trouble," Evie demurred.

"Evie, what kind of trouble could it be? It's a coffee-house for crying out loud. Now what can I get you?"

"Well, could I have a mochachino then? With extra whipped cream? I mean, only if it's really not any trouble," she added quickly, noticing Nate's amused smile.

"Yeah, you're low maintenance alright."

An absolutely glorious concoction arrived under her nose moments later, and she breathed in the smell of the homemade whipped cream. A taste of her drink a moment later confirmed her suspicions. She found herself very much able to fall in love with a man who could make her a delicious mochachino. *I am so easy*, she thought to herself, laughing a little.

Had Evie looked up at that moment she would have caught Nate staring quite openly at her, truly transfixed by her and unable to figure out why exactly. Her hair had been pulled into a low ponytail and he could smell the flowery scent of her shampoo from where he stood behind the counter. She was dressed in sweats that were indisputably too large for her slender frame, and she actually had a bit of whipped cream on the edge of her nose and didn't realize it. He watched as she laughed a little to herself and found himself staring into her huge blue eyes when she raised them up to thank him for the drink. He looked away, a little embarrassed to be caught staring like that, and started to fiddle around with the closest thing in his vicinity, which was the milk steamer. A near miss shortly thereafter by some misdirected steam and he figured he was ready to turn around and meet Evie's eyes again. It was either that or end up scalding himself.

The news agent had already left a pile of newspapers outside the door, and Evie had gotten up to retrieve them for him. "So where do you typically put these?" she had asked from behind a large stack of paper with half her head poking out. He had motioned with a slight tilt of his head to the small square table next to the entrance and couldn't help but think to himself she was unlike anyone he had ever met. Yes, she was certainly pretty, and he had been finding excuses to come into the common rooms of his flat anytime she was around so he could stare at her—in what was hopefully not a creepy, stalker kind of way—but there was more to it than that. She was also one of the funniest people he had ever had the pleasure of conversing with, but she was kind, too. As clichéd as it sounded, and even he had the good grace to be embarrassed by this thought, even though it *was* in his own inner monologue; she smiled with her eyes. There was just something about her eyes he decided.

Evie spent the next couple of hours trying to stay out of the way of Nate and Hannah as they poured coffees, both hot and cold, and doled out all sorts of breakfast cakes to the early morning commuters. They had developed a well choreographed precision behind the counter and Evie found that she was mesmerized by the way they slid around one another without coming close to damaging anyone or anything. And Evie also found out first hand why Nate had spoken so glowingly of Hannah when they first met. For starters, she called Evie a "pretty poppet," so it wasn't like it was a hard sell after that auspicious beginning.

"So, you're the pretty poppet who's been staying at Nate's all week that I've been hearing so much about. Your description did not do her justice, young man," she chided Nate as she gave Evie a big welcoming hug. Evie hugged back, delighting in this slightly older woman's joyful nature.

"So, Hannah, I hear you have two children. Both girls, right?"

"That's right. Josie is eleven, although she's living under the delusion that she's really sixteen, and my Rose is nine. I don't know how long you plan on staying today, but they'll come by the shop on their way home from school, so you can meet them yourself if you're still here."

"I was planning on staying the whole day. If that was alright by you, Nate," she added a bit shyly.

"Of course it is. You probably should know that you might end up getting roped into helping us out during the mid-afternoon rush, but at least you've been warned."

Evie did find herself managing the till around three o'clock when the City workers found themselves in need of a caffeine pick me up and the store filled up again, but she didn't mind. She kind of loved the idea of being part of a team with Nate and Hannah, and the next hour or so flew by. Shortly after four, Hannah's two daughters strolled into the café, laughing and chatting to each other before they caught sight of Evie, sitting behind the register.

"Oh, hello," said the older of the two, obviously Josie. "You must be Mr. Corgin's friend Mum told us about, Miss Evelyn. Nice to meet you." Her younger sister, Rose, just smiled tentatively up at Evelyn.

"And you two must be Josie and Rose. I've heard quite a bit about you two from your Mom today. It's a pleasure to finally meet you both."

Rose stared at Evie for a moment. "You talk funny."

Josie looked aghast at her little sister. "Rose, wait until Mum hears what you said. That's quite rude."

Evelyn just laughed. "No, it's alright. She's right." She whispered conspiratorially to the two young girls. "I have what is known throughout the world as a New York accent. And I was starting to get nervous I had lost it, because no one has mentioned it to me in quite a while. So thank you so much, Rose, for letting me know it was still there." She winked quickly at the solemn little girl, who rewarded her with a giant smile back, complete with a gap where her front right tooth should have been. "Quite alright, Miss Evelyn. I'm glad I was able to help you."

"There are my two little sweethearts," Hannah said, as she stepped out of the kitchen and caught sight of her daughters. "Have you been minding your manners with Miss Evelyn?" she asked brightly.

"They have been keeping me company and making me laugh since they arrived," Evie answered for them.

"Fabulous. Now girls, grab a seat and work on your homework while I finish up with some cleaning and prep work for tomorrow. We'll be out of here in the next twenty minutes or so."

When they left the shop at around four-thirty, there were plenty of hugs being doled out and hearty waves at the window as they walked away.

"Well, you certainly seemed to have made quite the impression on the Clayton women today. Hannah was singing your praises all day, and I don't think I've ever seen little Rose take to a stranger so quickly," Nate told her when they had vanished from sight.

"Oh, well, she reminded me of a slightly quieter version of my niece, Annie," she replied.

"Well done, anyway. It took about three weeks for me to even get a hello from her," Nate said.

"Well, of course," Evie answered quickly, before she realized what she was saying. "All little girls that age would be hard pressed to chat up a handsome older man."

Nate allowed himself a slight smile before asking, "So, you would classify me as handsome, then?"

"Why is it you couldn't just hear the word older?" was Evie's quick reply, followed up by an even quicker duck as a tea towel came hurtling towards her.

They spent the rest of their time cleaning and putting away dishes and coffee mugs, clearing off counters, and making the equipment gleam again. By six o'clock that evening, Nate was hanging up the CLOSED sign on the door, and switching off the machines and lights. He smiled warmly in Evelyn's direction. "I hope you had as much fun as I did today. Even if it was just work."

"Are you kidding me?" Evie gushed. "I love your shop, and Hannah...it was my favorite day here yet!"

"Yeah, mine too," Nate agreed with her. But Evie didn't know that the time frame he was referring to wasn't just the week she had been in London, but the whole time his shop had been open. "My favorite day here yet," he repeated as he locked up the store.

Eighteen

N ate and Evie were greeted by the sight of his answering machine blinking when they arrived home from The Olde Grind. Emily's voice drifted through the apartment, making Evie grimace slightly.

"Hello Evelyn, this is Emily calling. I just wanted to remind you that we're all set to go out shopping for bridesmaid dresses tomorrow. We should all meet at Charlotte and Michael's place no later then eleven o'clock. Oh," she threw out in what Evie thought sounded like an afterthought, but was probably in all likelihood the real reason for the call, since Evie and Charlotte had already touched base as to what time to arrive. "I'm not sure if Charlotte mentioned it, but we are going to quite a few upscale boutiques to look at gowns, so please don't forget to dress appropriately."

"Oh my God, she thinks I'm a fashion moron," was the only thing Evelyn could get out in her surprise over the ending of the message.

Even Nate looked surprised at this unguarded show of bitchiness on Emily's part towards Evie. The two of them just stared at each other for a moment, until Evie started to giggle at the sheer audacity of Charlotte's sister, and before long, Nate was joining in as well. They spent the next hour envisioning up the worst outfits they could think of, one of which included clown shoes, leg warmers, and genie pants a la MC Hammer.

Evie woke up early so she could shower and dress appropriately, whatever Emily meant by that, for dress shopping. She tried to figure out what Maura would wear when she didn't want to look like the frumpiest girl in the group. That, of course, made Evie giggle, because Maura was never the frumpiest girl in the group. After examining the contents of the closet, she decided she'd probably have to do some shopping for herself, after the bridesmaid dresses were picked out. Could she wear her Seven jeans again? The answer, she told herself as she put them on her body, was yes. She quickly paired them with a crisp white blouse without the slightest sign of a single stain. That in itself was a miracle and gave her hope for how the rest of the day would pan out. She dubiously double checked. *How did I manage to keep a white blouse so clean? Don't question it, Evie*, she told herself. *Just go with it.* She grabbed her oversized green leather bag, for a "splash of color" as her Mom liked to say, and threw on a pair of black loafers. She stepped back to give herself the once over in the mirror. Not bad, she thought. It's not going to win me any trendsetter awards, but nobody's going to accuse me of being a slouch.

As early as Evie thought she had risen, Nate had beaten her downstairs and offered her a cup of coffee when she came through the kitchen.

"No, thanks. I've got to get going if I'm going to be on time to Michael and Charlotte's place. Plus, I'm afraid I'll just end up spilling it all over myself simply because that's the kind of thing that happens to me. And I don't think coffee stains down the front of my white blouse were what Emily had in mind when she told me to look presentable," she quickly added, seeing the hurt look on his face. "Honestly, it has nothing to do with the fact you like your coffee strong enough to lift weights."

Even Nate had to laugh at that. "I'll tell you what...I've got to meet a potential new vendor for our scones. It's on the way to your brother's place. I'll give you a lift so you don't have to wander around on the Tube all day. I doubt being several hours late for your shopping expedition will endear you to the maid of honor any more than coffee stains will." He paused for a moment. "Funny, that's the type of thing you'd expect to piss off the bride-to-be and not her sister."

"Thanks so much. I was a bit concerned about managing the Tube all on my own. I was prepared to give it a try, though." She held up her map of the Tube, with her route already highlighted in bright pink.

"Every time I see someone carrying a highlighted subway map in New York, I feel so superior. I will never allow myself those uncharitable thoughts again. Let me just throw on some lipstick and I'll be ready to motor." Evie rolled her eyes at her choice of the word "motor." Even though she was becoming very comfortable staying here with Nate and they seemed to get along well, sometimes she would say something that sounded so ridiculous to her ears that she wanted to disappear. Wait until the girls hear that one. Evie grabbed some bright red lipstick out of her bag and started to apply it. At the last minute she fumbled her grip on it and realized with dismay that the open tube was about to connect with the front of her shirt. Before she could even react, Nate, who was walking next to her to grab his keys, caught the makeup with his left hand, never even breaking stride. She looked down at her pristine shirt. It was amazing. Not even a smudge. Of course, in making his unbelievable catch, Nate's hand had skimmed up the front of Evie's body just the slightest bit and she realized her face had turned the same shade as her lipstick. Nate noticed the red face, and smiled knowingly as he passed her back the cylinder. "I figured a smear of red down your shirt would be just as bad as coffee. You ready?" He headed out the front door before Evie could say or do anything in response. That was just as well, as her mind was a complete blank and she wouldn't have been able to come up with anything even remotely resembling a coherent sentence. Instead she looked at the lipstick in her hand and whispered to it, "You're my new favorite make-up," and followed out the front door herself.

Evie climbed in the passenger side of Nate's Volvo. *It's such a nice family car*, she thought. *I've really got to stop saying that to myself every time I get in this damn car*, was her next thought.

The twenty minute ride over to Michael and Charlotte's place went by too quickly for Evie. Not just because she enjoyed being with Nate, which was true, but because she was more than a little bit nervous at the prospect of spending the whole day with Charlotte's friends and sister. She was anticipating that Charlotte's friends would be just like her sister for some reason. She always felt a little underwhelming when she held herself up to comparison with Emily and figured the two other bridesmaids, Jacquelyn and Constance, would have the same effect on her self esteem.

It wasn't until Evie heard Nate say, "Hello? Did you even hear what I said?" did she realize he was talking to her.

"I'm sorry. Head in the clouds and all that. I didn't hear what you said. Do you mind repeating it?"

"I was just commenting on the fact you don't look too thrilled with what you've got going on today. I thought all girls loved shopping. Especially for dresses having to do with weddings. Even weddings that are not their own. Was I mistaken?"

"That's too much of a generalized sentiment. You're not taking into consideration that women are all individuals and we enjoy different things. I, in case my limited wardrobe didn't give it away sooner, am not necessarily one of those women who live to shop. It's just not my nature. My sister, Grace, though? Totally different beast. You give her a day without any kids and she's off to the races. Malls, boutiques, bodegas...it doesn't matter. As long as they accept some form of currency, she's in her glory. The phrase, 'To each his own,' has never been more truthfully applied."

"So," he looked at her thoughtfully as he asked, "What is it that you do like?"

"Me?" Evie mused for a moment on that. "I'd pretty much choose anything over shopping, but...a perfect day would include reading in bed, burgers and beers with the girls, maybe finding someone to play some tennis with. That would be a good day. And of course, a chocolate anything would find its way to me before the sun set."

"You know," Nate said quietly, "I'm a rather good tennis player. Maybe we should have a match one afternoon."

"Only if you promise not to be one of those men who say they're fine if a woman beats them, only to pout for an interminable amount of time when they lose."

"Why do you think I'll lose?"

"I've seen you play soccer. Remember? Last week? In the park?"

"We call it football over here."

"Fine then. I've seen you play football."

"They're two completely different sports."

"They're two sports."

"You, my dear, will have to eat those words shortly. When I beat you at tennis."

"I look forward to it. But remember...you can't be one of those guys."

"Well, with your attitude we're going to have to come up with some kind of wager to make it worth my while, so when I school you on how to play tennis properly there will be more than just bragging rights in it for me." He wiggled his eyebrows comically. It was then that they pulled up to Michael's flat. "I shall noodle on this while you're gone and come up with something. Probably something that will involve a home cooked meal."

"Great," Evie replied as she reached for the door handle. "It's been such a long time since I've had someone cook for me."

Evie was just about to get out of the car when Nate grabbed her hand and pulled her back in for a moment. "And don't let anyone make you think you're not good enough when you're out there shopping for bridesmaid dresses today. I'm not going to name names, but the fact is, you're better than them, and they know it. That's probably why maybe one in particular tends to act like a bitch. Consider it her defense mechanism. Remember that." He suddenly switched gears and cheerfully told her to tell her brother to call him later that afternoon so they could make plans to watch the game together the next evening. Evie left the car even more confused than if she had taken the Tube all alone.

———————

All right then, Evie thought to herself, as she rang the doorbell. *Into the viper pit we go.* Charlotte answered the door, looking radiant in a white, linen shift dress. With its A-line shape you could barely tell she was pregnant from the front, let alone the back. Strappy black and white polka dot heels completed her look and Evie immediately felt frumpy. *Only I could manage to feel like a schlub standing next to a six months pregnant woman* she chastised herself.

To Charlotte she said, "You look like you're a bride in training in your cute little white dress. I can't believe how put together you always look, regardless of how far along you get. I just know, when the time comes for me, and I'm heading into my six month of being pregnant, I will be living in sweats and oversized tees." Of course, it was that moment that Emily chose to stroll through the foyer and cast an appraising eye over Evie. "Oh, Evelyn, darling, you make it sound like that's miles away from how you normally dress."

Evie decided not the let the comment slide completely. She bestowed on Emily an enormous smile and said, "You do realize that Americans aren't fooled by the use of a term of endearment, like darling, into thinking that whatever follows it is going to be kind, right?"

Emily just raised her eyebrow and continued walking down the hallway. "Why don't you join us in the sitting room for some cocktails while we wait for Constance? Jacquelyn is already here."

Evie turned to Charlotte and asked if her brother was around. "I have a message from Nate I need to pass on first," she added.

"Sure, he's up in the nursery, putting the finishing touches on the baby's crib. Go ahead up."

"You're comfortable letting your baby sleep in something Michael is putting together? Did he ever mention the go-kart he tried to build when we were kids? Long story short, the brake fell off in his hand while we're on it, I fall off the back, and hung on for dear life while we're careening down a hill. My nickname was "Gravel Stomach" until Donny Smuthers flew over the handlebars of his bicycle three months later, lost his two front teeth and became known as "Incisor Face." True story.

Charlotte smiled serenely and just said, "Why do you think I have a handyman scheduled to pop in next week while your brother is at work? I'll be damned if I'm going to put our infant in what could be tantamount to a Pottery Barn deathtrap."

"I'm quite relieved to hear at least one of you is thinking like a parent," Evie said as she climbed up the stairs to find her brother. She hoped she could try to drag out her conversation with him a bit, in order to spend less time downstairs with Emily. Evie hated the way that girl could get under her skin so quickly with just a simple turn of her head.

Evie lingered as she passed some of the photos hung up on the wall in the hallway leading to the baby's room. They all looked professionally framed, but they had such a homey and welcoming feel to them. Charlotte and Michael, each as children, with their wide open smiles, and big innocent eyes, sharing the joy of the moment with the photographers taking their pictures. Evie couldn't believe how soon that wall would be adorned with photos of their own child. She stopped suddenly in front of a picture she hadn't seen in about twenty years. It was Evie, Grace, and Michael at ages seven, nine, and eleven, respectively. They had been at a family picnic, and as Evie stared at the photo she was reminded of how the grass had smelled, since it had just been mowed, and how there was a huge hole in the middle of the volleyball net that her Uncle Stanley always seemed to send the ball through. He kept saying it counted, and her Dad, his brother, always screamed at him that he was nuts, it had to go over. And it always ended the same way: her Uncle Stanley would say since they couldn't come to an agreement, why not just have a Do Over and her Dad would agree, muttering the whole time, "What are we in second grade? We're grown men, we don't have Do Overs." This picture, though, was a moment captured by their mother, when the three of them were unaware that anyone was paying any attention to them. They were having a watermelon pit fight and it was a fight to the death. You could actually see the seeds sticking to their arms and faces, like a life sized game of Battleship, marking each correct latitude and longitude. Evie had her mouth open as wide as humanly possible as she laughed as hard as a child could, and you could actually see the pit Michael let fly through the air, hoping to land a seed inside her mouth. Grace was reloading, shoving a huge wedge of watermelon into her mouth, her eyes wide as she realized the pit Michael had just released was going to be known as the greatest shot the world of competitive watermelon pit fighting had ever seen. Evie stood there smiling in front of the picture, forgetting why she had come upstairs in the first place, and found herself startled when Michael came out of the nursery.

"Oh, hey Evie. I didn't know you were up here. What's going on?"

"When did you get this picture?" she asked.

"Oh, God, I've always had that one. Mom gave it to me years ago because she knew it was one of my favorites. Charlotte found it in a box and framed it for me, though. Do you remember that reunion?"

"If you're asking if I remember Mom nearly having to do the Heimlich maneuver on me, to dislodge a watermelon pit from my throat, the answer would be a resounding yes. I had forgotten about that picture, though. It's great. It looks great here."

"Yeah, I like to think it reminds me to remember the little joys in life when things around me are stressing me out a bit." Seeing Evie's unbelieving face he quickly added, "I said I'd like to think it does, not that it works all the time."

"How's the crib coming along?" she asked nicely. "May I take a gander at your manual labor?"

"Yeah, check this out. I only have two screws and one wing nut left over. Pretty good, huh?" He pointed to an imposing sleigh crib, with three pieces of hardware on the floor next to it.

"Very impressive. Any plans to backtrack and try to figure out where they might have been left out of? Just in case they're for important areas or anything?"

"Please," he snorted. "Like I don't realize Charlotte has a handyman coming by next week to double check this, the changing table, and even the diaper genie? Which you should know, doesn't need to be assembled; you just drop in the special wrap so you're not overwhelmed by the scent of baby shit in your house."

"Well, I think she's a very wise woman."

"Of course she is. She's marrying me. And having my baby."

"Those weren't the arguments I was going to lead with, but, before I forget the reason I was wandering your hallway, Nate wanted me to tell you to call him so you guys can make plans to watch the game together."

"Oh, thanks." Michael said. "By the way, how have the past couple of weeks over at his place been for you? It's not weird or anything is it? If it is, we can figure something else out. I think Emily told Charlotte you could even stay with her if you wanted."

Evie almost laughed out loud at the thought of her and Emily being roommates for the next two months. *It would probably make for one hell of a novel* she thought to herself, *but even I'm not willing to do that for my craft.*

"Actually, things have worked out quite nicely at Nate's place. As long as I'm not bothering him, it seems like it'll be a good fit for me during my stay here."

"Yeah, I thought you guys would hit it off. Plus, I know he's the kind of guy to honor the unwritten code of guys. Don't hit on someone's sister."

"Oh, yeah, sure. I have not noticed any moves being put on me." Evie kind of stopped and looked at her brother. "But is that really a problem with you guys? Even now?"

"Oh Christ, Evie, don't tell me you're interested in Nate?"

"No, no, I didn't say that. I just didn't know that would be the kind of thing you would have a problem with, to be honest with you. I didn't realize you still felt that overprotective. I'm just a little surprised, that's all."

"Evie. Have you ever dated any of my friends? Ever?"

She tossed that idea around in her head. Sure she had crushes on some of his older friends, and some had even flirted back every once in a while, but now that she thought about it, nothing else had ever come of it.

"I guess not."

"No guessing about it. You never did. Neither did Grace. All my buddies knew I would flip out if they tried anything. And I never dated any of their sisters."

"But you dated friends of mine and Grace's."

"What's your point?"

"I love dealing with an enlightened man. I really hope you have a girl," Evie laughed. She figured she wouldn't push this conversation any farther. Sure, she might technically have what could be defined as a crush on Nate, but it's not like he shared those feelings with her and there was no sense embarrassing herself in front of her brother over it.

"I better go downstairs and see if the girls are almost ready to leave," she said. "I'll see you later," she threw over her shoulder as she headed down the staircase and followed the voices into the sitting room. Cocktails would probably be a good idea if her day was going to be anything close to what she was anticipating.

When she got to the sitting room, Constance still hadn't arrived. Emily was in a snit about it, which wasn't surprising. "I keep ringing her cell phone and it's just sending me straight to voicemail," she complained. "I can't believe she's forgotten to turn it on, again. I warned her not to be so absent minded about that today. She knows we have appointments for all these bridal shops. I don't know what she could possibly be thinking."

Charlotte just laughed at her sister. "Oh, really, Emily. Just calm down. We've got tons of time before the first appointment and you know she'll probably be here any minute. Who amongst us hasn't forgotten to turn their mobile on every now and then?"

"I'll be the first to admit I'm always being reprimanded over it," Evie chimed in for Constance's sake.

"Like that's a surprise," Emily muttered under her breath.

Jacquelyn looked relieved she didn't try to stick up for her friend and tried to change the topic of conversation. "Evie, would you care for some wine?"

Just for the hell of it, she decided to really try to get under Emily's skin. It was going to happen whether she planned for it or not, and she decided she might as well have some fun with it. "Actually, Charlotte, you wouldn't happen to have any beer in the house, would you?"

"Like your brother doesn't keep a shelf in the fridge strictly for his beer? Let me run into the kitchen and grab one for you."

Emily stared at her and rolled her eyes in disgust. "And I suppose you'll just drink it straight from the bottle like a typical American."

"Am I mixing up my stereotypes, because I could've sworn it was the French who have the reputation for rudeness?" Evie asked no one in particular.

Charlotte yelled out from the kitchen, "Hey, Evie, would you care for a glass?"

Evie stared straight at Emily as she replied. "Nah, I'll just drink it right out of the bottle, thanks." Evie was sure she saw Jacquelyn smirk a little to herself, but couldn't be positive because she quickly raised her glass of wine to her lips to cover it. Maybe there will be an extra ally in this bridal party aside from Grace, she thought to herself in surprise.

Emily started punching numbers into her cell phone with a ferocity that made Evie giggle to herself. *She totally wishes that was me,* she couldn't help but think. "Bugger...still no answer," Emily blew out a breath in frustration.

On cue, the doorbell rang, and Charlotte ran to answer it. "Oh, Constance," the other three girls heard her say, "I'm so glad you made it. Be forewarned," she continued, "Emily's on a bit of a rampage because your cell was off, but Evie, Jackie, and I were sticking up for you."

"Oh, did I not have it on? So sorry, ladies," she trilled as she walked into the room where the rest of the bridal party waited. "Oh, grand, a beer. Lovely. Charlotte, do you mind if I have one of those and pass on the wine? Will Michael be in a snit if his reserve is broken into?"

Evie couldn't wait to make herself helpful on this occasion. "Charlotte, let me, you sit down," she said, and practically ran into the kitchen. She came back carrying the bottle of Michelob Ultra and innocently turned to Constance. "I'm sorry, I should've asked before I came back out...would you like a glass for your beer?"

"Oh, don't bother with that," was her reply. "No need to dirty up glasses on my account. I'm not very high maintenance, am I, Char?"

"Nor keen on leaving your ringer on, Constance."

"Emily, please, that's quite enough" was all Charlotte said, but her tone conveyed a lot more. It surprised Evie, since she hadn't heard Charlotte use a cross word with her sister any time she had been around. *I guess everyone has their breaking point*, she surmised. Having her friends belittled seemed to be Charlotte's. She continued as if nothing had happened. "Contrary to how it might seem with the antics of our little general over there," and she nodded her head in Emily's direction, "we have about forty-five minutes before we even have to leave for our first appointment, so everyone just enjoy your beverages and I'm going to grab the salad I made for us, so we're not too hungry when we arrive."

Charlotte came out of the kitchen with a huge bowl of mixed greens, tomatoes, glazed pecans, strawberries, and blue cheese with a vinaigrette spread over it all. All the girls admired the presentation and then went to work making a dent in the bowl.

Constance broke the silence that had descended over them as they ate to ask the question Evie wasn't brave enough to. "I imagine that after we admire our skinny, salad-eating selves in whatever bridesmaid dress you pick out for us, we'll be able to hit a pub and grab some burgers, though, right?"

"As long as we all promise in writing to run a lap immediately following, so we stay true to the dress sizes we order, right, Charlotte?" Jackie leapt in with.

Evie was shocked. These girls are actually fun, she thought. They're not at all like Emily. This might not be half bad. Grace will be pleased by this development.

Nineteen

The rest of the day went as expected where Emily was concerned, but was quite a pleasant surprise in terms of the other girls. As for the shopping, Evie figured it was the standard shopping experience for any bridesmaid doing her duty for friend or family. She was just doing it on another continent. She was relatively certain there wasn't a bridal store in all of London they hadn't managed to cover. Charlotte chose their dresses at the second to last stop they had scheduled and, unbelievably, all the girls were in agreement that it was absolutely perfect. It made Evie wonder if it was simply exhaustion and all of the girls didn't have the heart to walk through yet another archway of tulle, but looking at the dress she dismissed the notion. It was the kind of dress you'd hope the bride would be kind enough to pick out. "Grace is going to love it, too," Evie assured Charlotte as she gave her Grace's measurements to order her dress. "Blue is her favorite color, and she looks good in any style...even after having two kids."

Evie was pleased with the dress as well. The crepe material hung as though it had been custom made and didn't have a single metallic thread woven through it. She gave it one more spin around the floor. It was a light blue that the saleslady, Wendy, called "Ocean," and Evie was thrilled with its simplicity. The dress hit their knees, and had a halter tie around the neck. The full skirt on the bottom was just perfect for dancing, she thought. And not a rhinestone to be found on the whole damn thing.

As Evie spun around the dressing room floor with the curtain open, Emily strutted by on her Jimmy Choos. Evie figured she would have been hobbling six stores ago, but not Emily. She had her black Donna Karen tank top back on with her white cigarette pants and her black, oversized sunglasses that Evie thought only Nicole Ritchie could pull off, perched on her head. Even Evie had to admit she looked stunning. As she passed by the curtain Emily threw out, "You know, if you ever want to join me at the gym while you're here you're more than welcome. They have a killer abs class you might find useful."

Evie did what any self-respecting thirty-two year old would do in the same situation. She stuck her tongue out at Emily's retreating figure.

The saleswoman came out from behind another curtained off dressing room and tutted after Emily. "That one will get hers one day, don't you worry," she whispered. "And she's obviously off her rocker if she thinks you need to work on your figure, honey. I know jealousy when I see it, and that girl is green with it." Evie could've wrapped Wendy in her arms for a big hug, but thought she'd frighten her if she tried it.

"Now, let's see," Wendy said, getting down to business. She pushed her white hair out of her eye with a quick flick of her wrist and simultaneously started to wrap Evie with the measuring tape to verify her numbers. "I think I'll order the eight for you and then we'll take it in around the chest and the waist. If you have anyone in particular whose eye you'd like to catch, you'll manage it in this number. It's quite a glorious color on you, love." This time she couldn't resist Wendy's motherly kindness and gave her a quick hug right there on the spot. And she was right...she surprised Wendy shitless when she did.

The good news was that they were finally done shopping for dresses, which meant they could finally allow themselves the luxury of getting to the closest pub and ordering up rounds of cider *and* cheeseburgers for dinner. Even Emily put her constant state of dieting on hold and joined in. Obviously the bad news was that Emily was still with them. Evie had been hoping something of a work or personal nature might get in the way, but nothing doing. The best she could do was position herself on the opposite end of the table and not let Emily's comments on the number of fat grams in french fries get her too upset. Because she was still ordering them, fat grams be damned!

Jacquelyn must've been having the same thoughts because for the first time that day, she just looked at Emily and snapped, "You know, I've been walking for the better part of four hours now, and I'd like to enjoy my chips in peace, if you don't mind. I'm just going to call it a tie between my input and output and leave it at that." Emily had the good grace to look slightly embarrassed at that.

Constance and Jacquelyn spent the next hour or so regaling the other three girls with stories from their trip to Greece that had kept them away from Michael and Charlotte's engagement party.

"It was seriously hedonistic, Charlotte," Constance was laughing. "Well, as hedonistic as Jacquelyn would let it get. On our one visit to a nude beach where we both decided to go for broke and go topless, Jackie got the worst sunburn of her life on her back because she wouldn't turn over."

"Every time I had convinced myself to just turn over, I'd start to flip, and just then I'd hear my mother's voice saying, 'Oh, Jackie, your nipples are showing.' Then I'd stop where I was and lie back down on my stomach. I couldn't make that pivotal half rotation. But aside from my prudish behavior at the nude beach," she continued, "we had a glorious trip. Dancing and drinking and sunshine and handsome Greek men...it was everything London was not at the time. Definitely what the doctor had ordered."

Constance turned quietly to Evie to fill her in on a little back story. "Jackie's boyfriend had broken up with her shortly before our trip. If ever a holiday came at a perfect time, this one did."

"Bladder issues and all that," Charlotte said, pointing at her stomach. "I've got to hit the loo for a moment." She looked back at her friends. "Hold on to any more juicy stories until I return."

Emily waited until her sister's form had retreated towards the back of the room and then suggested, "Speaking of dancing and drinking, we should talk about Charlotte's hen night while we're all here,"

Evelyn looked blankly around the table, wondering what the hell Emily was talking about. "Um, excuse me, but what's a hen night?"

"Right, you guys call it a bachelorette party," Constance informed her.

"Oh, fun...when are you guys planning it for?" she asked the table.

"Two weekends from now, if that's okay with everyone else," Emily said.

Evie couldn't help but smile at the news. "That's when my friends from New York are visiting. Is it alright if they're here and join us?"

"The more the merrier on a hen party," said Jackie.

"They're not trolls, are they?" Emily asked.

All three girls stared at Emily in amazement and Evie didn't even bother with a reply to the question. Instead, she turned to Constance and Jacquelyn and asked them what the plan for the evening was. Emily seemed to realize the question was rude, even by her standards, and did her best to insert herself back into the conversation. "Why don't you jot your e-mail down for me and when the itinerary is totally set up I'll send you an e-mail." She pushed a piece of paper in Evie's direction, which Evelyn quickly scribbled her address on, and passed it back to Emily before Charlotte returned to the table.

Evie had a feeling Charlotte's bachelorette party would call for yet another outfit, but at least this time she'd have Maura, Kelly, and Amanda to help her shop for it.

Twenty

"Kelly? Did I wake you?" Evie whispered into the phone.

"No...but if you did, whispering wouldn't help any."

"Yeah, I guess not."

"Hey!" Kelly suddenly sounded like she had a pleasant thought hit her. "Wasn't today the day you were picking out your bridesmaid dress? Or, maybe I should say tomorrow since you're so many hours ahead of me right now." She paused. "Or is it yesterday? You know, I don't really like this time warp space continuum thing you've got going on. It confuses me."

"You can't figure out time zones and I'm an idiot because I can't text message people. I think this evens us out a bit. I'll help you out a bit. It's one o'clock, Sunday afternoon here, so that makes it eight a.m. for you in New York. And yes, we did pick out our dresses, but it was yesterday. To be honest, we tried on so many I don't know if I'd be able to pick the one we ended up with out of a lineup."

"Well, what color is it?'

"Blue, I think."

"Are we talking navy, robin's egg, royal, aqua...you can just stop me when I hit on something close."

"It's a light blue, I'd say."

"Well, being a writer, I'd hope you could. Is it short, long? What do the sleeves look like?"

"It's short and in the end she chose a halter style for us."

"Shoes?"

"We're wearing them."

"Har har. I'll be honest with you Evie. When I get married, I'm going to expect a lot more interest from you when we're picking out dresses. Consider yourself warned. You're going to need to grow a vagina and get involved."

"Did you just tell me to 'grow a vagina'?" Evie laughed.

"Yes, I believe I did. Seriously, this is all the fun, girlie stuff. You should be bonding with Charlotte and you sound so, I don't know, disinterested. If I can sense it over a phone line, I'm sure she's getting it shoved down her throat."

"Oh, I don't mean to be a bitch. I'm just being particularly difficult right now, due to exhaustion. I would obviously know the dress in a lineup, and it's actually quite stunning. We all loved it. So, I guess it was worth walking all over London for. And it's really not Charlotte. I have to admit she's been nothing but nice the whole time I've been here. Her friends were also so welcoming to me. It was actually kind of like shopping with any one of you guys, especially since her one friend, Jacquelyn, was a red head like you. The only exception to that rule would be her sister, Emily. She is a complete nutter, as they say here. I honestly expect her to turn up with a fake moustache, twirl it around and laugh maniacally to complete my image of her as a nasty, crazed, sinister person."

Kelly started to giggle. "Did she tie you up to the rails again, right before the train came speeding down the tracks, filled with frontiersmen heading west for the Gold Rush?"

"Laugh all you want, but I tell you, the girl's a whackado. And you can quote me on that. You'll see for yourself when you guys get here in a couple of weeks. And just so you know, you should be planning on attending a hen party while you're over here."

"You're taking us to a chicken coop?" Kelly asked, sounding distinctly unimpressed.

"No, a bachelorette party. Which I believe is way better than a chicken coop, but that's just me. Also, I've got to get a general consensus from the three of you as to what you definitely want to hit while you're here, tourist wise. I've got some ideas, also." Evelyn and Kelly proceeded to try figure to out what spots they thought should be included in the tour.

"As long as we get to see the famous Nate's coffee house, I don't care where we go."

"Most people put Big Ben before a stranger's coffee shop, but suit yourself," laughed Evie.

Twenty-One

E vie rolled downstairs at eleven o'clock in the morning and was surprised to find Nate sitting on the couch, reading the paper.

"What are you doing here? Shouldn't you be at work?" she asked.

"Well, as the boss, I decided to give myself the day off. It's been forever since I had one, and it's absolutely perfect outside. Not a cloud in sight, which is kind of rare for London, so I figured I'd take advantage of it, and give you a whopping on the tennis courts. Do you remember our bet where the loser must prepare a home cooked meal for the winner?"

"Of course I do...I just didn't think you'd be so silly as to request it, to be honest with you."

"Well, I was getting a little worried that the sun would set before you had risen, but seeing as how you're up now, why don't we make today the day?"

"Sounds great. Just let me grab some breakfast and get dressed and I'll be ready to go. You might want to start perusing any cookbooks you have around here for some ideas on what you'll be making me tonight."

"I love witnessing first hand accounts of the proverb, 'pride goeth before a fall,'" Nate teased.

An hour later they arrived at the local courts that were close by Nate's apartment. They signed in at the ledger and were told that they would only have about a fifteen minute wait for the next available court. Evelyn took the time to eye up the court they would be playing on. Luckily, it wasn't grass. She was concerned that all of the courts in England would be like Wimbledon for some reason, and she has visions of herself sliding around like an ice skater, rather than a tennis player.

Nate gave her a sideways glance and came to a speedy conclusion. "You're looking nervous, Dunleavy. Are you sure you still want to go through with this?" he teased. "There's still time to admit defeat and just forfeit. Of course, that means you still have to cook tonight."

"I've faced much scarier opponents out here on the courts. I've played against Annie and Archie and they use me as a bulls eye, rather then aiming to stay in the lines. That's a match that would put the fear of God into a person. You...not so much."

"Trash talking. Impressive start. You won't get into my head with it, though."

The four older men who had just finished their last set nodded to Evie and Nate that they were done and the court was all theirs. The last one smiled at Evie, winked, and said, "My money's on you, sweetheart."

Evie grabbed her ponytail holder, wristband, and visor from the depths of her tennis racquet cover and set about readying herself.

"Wow, you sure do bring a lot of accessories to play tennis," Nate marveled at her. "I just need a racquet. Look at that...I'm done." He held his racquet up in the air to prove his point.

"I believe the phrase is 'jolly for you,' is it not?"

"Okay," Nate started, becoming serious very quickly. "I just have one hard and fast rule that must be heeded under any and all circumstances." He let a big dramatic pause fall between them before carrying on. "You must never, I repeat, NEVER, use the phrase, 'Homerun' if you over hit a ball. Or any other baseball terminology for that matter. 'It's out of here,' is another one that's off limits. I think you get the gist of what I'm saying. I abhor it when someone does that during the match. And inevitably, someone always does."

"Guilty as charged," Evie sheepishly admitted. "It just rolls off the tongue. I can't promise it won't happen today."

The two of them warmed up for a while, getting a feel for the court and each other. Evie was careful to swing easy and let her balls sail over the net a little higher than she normally would. She figured it made no sense to clue him into the fact that as soon as they started keeping score she was going to be hitting the same balls Nate was able to return so easily in the warm up, low, fast, and angled all over the court so he didn't have a shot in hell of returning them. Poor Nate. But there was no way Evie was going to cook that night. She was a terrible cook.

Halfway through the second set Nate just stopped and stared hard at Evelyn from the service line. The back of his shirt had turned a shade darker where the sweat had been accumulating and he was noticeably winded. Evie on the other hand, looked as fresh as she did when she started. The only concession to that fact was the damp wristband she wore that was used to mop her forehead every couple of points.

"I don't get it," he complained. "I thought you told me the last time you played a singles match you were in high school. How can that be true when you're absolutely destroying me?"

"It is true. But did I not mention I play doubles every week in a league in the city? It must've totally slipped my mind." She effortlessly tossed the ball over her head and sliced in a serve that Nate barely got his racquet on, but one quick backhand down the line and the point was hers anyway.

The rest of the match followed suit and Evie handily won three straight sets. "That was fun," she joyfully exclaimed as they shook hands when they had finished. "Now, remember what my rule was. No moping now that you lost. I would be very disappointed if you turned out to be one of those guys."

"Well, I guess we should get home. Seems like I need to do some grocery shopping after I shower, since I now have a meal to prepare tonight."

A few hours later and Evie was being summoned to the kitchen table where Nate had gone to a lot of effort to make her victory dinner. The candles that he had lit and strewn around the granite counter tops were giving off a hazy, and rather complimentary, light. He had even gone to the trouble to cut a few blossoms from the hydrangea bushes growing outside his front door and set them in a crystal vase on the table, much to Evie's surprise. A bottle of merlot had already been opened to breathe and a salad at each place setting was waiting for her arrival.

"I am very pleasantly surprised," she told him, turning quickly to watch him take the garlic bread that had been warming in the oven out before it burned. "I think we should have a rematch. If only so I'm guaranteed another meal like this"

"Fool me once, yada, yada, yada," was his reply. He picked up the wooden spoon sitting on the counter top and started to stir his sauce. "I have made the House Specialty for us tonight. It's not very fancy, but it is very satisfying and delicious. Or so I've been told. I call it Pizza Pasta. It's pasta that's topped with a sauce made from cream, tomatoes, and pepperoni. And of course, a few secret spices, which cannot be divulged to anyone." He carefully prepared two plates with the dinner while he spoke, and set everything down at the table, where he held out a seat for Evie. "Mademoiselle."

Evie sat down, smoothing a cloth napkin onto her lap as she did so. "I totally feel underdressed. If I had known you were going to go to so much trouble, I would've at least thrown on a little more makeup for the evening."

"You look gorgeous," Nate said sincerely. "You don't need anymore makeup."

Evie suddenly felt self conscious with Nate looking at her like he was about to say something else, so she quickly scanned her brain for a neutral topic they could speak about before he could do so. The task was harder then it would seem since the only thing that was springing to her mind was how unbelievably gorgeous he looked in his frayed jeans and long sleeved gray tee shirt. And how she hated the fact he was her brother's good friend, and thereby off the table, so to speak, for her to think about in romantic terms. *Not that he would really be interested in me anyway,* she reminded herself for about the thousandth time since she had arrived in London.

Nate himself was thinking about a table, but more to the point, envisioning the table they were sitting at being used for something other than eating and was close to revealing his true thoughts when Evie started talking. "So, you're sure you really don't mind the girls staying here for the long weekend coming up? We do tend to get a little noisy when we're all together."

Nate stopped for a moment to look at Evie, pondering not so much her question, but her timing. Every time a spark seemed to pass from one to the other she did her best to throw out any line of conversation other than the one he wanted to explore. Was he misreading the signs, he asked himself for the thousandth time since she had arrived? Did she not feel the same connection he did? If that was the case, there was no sense in looking like a fool, so he answered her actual question and let the unanswered ones remain unspoken. Even though he'd much rather gain some insight to the ones swimming around his head every time he glanced in her direction and saw her quickly look away, blushing slightly.

"Of course I don't mind," he answered a little heartier than necessary; to try to throw her off the trail his thoughts had just taken. "If for no other reason than I'm sure they have some embarrassing stories about you they could share."

"Are you saying that the stories my brother has so kindly been sharing haven't been embarrassing enough? You now know that I wrote to Donny and Marie no less then thirty-seven times in my youth. What more do you want?"

"I'm thinking more contemporary stuff might be worth my while. Don't get me wrong, it's not that I haven't enjoyed the stories Michael's divulged so far. The fact that you stole your mother's wedding ring to validate your Nancy Drew Mystery Club was a particular favorite of mine. I really had no idea that a seven year old girl could be so diabolical, but I'm ready to explore another decade now."

"Maybe they should stay at a hotel," Evie mumbled into her pasta.

Twenty-Two

"Guys, over here," Evie shouted as she saw her three friends coming through customs at Heathrow. They all raced towards each other, laughing at how silly they must look.

"We could totally be a clip from *Love, Actually* in one of the airport scenes that bookend that movie," Kelly snickered. Evie didn't care what they looked like to anyone strolling around the terminal. She was delirious with joy at finally seeing her three best friends.

"Guys, I am so glad to see you again," she proclaimed as she gave each girl a bear hug. Your New York accents are so soothing to the ears."

"You do not hear that all that often," Amanda said.

"Well, you should. It's a cochlea delicacy."

"I've missed you and your fancy words," Maura said. "It's so aggravating when people only use words that you already know."

"Then you should go visit my Mom when you get home. Remember how I told you she tried out all the British phrases she had ever heard or read when she was over for the engagement party? My Dad says she's still carrying on with that at home, and it's starting to drive everyone nuts. He's afraid it's here to stay, and he says he's had enough of being called a git every time he doesn't put his clothes in the hamper."

"I'm not ready to think of going home," Kelly declared. I've got five days and four nights of fun on another continent. "I refuse to give into jet lag, so you just say the word and I'm ready to hit the pubs with you."

"You've got more moxie than I do," Maura told her. "Any chance that those of us who wanted to, could take a quick snooze before hitting the town?"

"Why don't we head back to Nate's place and if anyone wants to get a little shut eye they can, and if anyone wants to hit our local, we can do that as well."

"*Our* local?" Amanda inquired with a seriously steep eyebrow raise. "Isn't that chummy? I thought you said that there wasn't anything going on with the two of you."

"There isn't. I would say that in regards to anyone who was my roommate; romantic interest or not. Not that there's any romantic interest on anyone's part, though," Evie hastened to add. "I don't need you guys being all goofy and embarrassing me, thank you very much."

Maura just laughed slyly. "You're so adorable when you get flustered. Obviously there's nothing going on. You've just been describing him as a chivalrous dreamboat since you've gotten here, so why would you be attracted to him? That'd be pure lunacy."

"Sarcasm is duly noted...now into the car."

———

"Your driving is very impressive, Evie. You're staying in all the lines."

"Kelly, sometimes you'd never guess you were an elementary school teacher. But thank you for the positive reinforcement. You do realize I'm driving a car, though, not coloring in a coloring book, right?"

Evie drove them skillfully back from the airport to Nate's flat, and they were all rightly impressed. "In all seriousness, that was some really good driving, Evie. You don't even drive this well in New York and now you're dealing with steering wheels on the wrong side of the car, and driving on the opposite side of the road. How did you manage to get so good?" Maura asked sincerely.

"Actually, Nate's taken me out a couple of times in an old school lot that's close by. He's a really patient teacher." She had the good grace to blush as she said it. Presumably because she knew the ribbing her friends would give her, as soon as the sentence was out of her mouth. But to her astonishment and relief, nobody said anything. However, she missed the knowing looks her newly arrived friends gave each other as she stepped out of the car.

"She is totally nuts for this guy," Amanda whispered to Kelly right before exiting out the back door of the car.

The girls all piled into the flat and instantly started laughing when they spotted the picture frame on the foyer table. Nate had taken Evie's photo of the four of them in Central Park that usually resided on the nightstand in her room and placed it squarely on the table so it was the first thing that greeted them. He had also hung a small paper banner, not very artistic, but extremely endearing, that read, "WELCOME FRIENDS OF EVIE'S." Next to that sat a big bowl of Cadbury Flakes, which had quickly become one of Evie's favorite snacks ever.

"We haven't even met him yet and I just want to eat him up he's so delicious," Kelly said. "What a lovely reception."

Evie felt a burst of pride from Nate's small gestures of welcome. She knew not too many guys would have felt comfortable having a pack of unknown guests take over their home for a long weekend, and here he had gone above the call of duty with homemade banners and tiny touches of kindness.

Amanda, who had moved on into the kitchen area to grab some water, yelled behind her, "Evie, there's a note here for you on the counter."

Evie read Nate's message as her friends started in on the Flakes Maura so sensibly carried in to the kitchen with them. She absently grabbed a piece of the chocolate as she relayed what Nate had written. "He just said for me to call him and let him know how we plan to proceed. Option one being naps, option two being drinks in, right away. It's your call ladies."

Maura reiterated her need for a bit of a rest. Amanda agreed with her, but Kelly was still gung ho about making the most of her time in London. "I'll sleep when I get back to New York. Why don't we go someplace close, so it'll be easy for us to come back and get these two layabouts at a designated time and I can see if I can find myself a nice English bloke like you've managed to come across?"

It was decided that Evelyn and Kelly would return in two hours, which would hopefully be enough time to rejuvenate Maura and Mandy. Evie showed her two soon-to-be slumbering friends up to the room they would share. Their guest room had two twin beds, both with blue plaid comforters that they climbed gratefully under, after barely removing their shoes.

"Seriously, Evie, no matter how hard we beg, you must promise to make us get out of these beds when you come back for us, or we'll be so thrown off kilter sleeping wise we'll never manage to be even remotely on schedule," Maura warned. "And then you won't have your whole posse in 'I got your back' form for the bachelorette party with Emily."

"I will physically tip these beds over to ensure that doesn't happen. We will see you in two hours."

Evie then had Kelly follow her to her room, since they would be sharing it while the girls were in town.

"My room only has a queen bed, so you better have learned to share blankets better than I remember, or I'm kicking you out."

"Or maybe you could just give me the bed and Nate would let you share his bed while we're here. He seems to be such a fabulous host, I'm sure he wouldn't mind the slight inconvenience."

"Don't be ridiculous," Evie muttered, wondering why she felt her face becoming flushed all of a sudden.

"Then maybe he'll let me share his bed," Kelly teased.

"Don't be even more ridiculous," Evie muttered, wondering why she felt so annoyed by this obvious attempt to read her feelings.

"Hey," Kelly said suddenly, seeing something in her eyes Evie wasn't ready to show. "I was just kidding there, you know."

"Of course I know. It doesn't matter anyway. Now, did you want to freshen up, or just head right out?" Evie spoke quickly, afraid of giving away any more clues about how she was starting to feel about Nate. She didn't want to examine it too closely herself, let alone dissect it ad nauseum with her well meaning friends.

"Well, what's the dress code? Do I pass muster?" Evie glanced at Kelly and told her she looked perfect. A tall, slim redhead in jeans with a white, eyelet shirt with spaghetti straps was going to be a very welcome addition to the mostly male crowd, who favored their rugby shirts dirty and their pints followed up by a whisky chaser.

"I feel the need to remind you that this is not some fancy gin joint we're heading to, or hip new club. When I say "our local" I mean that with every unspoken caveat there could be. I don't even want you picturing something quaint like "Cheers." It's just short of squalor. It's very unlikely we'll find any Prince Charming types in the vicinity."

"It sounds like yours is," Kelly couldn't help but say. But seeing how Evie's face seemed to shut down at that, she quickly added, "All that matters is we get a chance to catch up anyway. I was only kidding about being on the prowl." As Evie gave her a look of disbelief, she amended, "Well, maybe kidding is too strong a word."

———————

The Wednesday afternoon crowd was exactly what Evie was expecting for The Ale House as the two girls walked past the small crowd of university guys staring at a television that had on a rugby game. They only heard one lone wolf whistle as they made their way to the bar to order their drinks.

"I guess Gloria Steinem would choke on her own spit to hear me say it, but just one cat call is depressing. Does that mean we're losing it or that men in general are behaving more like gentlemen these days?" Kelly wondered.

"For the sake of our egos, let's go with the line of thinking that Miss Manners herself was over here earlier this afternoon, giving etiquette lessons and instructions for the proper way to show respect towards women."

"Maybe I can just let the strap of my top fall a little bit down my shoulder and we'll get some attention that way?" Kelly suggested.

Evie held up her right hand in a fist and said, "Feminists all over the world rejoice. We have found our savior."

Kelly just shook her head, saying, "I don't believe the Malcolm X hand gestures go with the rhetoric you're spouting. He'd be extremely disappointed I should think."

"As would your Mom if she saw you sitting here letting your bra strap show."

"True, but it's a bit harsh of you to remind me of that, wouldn't you say?"

The girls ordered their drinks and crossed to the far side of the bar where they could converse in peace and catch up a bit before the night got away from them.

"So," Evie started with, "what's your take on Garrett? Have you guys had a chance to meet him?"

"Yeeaahh..." Kelly seemed reluctant to say much more but the way she drew out her one word answer was telling enough.

"I'm guessing from the sound of it, he didn't pass muster."

"Weelll..."

"Oh for Christ's sake, Kelly, you're taking one syllable words and making them last for thirty seconds. At this rate it's going to take you nine hours to tell me he chewed with his mouth open or something equally horrid. What's going on?"

"The thing is, well, it's kind of awkward." She paused before continuing. "He made a pass at me." Kelly stared at Evie waiting for her to say something.

Evie almost did a spit take with her gin and tonic and just looked back at Kelly. "He did what?" she asked slowly. She needed verification that she had heard what Kelly said correctly.

"I know, it sounds like a truly bad eighties movie. Something that Molly Ringwald would shine in, but unfortunately, it's true."

"Oh no. What did Mandy say? Did she physically hit him, or just use her cold voice when she broke up with him?"

"That's the other thing. Maura and I decided not to tell her. Yet," she quickly amended seeing the look of astonishment cross Evie's face. "Here's the story. Maura and I met them out at Due South two nights ago, or maybe it's three now, since I don't know what day it is, but irregardless, we met them out for a quick drink. Afterward, they were going to go out to dinner and Maura and I were going to go back to our apartments since we still had to finish packing for our trip. So anyway, everything is going fine and he seems nice enough. Then Amanda goes to the restroom to freshen up and Maura goes with her. And that's when things got weird."

"Weird, how?" Evie asked.

"Well, he started off nicely, just saying something like, 'Wow, I can't believe you don't have a boyfriend,' that kind of stuff. Then he took it to a whole other level when he said, 'I mean, a fiery red head like you? Man, you must be a real tiger in the sack. What I wouldn't give to find out for myself.' And yes, those were his actual words, and yes, I get nauseous just repeating them now, a couple of days after the fact, so you can imagine what I felt like when I heard them the first time around."

"Oh, Kelly, he sounds like such an asshole. He actually used the phrase 'a real tiger in the sack?' That's the most ridiculous thing I've ever heard. What happened then? And how did you and Maura decide to keep it to yourselves?"

"Well, as you could imagine I was caught so off guard that I didn't know what to do. Luckily, at that point Maura and Amanda came back from the bathroom, so I just told Maura I was going to take off to finish off my packing. She came with me and I told her what happened after we left. To be honest, we did think about storming the restaurant in indignation and grabbing her away from him, but in the long run we didn't think that would be our best course of action. So then we thought about waiting outside your apartment to hijack her when they came home, but we didn't know if she would even stay there that night. And we didn't want to call and tell her this over her cell phone. In the end we figured she'd have an awful time on this vacation if she broke up with him the day before we came here and that we'd sit on the information until we got back to New York. This way we can tell her in the privacy of her own home where she can have any sort of reaction she wants. Without him being privy to it. You've got to promise not to say anything to her, though, Evie. It'll ruin her trip."

Evie thought about her smiling, trusting roommate and wanted to cross the Atlantic and pummel this Garrett who had such bad taste in television. "Fine. But just for the record, as soon as she said he liked *Desperate Housewives* I had him pegged as a jackass."

"Didn't we all?" Kelly agreed while rolling her eyes at the thought of a guy naming that as one of his favorite shows.

An hour and a half passed in no time at all and they were settling up at the bar in order to make it back to the flat in time, when Evie's cell phone rang. "Oh, Nate's calling from work. Let me just take this and then we'll head back to wake up Maura and Amanda."

Nate started talking before Evie could even get a hello out. "Evie, listen, it's Nate."

"I know Nate. I have caller id."

"Oh, yeah, well, anyway, I have one of my regular customers here and you're never going to believe this, but, he's got four tickets he's looking to sell for the Coldplay concert on Friday night. And Amy Winehouse is opening up for them."

"Get out."

"Do you want me to get them for you and your friends or do you have other plans?"

"Well, I'd say yes, but hold on while I ask Kelly and we'll just have to make an executive decision for the other two." She turned to Kelly. "Okay, Nate can get us four tickets to see Coldplay for Friday night if we want them. We just have to tell him a definite yes or no right now. What do you think?"

"Granted they lost major street cred when Chris Martin married Gwyneth Paltrow and named his children Apple and Moses, but...YES!! They still make awesome music."

"Nate?" Evie asked into her phone. "Tell him we'll take them. Thanks so much. I'll give you the money when you get home later."

"What are you guys up to now?" Nate asked.

"Well, at this exact second, Kelly is doing what I can only assume is her victory dance as the proud owner of Coldplay tickets, but she would not be a serious contender on *So You Think You Can Dance*. By the way, you may not want to come to The Ale House for a couple of days, as that's where said dance is occurring. But we were actually going to head back to your place to wake up Maura and Amanda. Now we'll get to wake them up with the delightful news of our new and improved Friday night plans."

"Alright, then. I guess I'll just meet you at home with the tickets. I should be heading out in about half an hour or so."

"Great. Thanks again, Nate. This is such awesome news. The other two are going to be ecstatic as well."

———————

"I don't think I've ever been woken up in such a lovely manner," was Amanda's take on the news of the tickets.

"Well, then I'd say you need a new boyfriend," was what Evie shot back with, before she even thought about it. She looked at Kelly's stricken face and whispered, "Completely spoken without any premeditation. Just a joke." Kelly visibly relaxed and realized it's exactly the kind of thing Evie would say even without the knowledge that Amanda's boyfriend was a bonehead.

"And guess who's slated to open up for them?" Kelly threw out. "Amy Winehouse."

Evie was surprised at how excited her friends were at that news. "Wait a sec. You guys have heard of her? I thought I was going to look like a total hipster and be the only one who knew who she was."

"Evie," Maura explained patiently, as though talking to a small child, "New York City is very much involved in the music industry. As a matter of fact, I'm pretty sure I suggested that you download her album on your iPod before you even left."

"That actually would've been very helpful had I listened to you. There was a bit of ridicule thrown in my direction when word got out that I had asked Charlotte if she was anything like our Britney Spears. She was a bit surprised when I said I hadn't a clue who she was."

Amanda just closed her eyes at the indignity of it all. Partly in pity, and partly in disgust. "First of all...please stop using the plural possessive when referencing Britney Spears. This is not *The Sisterhood of the Traveling Pants* where everyone gets Britney for a week. Secondly, oh, good God, you must've been laughed at pretty hard over that one. Let me put it to you this way: if Zach Braff was looking for some music to include on a soundtrack for a new movie he was making, he would consider her to be way too mainstream."

Kelly tried to make Evie feel better. "Well, if they were talking crazy ass party antics they have more than a few similar personality traits." She continued on, "Just not even close on a talent scale, though, honey. That's where it'd be an embarrassing comparison."

"So I've been told," Evie replied, dryly. "Now we should stop talking about this, because I don't need Nate to have another go around with this conversation. Once was enough for me, thanks."

"You might want to rethink referring to yourself as a hipster, then," was Maura's sage advice. "Because you are opening a whole other door for ridicule to run through if you don't."

"Another no-no would be a hep cat," Amanda couldn't help but add.

"Unless you were going to a reading of some beatnik poetry, of course," Kelly said.

"Remember when I told you all how much I missed you when we were at the airport? Not so much anymore."

Twenty-Three

A ll four girls came out of the concert hall on what Kelly referred to as a "music high." Everyone else pouring onto the streets from the show obviously felt the same way. The streets seemed alive, and everyone was buzzing from the performances.

"That was the highest head of hair I have ever seen in my life," Maura emphatically stated. "I mean, seriously, it's like gravity does not adhere to its own rules in regard to her hair. How is that even possible?"

"And Coldplay? Majestic is the only word that springs to mind right now," Amanda said.

"How many pounds do you think her hair weighs? And do you think it's hard for her to hold her head upright?" Maura couldn't seem to let go of the topic of Amy Winehouse's beehive.

"Personally, I was more intrigued by the fact she could still stand after all those shots she did on stage," was Evie's take on the singer. "And," she said after a brief pause, "I think her hair weighs more than her actual body. Or at least half of her body. Let's just say from her waist down for argument's sake."

"So where are we meeting your brother and his posse?" Kelly asked. "I can't wait to brag about the concert."

Maura looked at her quickly. "Isn't that the kind of behavior you try to dissuade your young students from using?"

"Yeah, but this is something that is actually good. We just got to see Coldplay and Amy Winehouse. They're usually bragging about things like who can make the loudest arm fart. I mean really, who gives a crap about that?"

"Brag on, you braggerty braggart." Amanda was using her "I'm feeling the effects of all the alcohol I've drank" loud voice, so several people turned to look at the girl making up words, solely for the sake of alliteration. She giggled. "I think you will find several people trying to fit that phrase into conversation come Monday morning back in the office."

"They're all waiting for us at some club called Fabric. I don't think it'll take us that long, once we grab a cab."

When they arrived at the club, Evie pulled out her cell phone to call her brother. "He said something about some of his friends having some kind of membership thing and to call him when we got here. This way we won't have to wait on the queue. There's some kind of special entrance so members get to avoid standing around. Michael said it was like the Disney fast pass, except the reward is getting a drink in a shorter amount of time, rather than getting on Space Mountain quicker." Evie noticed her friends staring at her. "I know; it's totally weird that a grown man without any kids would love Disney World so much, right? I tell him that all the time."

"Nooo," Amanda said slowly. "I think we're more confused by your sudden use of the word queue over the word line. You're starting to sound a lot like you said your Mom did while she was here."

"If you start saying loo, I'm going to punch you," Kelly promised.

"I said loo in New York."

"And I always wanted to punch you when you did. Weird, huh?"

Michael's friend, Brian, came out and ushered them through a separate door and nodded at the two gentlemen manning the entrance. He led them to a back room where Michael and a bunch of his work friends were laughing loudly, and watching a soccer game. Or football, depending on what country you originated from. Evie was constantly in a state of turmoil trying to figure out what she should refer to it as. She felt like a poser if she called it football, but it was becoming rather tiresome having every English person she came in contact with explain to her as if talking to an imbecile that it's not called soccer here. She was relatively certain she would soon be calling it football, just as a way to silence that conversation forever. She scanned the faces, trying to see if Nate had shown up as well. When they had left him earlier, he hadn't figured out what he was going to do. She felt a little defeated when she realized she didn't see him, and her face fell for an instant, but she quickly regained her smile. But not quick enough that her friends weren't able to notice Evie's quick scan of the crowd and the momentary look of disappointment cross over her features. Eyebrows were raised between the three of them in what to a passerby would seem like a bizarre Groucho Marx impression.

Evie and Amanda offered to buy the first round and made their way up to the bar to place their drink order. They wound their way back to the table with their arms full of gin and tonics, and pints of lager and ale to disperse to the crowd. Maura was in full beehive description mode, hands gesturing up above her head and a look of wonderment on her face. Three of Michael's friends had a look of wonderment on their faces watching Evie's gorgeous friend. Kelly came up to the other two girls and laughed. "She never has a problem attracting members of the opposite sex, does she? They're enraptured."

"It must be a curse to walk around with black hair, green eyes, and a killer body," Amanda said. "If I didn't have Garrett, I'd totally be jealous." Evie and Kelly tried not to look at each other after she said that.

After an hour or so, Evie found herself in line for the bathroom, talking to the bartender. He had originally asked her what she wanted, not realizing the line for the ladies room had started to snake out by the bar, and she was just the end of that line, not the beginning of the drinks line. This led to the standard barroom debate over the unfairness of the discrepancy between wait times for the men's and ladies rooms. What Nate saw when he walked into the club was Evie laughing with the bartender, and he was surprised by how much he didn't like it. He gave the bartender a once over and figured he was just the type of guy a girl would find attractive. Dark hair and eyes, to go with a tan no one who lived in London could actually be the owner of naturally, and a crisp white shirt teamed with his black pants. He then studied Evie from the distance and couldn't imagine anyone not being attracted to her. Her dark hair was loose and slightly curly for a change and he could see the jolt of blue her eyes gave off when she laughed even from where he was standing. He thought she looked perfect in her simple black skirt and a black and white geometric top, with tall black boots. He laughed to himself when he recalled what a shambles her room had been in when she left, clothes thrown all over the floor, in her attempt to find the perfect concert/club outfit. And he laughed again to himself when he recalled how she ran all over the flat saying exactly that. "I need help figuring out the perfect concert slash club outfit. Can I get some feedback in here, please?" For all her talk about not having a clue in regards to fashion, he thought, she always looked great. Even in the old tee shirt and sweats that tended to be her staple when she read the paper in the morning. That was actually when Nate thought Evie looked her most amazing.

Even though he had no right to feel territorial, he marched over to where she stood at the bar, and gave her a quick squeeze. He figured it was short enough that Evie wouldn't think it was strange, but long enough that the bartender would assume they were together and back off. He thought this was the oddest kind of math he had ever attempted.

"Oh good, Nate, you're here. I was beginning to think you weren't going to make it tonight." Evie tried not to let her mouth drop open when she turned to see who had come up from behind her. He was so good looking and she noticed a few other women at the bar give him second and even third glances. With his vintage Rolling Stones tee shirt and a pair of Levi's, he made all the other guys wearing their trendy blazers or bright colored cashmere sweaters look overdone and almost girlish.

"Michael and his friends are over in that corner. I'm hoping that a stall in the ladies restroom might potentially open up this millennium. Wish me luck," she said as the line moved up a fraction of an inch.

"So how was the concert?" he asked.

"For me to say, I'd have to come up with a superlative that eclipses awesome, fabulous, mind blowing, and life altering."

"So it didn't suck."

"No," Evie laughed easily. "It most certainly did not suck. And the girls had a blast. Even for a bunch of jaded women from New York, this was one for the record books. Thanks so much for getting those tickets."

"I was just in the right place at the right time. No thanks needed. Although if you felt obligated, I wouldn't say no to breakfast in bed." He raised his eyebrows in a comically leering manner.

"Aww...like your Mom used to do when you were home sick as a kid?"

"You have just ruined the concept of breakfast in bed with a beautiful woman for me forever. I hope you're happy," Nate concluded with a pout.

"Oh yea, the line's really moving now," Evie clapped happily as three girls went into the bathroom together and she got to move up several feet.

"You know, if you want to hop into the men's room, I'll stand guard for you."

"So many bad flashbacks for that one seemingly innocuous phrase. I'll just wait my turn, thanks."

"That sounds like fodder for a late night talk, if ever I heard one."

"Do I sound mysterious if I say 'no comment?'"

"No, just like you had an easily distracted boyfriend in college, who'd forget you were in there one too many times."

"Did you go to NYU, also?" she laughed. "You know, you don't have to stand here and keep me company. Michael's over that way."

"Yeah, I know. I saw him when I came in. I wanted to say hi to you first, though. Can I get you a drink for when you finally emerge from bathroom hell?"

"That would be great. I've been drinking gin and tonics so far tonight, but I think I should get something without ice. It's quite possible that by the time I manage to make my way back to all of you, the ice will have completely melted and it'll dilute the drink so much it would be like drinking a glass of water. God forbid. So to prepare against that, I'll take a glass of merlot. Thanks."

"That's what you Americans call thinking outside the box, is it not?" Nate asked wryly, as he left her standing in the line.

When Evie finally managed to meet up with everyone she made a beeline towards Nate. She wrapped her arms around him to grab the glass of wine that he never put down, in the hope that she'd reach for it in the sort of fashion she did. He decided to make her work a little bit for it and held it aloft, over his head.

"I know your mother taught you to not to grab for things and to use words like please and thank you," he teased her.

"Mom would be so disappointed," Michael agreed.

"Michael. You have known me for thirty-two years. I thought you would've come to the realization that rudeness is a character trait of mine. I'm flawed, you know."

"Of course I know you're flawed. But Mom would still be disappointed."

"That's true. I apologize for my appalling lack of manners, Nate. I would like to thank you for so kindly buying me a glass of wine, and I would really like to drink it now."

He stared at her, waiting.

"Please?"

He smiled and lowered his arm so she could now reach the glass. When Evie had retrieved the wine from his grasp, she punched his arm. "Is that rude, too?"

"Little bit."

Kylie Minogue was now playing from the DJ booth and Nate grimaced.

"Hey, it's your *I Will Survive*," Evie said, speaking into his ear, so he could hear her above the music.

He smiled at her, loving the fact that she had remembered that trivial detail from the engagement party. That was a sentence that only the two of them would fully understand, even if she said it over the DJ's microphone to the entire, crowded club. And he wanted to share even more shorthand sentences like that with her. But it wasn't that easy when her brother was one of his best friends. It was a tricky line to cross, not to mention she'd be heading back to New York City after the wedding. He couldn't let himself fall for Evie; it would just lead to heartbreak, and he definitely didn't need that.

While Evie and Nate stood flirting gently almost directly across from her oblivious brother, Amanda, Kelly, and Maura were taking notes. Literally. On a cocktail napkin.

"Seriously, Maura. How do you manage to fit a pen into that tiny clutch? I swear to God, it's like Hermione's magic bag that fit in everything *and* the kitchen sink in *The Deathly Hallows*," was Amanda's take on the situation when Maura pulled out a pen that was twice as long as the bag was.

When Maura and Kelly looked at her in scorn over her comparison, she indignantly shot off, "What? Evie's the only adult in our group that can read and enjoy the Harry Potter books? They're good," she added defensively.

"Alright, let's get to the important stuff," Kelly said quickly. "We need to figure out a way to have Nate and Evie go home alone. Anyone have any ideas?"

"Well, we could plead exhaustion," was Maura's first thought.

"It does make sense; we all could be fighting jet lag," Amanda said.

"Which is the only way to explain why we thought we'd need to actually write this all down," Maura laughed, crumpling and tossing the napkin into an empty glass. "Let's be honest, we're more Maxwell Smart than James Bond, anyway."

The three girls turned to their friend and got Evelyn's attention. When she walked over to them, Maura spoke for them all. "Listen, Evie, would you mind terribly if the three of us called it a night now? I think everything seems to have caught up to all of us and we figure we should try to get some sleep so we're ready for Charlotte's bachelorette party tomorrow night."

"No, that's fine. Let me just say goodbye and we'll grab a cab outside."

Maura, Kelly, and Amanda looked worriedly at each other, and this time it was Amanda who spoke.

"You know, Evs, you don't have to leave just because we are. We have the address and I'm pretty sure we can manage a London cab. You've been adjusted to the time change for ages now. No need to tag along with the jet lagged crew. Why don't you just give us your key and you can go home with Nate?" Before Evie even had a chance to respond, Amanda was yelling in Nate's direction. "Hey, Nate. If Kelly, Maura, and I were to leave right now and took Evie's key with us, would you be okay with her coming back with you?"

"Sure thing."

"Are you guys sure you don't want me to come back home with you?" Evie questioned them. "It's really not a big deal. We're going to be out all night tomorrow. I could probably use the extra sleep myself."

"No," Maura said firmly. "We'd feel bad taking you away from this time with your brother and his friends. You'll be back in New York City with us before you know it, and we don't want you to miss anything because we're a little sleepy."

"Well, alright then. I'll see you back home, I guess."

Kelly fought back her knee jerk response of throwing up her hand for someone to high five, and barely managed to catch herself before she started flailing her digits over her head. On their way out the door, Maura just turned to her and said, "A high five? Seriously, Kelly?"

"I know," Kelly laughed. "I'm the bad cliché of a high school football team that wins the state champs. It was instinct. You don't think she saw, do you?"

"No, she was already ogling Nate by that time," Amanda pointed out.

"At the rate that that's occurring, I'm starting to think she believes that he's better looking than us."

"Bugger off and speak for yourself, Maura. I'm still hot," Kelly teased. Then she stopped in her tracks. "Shit. It really *is* easy to fall into the trap of using English slang."

Amanda flagged down a cab driver and gave him the address of Nate's flat while they hopped in.

"Sure thing, poppet. We'll be there shortly."

Maura looked wistful as she turned to her two friends. "Poppet," she sighed. "Now why couldn't a New York cabbie refer to us in that manner? It's so quaint."

———————

If Evie or Nate were surprised by her friends' sudden departure, they didn't give it too much thought. They stood talking to one another for a short time before Evie's brother appeared at their side.

"Don't you two ever get tired of talking to each other?" he teased. "Seriously, Nate, don't feel like you have to babysit her or anything. I'd say you've done your part by giving her a room in your place."

Evie felt a twinge of resentment towards her brother. She puts her life on hold for a couple of months as per his request, and he repays her by trying to take away the cute guy she's talking to? Should she be thinking of Nate as just some cute guy to flirt with? Of course not. He's her brother's good friend, so of course Michael would have no reason to think she'd be intentionally flirting with him, so technically he doesn't realize what he's doing. *But I am still unable to give him a free pass,* she thought to herself.

Nate seemed nonplussed by Michael's sudden interruption. "Mike, you know I think your sister's a riot. It's never a chore to talk to her. Although," he continued, looking at his watch, "I think we should probably get going anyway. I didn't realize how late it is, and, with the risk of sounding like a babysitter, you have a big bachelorette party tomorrow night, so you should probably get some rest."

"You're probably right. Charlotte will be all glowing and rested, having stayed in tonight, like a wise woman, and I'll be the ogre with bags under my eyes. Michael, tell your bride-to-be that I'll see her tomorrow evening. Let me just grab my purse so we can head out."

When they exited through the door, Nate looked down at her and carefully asked, "I know you're hoping to avoid the dark circles under your eyes for tomorrow, but any chance you'd be up for a quick stroll around the block to clear our heads? This weather is just too gorgeous to let it go to waste."

"That actually sounds perfect."

Each of them tried to steal furtive sideways glances at the other as they sauntered off, not really caring where they were going; sometimes successful, sometimes not. "So tell me, Evie," Nate asked her, "Have you ever dated any of your brother's friends?"

"No, I haven't." She paused. "You know, I had never given it too much thought until recently when he and I had a conversation about this very thing. I didn't realize how against it he would be until he started telling me about this 'guy code' and all his friends from high school and college knew dating Grace or I was off limits. Of course, the same rule did not apply in reverse, as a string of mine and Grace's friends who were left nursing broken hearts would attest to."

She was getting a little nervous as to where this conversation was heading and had the good sense to realize if she ever wanted to have such a talk with Nate, she'd want to do it in a more sober condition. But unfortunately her sense was not that keen at the moment to realize how curt the response she chose was. "He's probably right, anyway. I'd hate to be the reason for a rift in a friendship of his."

"No, of course not," Nate thoughtfully replied. "I've just always been someone who lives by the old adage, 'Never say never' myself." After a few moments of the two of them walking silently side by side, he said, "I guess we should try to flag down a cab and get ourselves home. Thanks for the walk, Evie. It was enlightening as usual."

Twenty-Four

E vie and her friends were the last to be picked up by the limo for Charlotte's bachelorette party as Nate's apartment was the closest to their first stop. This was the place that Maura was the most excited to get to.

"Ladies, we're going to be taking private salsa lessons. I tell you, Evie, you may not be the biggest fan of this Emily, but that is a seriously great idea to get things started."

Nate looked up from his couch and felt the need to put his two cents in. "She's right, you know. You never know when you'll need to salsa dance to save someone's life. It's probably more important than the Heimlich maneuver."

Evie swatted him on his head with her magazine as she walked behind the couch. "Oh, yeah? What about when I go to Argentina, and I'm in a sweaty bar, with a palm leaf ceiling fan as the only form of relief from the heat, circling slowly overhead, and a handsome local looks at me deeply and says in a sexy Spanish accent, "Excuse me, senorita, but do you salsa?""

Nate just looked at her. "How is that comparable to saving someone's life?" he asked her dryly.

"Well, it's not exactly a knife and scalpel procedure, but I'll meet a cute Latino. So it's more life affirming than life saving. But close enough for me."

Maura and Amanda nodded in agreement. Kelly laughed. "The palm leaf ceiling fan is a nice touch. I like your attention to detail. I can totally feel the heat and humidity bearing down on me. As a matter of fact, I think my hair started to frizz when you said that."

"Well maybe when the four of you return tonight you can give me a demonstration and I'll let you know if that changes my mind on how important the salsa is."

"I was going to put this magazine away, but I'd say you deserve another rap to the noggin for that comment," Evie said while crossing back behind the couch again. Nate was obviously expecting some kind of retaliation because he was ready for her and neatly stopped her wrist in its track before the magazine landed on its intended target. He easily flipped her over the couch, and she laid there a minute, laughing, enjoying the feel of his hands on her arms, and the back of her head on his thigh. *I like this guy so much*, was all she could think. And immediately banished it. *He's my interim roommate, and one of Michael's best friends, and he would never look twice at me. Stop it.*

Maura's stifled laughter brought her back to her senses and reminded her there were other people in the room and that she had probably laid there for about ten seconds too long if she really wanted her friends to believe that she didn't have any feelings for Nate. She tried for light and breezy as she smoothed her hair. "Now you've probably ruined all of Amanda's hard work of curling my hair. You'll have to answer to her, mister."

"Nah," Amanda answered quickly. "Now it just looks like you have that sexy bed head kind of vibe. Don't you think so, Nate?" she asked innocently, not at all innocently. Kelly, Amanda, and Maura were all waiting for his answer, because they were trying to get a read on his feelings for their friend by how he responded. None of them even knew what they were hoping he'd say, they all just thought they'd know it if they heard it. Kind of like how people describe finding the wedding dress of their dreams: you just know it when you put it on.

"I think the hair looks great, but you could shave it off and as long as you smiled, no one would even notice. It's your smile that knocks people out."

So *that* was what they were hoping for.

———

When all was said and done twelve girls filed out of the stretch limo in front of the dance club where they were to be given their private salsa lessons at eight o'clock that night. They were all giggling, partly due to excitement, partly due to the two empty champagne bottles they finished in the limo on the forty-five minute ride over.

"I hope the champagne hasn't dulled my senses too much," Maura said. "I'm usually quite graceful on the dance floor, you know. I've got particularly good eye/hand coordination."

Evie looked at her quickly, and glanced over at Amanda and Kelly. "I'm just going to make sure nothing has changed drastically in the month or so that I've been away. Maura still has to stop on the street when she's dialing her cell phone, right?"

"Oh, that's right," Maura said, stopping suddenly. "I actually *need* the alcohol to enhance my coordination. In that case, I'm going to be superb," she said, twirling around the room they entered.

Their instructors, Lena and Ernesto, wasted no time getting the one hour class started. They whirled around the room to a collection of songs from artists like Mark Antony, Ricky Martin, and Buena Vista Social Club to get them in the mood. Lena and Ernesto shouted at them to, "Sway," and "Feel the Music." Kelly, who was Evie's partner, started to laugh after their attempt at what they termed a salsa "free style" during a particularly long bongo segment. "I couldn't tell you one single rule of salsa dancing, but I am having a blast."

At the end of the hour, all the girls gathered around a table that had been laid out with Coronas, tequila, chips and salsa (which happened to be the name of the lesson plan, which Amanda found to be hilarious when someone told her. "Get it guys?" she asked, turning to her three friends. "Chips and *Salsa?*" That's fantastic.")

All the girls dove into the alcohol, except Charlotte who nursed her seltzer with lemon. Emily started doling out shots of tequila to everyone else. When Evie demurred, saying, "Tequila is not my friend," Emily responded with, "Really, I thought you Americans all partied like rock stars, as the saying goes."

"Some of us party more like Boy Bands," was Evelyn's answer.

"This American could be persuaded to have some tequila, though," Amanda said, while grabbing the shot glass out of Emily's hand. After a cough, a gasp, and a sputter, Amanda got out, "That hurt. I officially drop my Rock Star status to Boy Band as well."

Evie was talking to Constance and Jacquelyn when they were told the next group was coming up and they should go downstairs to the actual club and "practice their moves on the dance floor."

"That should be interesting, since I don't actually remember anything they just taught us," was Constance's comment.

Kelly, who had just walked up to their group agreed. 'I know what you mean. I'm afraid I'll end up reverting to my old standby move of The Sprinkler and Lena and Ernesto would have full on coronaries if they were to catch sight of me doing it."

Maura ran past them all on the staircase, shouting at them with her head thrown over her shoulder, "Last one to do The Running Man is a rotten egg."

Emily walked behind everyone, muttering to herself. "Front, middle, back, middle. Count it out. One, two, three, five, six, seven."

————

After a half an hour of Emily dancing salsa like a pro and the eleven other girls doing whatever came naturally to them, Maura spied Amanda out in the lobby using her cell phone. She motioned to Kelly and Evelyn to follow her out and see what was up. "I really hope she's not calling that asswipe, Garrett. I've got a bad feeling about this."

The three of them arrived in the vestibule in time to hear Amanda partly slur out, "Hi baby. 'Sme, Amanda. We're at the bachelorette party for Evie's sister-in-law and I just thought I'd call. Umm...oh hello there. Did I wake you?" In an instant the girls saw Amanda's smile evaporate off her face. "Why do I hear a girl's voice in your apartment? Who's there?" Her tone was decidedly more sober. "Garrett, you're not at work. I called your apartment, not your cell, so don't tell me you're at the office with a co-worker. I'm not that drunk and I'm not that stupid." She interrupted him while he was obviously trying to talk his way out of trouble.

"I'd say that to use the phrase 'this obviously isn't working out' would be the understatement of the year. I'll be by to pick up the key to my apartment next week. Carry on."

Amanda still had her back to her friends while she dabbed viciously at her eyes and then ran her fingers through her hair. "I know you guys are there. Just give me a sec, okay?" She let out another deep sigh and turned around. "Finding out about your boyfriend's infidelity is a huge buzz kill. I'm going to need something stronger."

Maura put her arm around Amanda's shoulder. "Carry on? That was brilliant. Let's go get a drink and met some cute ruggers. Is that what they call rugby players, Evie?"

"I'm not sure, but I say we go with it. Makes sense."

By the time they returned to their group it had been decided they would head to Dickens, a favorite pub of Charlotte's that was in the vicinity. Evie thought it was a great idea. Charlotte looked tired and she was sure all that dancing was beginning to wear her out. They'd get her a comfortable seat if possible, so she could try to get her second wind.

They filed into the limo, even more unstable than when they arrived, and the kindly driver just tutted after them as they got situated. He poked his head in after the last one fell into her seat. "Now, ladies, it might not be my place to say anything, but you should have a glass of water every now and then tonight. You don't want to be feeling too awful tomorrow morning."

Amanda raised her bleary eyes to the gentleman. "I just called my boyfriend in America and found out he was cheating on me."

"You may get pissed, my dear."

"I know; I am. I'm so angry right now."

"No, sweetie," Evie said in her ear. "He means you can get drunk. That's just how they say it here."

"Damn right I'm going to get pissed, then. To Dickens," Amanda crowed.

"To Dickens," they all shouted back at her...even the driver.

When they entered the pub, they realized it was the right call. There was a decent crowd of people there, yet they still managed to grab a couple of bar seats. That was mostly due to Charlotte throwing her belly around a bit and complaining how badly her feet were hurting her at the moment.

"Oh, here now luv, why don't you take my seat and take a load off. I wouldn't be able to watch the game comfortably, knowing you were standing there," one nice guy told her.

Charlotte sat down gratefully, and groaned in pleasure. "You have no idea how happy you just made me. My girlfriends took me to get salsa lessons for my hen party tonight." She laughed. What kind of idea is that for a seven months pregnant woman, I ask you?"

"A fabulous one," Jacquelyn laughed at her. "The hen party is not about the bride, as you well know. It's about her friends. Now I'm going to buy your knight in shining armor here a drink for so graciously offering his barstool to you before he thinks we have no manners at all."

"And that's the last we saw of Jacky," Evie laughed to Amanda, who was standing beside her.

It turned out Jacky's new friend actually *was* part of a rugby team, and he was there with some of his teammates, who had no trouble mingling with Charlotte's hen party.

Amanda, in particular, had her radar on. "What do you think of that guy?" she asked half of the bachelorette party, and pointed to a man wearing a flannel shirt with a pair of jeans and work boots. His dark hair was still slightly damp, either from a recent shower or it had started to rain while they had been inside drinking, and he had a dimple in his left cheek. "He's the complete opposite of Garrett, in that Garrett would never wear flannel and work boots, so that's a positive for him. It also doesn't hurt that he's totally gorgeous."

"Go for it," a few of the girls cajoled Amanda. "Yeah," Charlotte's friend, Marni, added. "You just need to throw the cat around a little and you'll start to feel better."

Kelly turned to Marni with a gleeful expression on her face. "You do know you have just introduced me to the greatest line I've ever heard, right?"

All this was more than enough encouragement for Amanda. She fluffed up her slightly limp bob, and straightened out her one piece, peasant inspired, red dress before grabbing two shots from the bar in front of Evie. "If these aren't ours, please send my apologies and two new shots to whomever they belong to," she said, managing to look quite graceful wending her way through the crowded bar, even in her red high heeled sandals with many drinks in her system. Her friends cheered silently as she managed to arrive next to "Hot Flannel Man," as he would forever be known as, even when they learned his name was Ben, and proffered her introductory shot.

"Well," Emily said in a voice that could only be described as something halfway between sneering and full of respect, "your friend seems to bounce back awfully quickly. I can't decide if that's trampy or admirable."

Kelly raised her glass in Amanda's direction, even though she couldn't see her through the crowd, and said, "A little bit of both, bless her soul. Here's to resilience," and finished the remainder of her drink.

Emily gave a half smile, raised her drink, and added her own two cents. "And let's not forget to a hot rebound guy."

"You must drink to a hot rebound guy," Constance agreed, as they all drank again.

Emily looked a little nervous as she walked up to the group at the bar, having just made a phone call. "Well, alright then," she began and waited for everyone to give her their attention. When they did, she started speaking again. "Okay. Here's the situation."

Evie couldn't help herself and blurted out, without a moment's hesitation, "My parents went away for a week's vacation." She was actually kind of horrified until Maura piped in with the next line. "They left the keys to the brand new Porsche," and started to snicker. One of the guys from the rugby team that had been flirting with their bachelorette party was walking by and finished off the stanza for them. "Was it mine? Hmmm. Well, of course not." He didn't even break stride as he headed towards the door marked Bucks.

"Damn," Kelly said appreciatively. "He totally had the pauses in all the right places. That was a spot on rendition. I did not expect Will Smith early nineties to translate in London, quite frankly. It's good to know that in today's world, there are still some things that can bring us together." She shakily picked up her lager and tried to aim the rim of the pint glass in the general direction of her lips. She more or less managed to get most of the beer in her mouth rather than on her shirt, but Evie was sure if she attempted this too many more times, the ratio was going to switch. Much to the detriment of Kelly's silk camisole that was probably more expensive than anything else she brought with her for the weekend. *It's weird how some of the most expensive pieces of clothing are the ones that have the least amount of fabric,* Evie thought to herself, going off in a mini tangent inside her own head before she realized that Emily had started to speak again.

"If I might address the rather serious situation that has apparently arisen without anymore outbursts from our dear American friends, I'm afraid to say the limo driver has apparently decided to move the car from the premises and apparently has his mobile turned off."

Constance turned to the four girls. "Dear American Friends, you do know how pissy Emily can get when one's ringer is off."

"Apparently," was all Maura had to add to set the five of them off into fits of giggles.

Emily glared in their general direction and moved off to talk to her sister. All they heard was, "Charlotte, if you had just let me get the walkie talkies like I wanted to this never would've happened."

Poor Charlotte had to take control of the situation and try to calm Emily down. "Em, relax. The driver probably just went to get a cup of coffee or a bite to eat. We told him we would be here for awhile. Let's not get ahead of ourselves. I don't think we're stranded. Besides, what's the worst that could happen? We're in the middle of London, for Christ's sake. We'll just grab taxis. No one's in a rush to get home, so stop fussing and let's just enjoy the night. Now I want you to take a look around and see if there's anyone you fancy and we'll try to work a little magic in that direction, okay?"

Evie was startled to overhear Emily's response, because it was so tender, contrite and...sisterly. She had never thought of Emily in terms like that. "I'm sorry, Char. I just wanted your night to go perfectly. Well, as perfectly as it could go for a just about seven month's pregnant bride-to-be on her hen night," she laughed.

Evelyn would never have guessed that Emily came equipped with even the slightest bit of a sense of humor. "The ice princess melteth," she mumbled to herself.

"You say something, Evs?" Kelly asked.

"Um, yeah, I'm going to get shots. I'll be right back." When she returned with a tray of shooters for the entire group—something yummy and pink was all she asked for—she made a point of giving Emily a genuine smile and saying, "You worked really hard on this night. It's been a lot of fun. Thanks for organizing it."

She was rewarded by a smile from Emily that was as real as it was caught off guard. "Cheers," she said as she raised her shot to her lips and finished it off in one swallow.

A few hours later, Charlotte had taken charge of her friends, and was ushering the majority of them into the limo, for the last time that night. The exception being Jacquelyn and their other friend, Marni (she of the greatest line that Kelly had ever heard), who were going for a late night snack with the rugby player who had kindly given up his seat to Charlotte, and another teammate of his.

"Don't worry Connie," she had assured her roommate as she left, "we're just getting some chips and then Marni and I will cab it home together. We'll see you in a little while." She gave a quick wink to Amanda, "To hell with blokes who don't appreciate the great women they've got. There are plenty of other guys out there."

Amanda held up a scrap of paper with Ben's number on it, "Amen to that, sister. Maybe I'll move here," she added, looking thoughtfully at the piece of paper she held in her hand.

Thankfully the accounting rule of LIFO that Evie somehow remembered from high school applied to limo rides as well. "Last in first out! That means we get home first," she shouted gleefully to her friends.

"I can't wait to put on my baggy pajamas and get out of this halter top and skirt," Maura said, rubbing her shoeless feet. "If I had to take one more step in these heels, I would've had to go barefoot in that bar...and that's just gross."

Everyone else agreed that the thought of comfy p.j.'s was the only thing keeping them going.

The limo driver pulled up to Nate's place and the four friends somehow managed to extricate themselves from the car without falling head first onto the pavement. The limo driver smiled benevolently at Amanda and said, "Don't forget the aspirin and water before you go to sleep, young lady, or you'll be having some big regrets come tomorrow morning."

"So, do you think I should call Ben tomorrow?" she asked him in a confiding manner. "Even though I leave the day after tomorrow?"

"Luv, he'd be lucky to talk to you," was his reply.

Twenty-Five

A manda woke up in a condition that Evie claimed could only be described as still drunk, and the other three girls were definitely a little worse for wear. So to say that they were delirious with joy over the breakfast feast that Nate had prepared for them would be like saying puppies are kind of cute.

Maura looked at the table, laden with pancakes and bacon on one side, and muffins, juice, and coffee on the other and sighed in happiness. "This really is our own slice of heaven right here in the Queen's backyard. Many thanks to our gracious host."

Nate nodded his head in acknowledgement. "I had a feeling something like this might be in order after the big night out last night. So how was it? Was the bachelorette right pissed?" he teased.

"Oh, God yeah," Evie replied with equal sarcasm. "For a woman who's seven months pregnant, Charlotte can really hold her liquor. Although she did get a surprisingly large number of double takes from the other patrons when she was doing all those shots of lemon drops, which I found weird. Even the rugby players seemed to have a hard time wrapping their head around it."

Amanda just held her head and took a small bite of a muffin. "Please stop talking about alcohol. The only silver lining in this unholy cloud that is my head is the fact that I don't have to board a plane today. I would have to change my flight if that were the case, because the idea of actually flying is just not feasible."

"Sweetie, how are you doing?" Kelly asked. "And I don't mean your head or stomach. I mean your heart."

Nate threw a questioning glance in Evie's direction who just mouthed, "I'll tell you later," back at him.

Amanda gave her first genuine smile of the morning to her big hearted friend and said, "I think you are the only person in the world who could ask that question and not end up covered in vomit." She paused before continuing. "And to be honest, my heart hurts less than my head or stomach, so I'm guessing that's a good thing. Ew, forgive me for using the Martha Stewart catch phrase. But thanks for asking."

"You only get penalized for using the Paris Hilton catch phrase, Mandy. You get a free pass for Martha," Evie reminded her.

The rest of the morning was spent in their pajamas, rehashing all the funny moments the evening had offered them, with Nate laughing along to the stories they shared, until he left to relieve Hannah at the coffee shop at noon. "Remember what I said, Evie. If you're really bored you can always bring the girls over to the store. Of course, you should prepare them for the fact they could be pressed into service like you always are, but we do have fresh coffee and scones for consumption."

"After everything I just ate," marveled Maura, "I am truly shocked and dismayed to realize that I could eat some scones right now."

"Alright then. Maybe I'll see you guys a little later," he called out as he walked out the front door.

"How cute is it that he drives a Volvo?" Kelly asked when the coast was clear. "This gorgeous hunk of a guy, out driving a safe, family vehicle? It's adorable."

Evie just muttered, "Who even thinks like that?" while her cheeks flushed a bright red.

———————

No one was very surprised when they decided to head to Nate's coffee house about an hour or so later. After all, he was offering them free treats and coffee, and they were all hung over. No brainer!

Evie decided to use the Tube with her friends after eliciting promises from them all not to scoff at her highlighted map. "Believe me, I know I would be the first person to laugh if I saw one of you holding this thing up, but trust me, if I don't have this on my person, we'll never get anywhere. We'll just ride the rails all day and night and there will be no coffee or crumb cake for anyone." That seemed to do the job of keeping everyone silent, at least in front of Evie.

They arrived in front of The Olde Grind, no worse for wear; just really craving a jolt of joe to pep them all up.

When they walked into the shop Nate and Hannah both had big smiles for the girls, but Hannah noticed that Nate's eyes lingered on Evie far more than anyone else and stayed there for quite a while. Hannah smiled knowingly at Nate and turned her attention quickly to Evie, who was introducing her friends to Nate's second in command. They spent the next three hours sharing stories from the previous night's bachelorette party with Nate and Hannah, while Amanda kept her face in her hands for most of the rehashing, claiming no knowledge of what they were talking about.

"I don't even know if I ever told you last night, Mandy, but the shots you grabbed from the bar to introduce yourself to "Hot Flannel Man" actually were not from our personal stash like you originally thought, but belonged to two guys who were bus drivers for those cool double decker buses," Evie told her.

"Presumably off duty," Maura added.

"So I think that would make you some sort of international thief," was Kelly's take on the situation.

"Even if the shots were then paid back?" Amanda challenged.

"Alright, so you're not exactly a fugitive from justice, but it would make a nice story," Kelly answered.

Maura laughed. "You just better hope we don't turn you in to Interpol before our flight leaves tomorrow. You might not be allowed into the Continental frequent flyer lounge."

"Oh," Kelly moaned. "Don't remind me that we leave tomorrow. That means I have less then thirty-six hours before I am drowning under a pile of finger paintings."

"Oh, please," Evie said. "Like you are not totally excited to get back to the classroom and engage those budding minds like you like to say."

"Fine, but that doesn't mean I can't wish that we still had a few more days to hang out with you."

"I do too, but you'll see. I'll be back in New York before you know it. Michael's wedding is a little less then a month away. It'll be here before any of us know it," Evie promised. She was startled to realize that as the words were leaving her mouth, she really didn't get any sense of excitement at the thought of going back to New York. And at the exact same time, Nate was thinking the same thing. Neither noticed how both faces fell for a moment, before plastering on their false smiles. But that didn't mean the other four women sitting around the table didn't.

Twenty-Six

T he following day came too quickly for Evie, and she was having trouble concentrating on the road to Heathrow.

"What the fuck is wrong with that lorry driver, anyway," she mumbled to herself, as she swerved to avoid a near miss with an oncoming truck.

"You do know you just called that trucker a lorry driver, right?" Maura teased her good naturedly.

"Did I?" Evie responded distractedly. "That's odd."

"Yes, yes it is, since you are an American. I thought when you came over here that you could possibly fall into the misguided footsteps of Madonna and Gwyneth Paltrow and suddenly start using an English accent. Wasn't expecting a full on change of vocabulary, though, I have to say," was Amanda's take on the situation.

"Serves me right for making so much fun of my Mom, I guess. As soon as I'm back in New York I'm sure it'll stop all on its own accord. Right?"

"Absolutely," Maura agreed. "When do you get home anyway? Have you set a date?"

"No, I haven't booked my return flight or anything like that. The wedding isn't until the end of next month and I just haven't focused on anything past that. I suppose I should start thinking about it, though. I'm sure Nate is probably anxious to get his home back and lose the permanent house guest."

"No, I definitely did not get that vibe at all," was all Maura said on the matter.

A slow smile spread across Evie's face. "Really? Well, at least I'm not wearing out my welcome," she added, before mentally telling her face muscles to relax and stop grinning like a fool.

———————

The goodbyes were much more subdued than the raucous hellos from five days earlier. They lingered for as long as they could before the three girls had to head to the gate for their departure.

"Alright, now," Evie said. "I am really going to miss you guys, but I'll be home before we even know it." She turned quickly to Amanda. "Are you going to be alright, after everything's that just happened?"

Kelly and Maura each put a protective arm around Amanda and said in unison, "She'll be fine."

Maura smiled serenely and said, "I think we'll both have to go with her to get her key and other belongings. And when we do, I'm sure it wouldn't surprise you at all to hear that Amanda had a bit of trouble finding some of her possessions and in that time span, somehow, Garrett's TIVO was changed so it no longer recorded episodes of *Desperate Housewives*. It'll be weird, I know, but these things happen from time to time. Technology is not always perfect."

"I'll be sad not to be there," was all Evie could say before her voice started to give away her emotions. "I'll miss you guys," she said quickly as she gave them each another hug before they headed down the corridor for International flights.

Maura looked like she wanted to say something else and was having a debate inside her head as to whether or not she should, so Evie decided to let her off the hook and ask her what it was.

"Penny for your thoughts?"

Maura smiled at the invitation and just whispered in her ear, "Just do me one favor please. Wait until *after* Michael's wedding to set up your return flight. I just think it's important that you not have a set date in your mind for the next month looming in your head."

"What difference does that make?"

"I have no idea, but I just want you to promise me," she said earnestly.

"Alright," Evie agreed. "I promise."

"We'll see you when we see you," chirped Maura and Evie waved one final time before heading out to the car park. *The parking lot she quickly corrected herself. It's called a frickin' parking lot. Tonight*, she promised herself, *was all about pajamas and staying away from alcohol!*

Twenty-Seven

W hen Evie got out of the shower, she threw on her flannel pajamas and brushed out her hair. She was totally looking forward to a quiet night in watching a movie and reading some of those tabloid rags she picked up with her curry before she came home. It was shocking to her, but the British tabloids were somehow even more intrusive than the American ones. How was that possible? But more importantly, how could she have lived in New York City all these years and never tried a take away curry before? It was incomprehensible to her. And kind of unforgivable she reproached herself. *What the hell else am I missing out on* she wondered?

She threw her damp hair up in a butterfly clip and watched as it fanned out behind her head. Magazines in hand, she headed to the living room, only to stop short at the sight of Nate sitting on the floor in front of the television already. Sweatpants and a graphic tee-shirt with a frayed hem didn't really scream "Big Night on The Town" to her. She looked at him, puzzled, the furrow above her brow proving how confused she was.

"I thought you were going out tonight? Boys on the hunt and all that, right?" she asked.

"I was kind of hoping you wouldn't mind the company. To be honest, the idea of heading out to the pubs and trying to be debonair and charming felt slightly overwhelming to me tonight. I'm exhausted. No energy to try to sell myself to some poor unsuspecting young lady. Plus, you talked up the virtues of a night of temperance so aptly; I find the idea rather appealing." He gave her his best sad-sack smile and waited for Evie's response.

She considered her cherry blossom flannel pajamas and half snorted, half sighed. "If we can avoid all talk of my attire, I would be delighted to have some company during my self imposed night of detoxing. I've only got a curry for one, though. And I'm not a big fan of the idea of sharing frankly. I've got a bit of the Joey Tribiani in me if you know what I mean. Oh, and one more rule...I still get to pick the movie. And it's going to be the Joan Allen/Kevin Costner vehicle, *The Upside of Anger*."

"Your pajamas remind me of a cherry flambé, in a good way, I can't say I get your Joey Tribiani reference, and I loved *Bull Durham*, so I'm sure this will be just as good."

"You obviously don't read movie reviews but more importantly you didn't say where you stand on the point of my not sharing the one curry. Emphasis on the word one."

"Well, I saved the best for last." Nate held up two pints of Ben and Jerry's ice cream. One Chubby Hubby and one Phish Food. "I'll share mine if you share yours."

"Your status has immediately jumped to Best Detox Partner Ever! We should probably eat your stuff first though...so it doesn't melt."

"I do have a freezer, you know," Nate mentioned.

"My detox, my rules."

Nate produced two spoons from beside him on the rug. "I was hoping you'd say that. I didn't bring bowls, though. I'm going to go on the assumption you don't have cooties and we can eat right out of the pint containers. And that'll make two less dishes to do later."

"You do have a dishwasher, you know," Evie reminded him in the same sing-song manner he reminded her about the freezer.

"Fine, I'm lazy and don't feel like getting up to gather two bowls for us. Unless you do, of course?"

"Spoon please."

With spoons in hand, they set upon the task of making the ice cream disappear. After a couple of minutes of silence, Nate broke the quiet with a question.

"Do you have a time table for your detox set up or is it done all very willy-nilly?"

"This being my first imposed moratorium on the consumption of copious amounts of alcohol, I'm going to go with the wily nily approach to guide me through. I don't think you want to be too rigid on your first outing. It might make you averse to trying it again, and I've come to the sad realization that perhaps a night in every once in a while, will not only *NOT* kill me, it might help me live longer."

"I could learn a lot from your wisdom, sensei."

"Right? Like did you know that a goldfish only has the capacity to remember something for three seconds?

"I did not know that. That is weird wild stuff," Nate said in his best Johnny Carson impression.

"That is quite possibly the worst Johnny Carson impression I've ever heard. You might not be aware of this, but Johnny Carson did not speak with a British accent."

"Really? I thought I nailed it. So tell me, Evie. Are you sad now that your friends have left?"

Evie thought carefully before she answered his question. "You know, I don't know how to answer that, exactly. Of course, it was wonderful to see them all again, and I had so much fun while they were here. But I don't feel as," she paused, searching for the right word, "ALONE, I guess, as I thought I would when they left.

Which is kind of enlightening for me. I mean, I have always seen myself as almost unable to function without them, to tell you the truth. I'm kind of proud of myself that for this set amount of time that I've been away, I've not only been able to function, I've kind of thrived. It's exciting to explore a new city without any preconceived notions and without anyone else's agenda but my own. Well, my own and some upcoming nuptials, of course, but hopefully you know what I mean. And it's nice to see that no matter how much time may pass where I don't see my friends on a daily basis, we're able to pick right up from where we left off. It's made me appreciate my friends even more, and at the same time, appreciate the fact that I'm still able to grow as a person, alone." She laughed a little self consciously. "That probably sounds like a bunch of Dr. Phil mumbo-jumbo, but hopefully you get the gist of what I'm trying to say."

"I guess you've finally realized that it's okay to live your own life on your own terms, and still feel good about the relationships you have with those around you."

"Who's the sensei now?" Evie teased.

They wordlessly switched their pints of ice-cream, to swap flavors. "Great," Evie complained, "I've talked so much you've managed to eat more ice cream than I have. Now I get to ask you a question that will hopefully spark such animated conversation on your part, I'll be able to catch up. Okay, what's the craziest breakup story you've ever heard that you're at least ninety-nine percent sure actually happened. In other words, the story had to have come from a reliable source."

"Actually, I know this bloke from university that almost accidentally killed the girl he was trying to break up with."

Evie eyed Nate suspiciously. "Accidentally? How exactly does that happen?"

"Well, they had a huge row in a pub and Evan, that's my friend's name, got so pissed, both drunk, as in my vernacular, and angry, as in yours, that he made the huge mistake of screaming at her, 'That's it. I never want to see you again, you stupid bitch. It's over.' He then made the bigger mistake of storming out of the pub and getting into his car. Unfortunately for him, he was so drunk he put the car in drive when he meant to throw it in reverse. Things got a little worse when the girl, Renee, ran out of the pub screaming at him that he couldn't dump her, she was dumping him, and he slammed on the gas, thinking he was going to go backwards, and instead ended up making a beeline straight at her. Luckily, he realized in time what was happening and swerved into a parked car to avoid hitting her at the last moment."

Evie just stared at Nate while he told this story, a half smile on his face. "What's even remotely funny about that story?" she asked when she realized he was starting to chuckle.

"I'm just trying to decide if this falls into the category of a breakup story, per se, since right after that, they ran for each other as if their lives depended on it and he proposed to her on the spot. It's been eight years and they're still married."

They switched pints again and this time it was Nate's turn to frown when seeing the damage Evie had inflicted on the carton while he had been speaking.

"Okay, then," he managed to sputter while at the same time throwing a heaping spoonful of Phish Food into his mouth. How about you? Worst breakup story you've heard?"

"This one is so easy. It actually happened to a girl I went to grammar school with. She married her high school sweetheart and had no clue he had the bad habit of constantly cheating on her. He also happened to be in the Coast Guard and had an affair with a higher up. You may not know this, not being an American citizen, but that is part of our military and thus subject to the same strict moral codes imposed on the other branches. The affair became public knowledge to everyone but his wife, and he was actually court martialed and sentenced to six months in jail. At this point, you may assume that he sucked it up and told his wife. After all, he was heading to jail. What other option is there you may ask yourself? The option of telling her he was going on a submarine for six months and would not have any contact with the outside world for that duration of time would be the answer."

"I did not see that coming," was all Nate could manage to get out in his surprise.

"Who would? So he actually served his jail sentence and came home, his wife none the wiser."

"It's a great story, one for the ages, really, but where's the breakup part?" asked Nate.

"I'm getting there. Now, back when I first heard this story from a mutual friend a couple of years ago, the sticking point for me was that she would buy the fact he couldn't contact her for that long just because he was in a submarine. Turns out that was the believable part. They do go for months at a time, submerged, without contacting the outside world. What my friend told me actually should've tipped the girl off was the fact the Coast Guard doesn't have any submarines. That's just an aside, really, in case any of these thoughts were swirling around your head. But to stay on topic, she finally found out when she got a phone call from his parole officer. She first thought he introduced himself as Petty Officer William Butler. A title used in the Coast Guard. He actually said, "This is parole office William Butler. I'm assigned to your husband's case." From what I heard they actually spoke on the phone for about ten minutes before she realized they were having two separate conversations. Hers based on the fact of who she assumed he was and his on whom he assumed she knew him to be. When her husband got home, he found all his stuff on the driveway, a la *Waiting to Exhale* sans the burning flames shooting around all over the driveway. Her Dad was a fireman and she was a little too nervous over the possibility of setting her house on fire by accident."

It took Nate a moment to even speak, as he was intent on just trying to let the story sink in. "That could quite possibly be the greatest story ever told, as long as you are not the wife. Have the years that have passed allowed her to view it with any humor at all?"

"From what I understand, I'm not going to lead with that question at our next reunion, should she be in attendance."

"No, I suppose not."

At this point, neither container of ice cream held anything and the tops were starting to fray a bit where the spoons had been invading. Evie just looked at Nate sadly. "I'm too full for my curry right now."

"Me too," Nate agreed, patting his belly as though he was practicing to be a sidewalk Santa. "Why don't we digest a little bit before we even attempt it? What are your thoughts on taking a quick walk around the block to help that along? Does detox need to be done completely indoors?" he inquired.

"No, no set rule against sober strolls." She stared dubiously down at her pajamas. "I'm not quite sure where the rules stand on strolls in pajamas...because God knows if I'm too lazy to grab a bowl in the kitchen, I'm too lazy to change."

"I say you risk it. Who's going to see us anyway? It's ten o'clock on a Monday night. The young ones will be at the pub by now, which we won't walk by for fear of temptation, and the old ones will be in bed.

"You're sure you won't be too embarrassed to be seen with me?" she teased.

"I don't think I'd ever be embarrassed to be seen with you," Nate answered seriously.

Evie immediately went into her "joke to protect yourself mode."

"That sounds like a challenge you don't want to issue, buddy. I rise to occasions like that." Was it her imagination or did she notice a flicker of disappointment cross Nate's features as she once again stopped any potential opening for a conversation about the flirtations that had become more and more frequent between the two of them. She dismissed it just as quickly. Nate was an unbelievably gorgeous, single man in the middle of one of the most bustling cities in the world. There was no way that he would take even the slightest interest in her. It was just that European hospitality she heard so much about. Hell, she thought, in *Four Weddings and a Funeral* people would invite strangers to their life altering events without the slightest thought. That's all this is, she firmly told herself.

Nate matched her joking tone immediately and smiled easily at her. "I fully trust you that you have no shame, so please don't take my offhand comment as an invitation to make us look like fools," he said as they headed out the door.

―――――――

The night was crisp enough that they could see the hazy outline of their breath with each exhale. Evie loved the fact that the night could cool off so much it could feel like the middle of fall, even though the date on the calendar read the end of July. They wandered away from the apartment at a leisurely pace without any set route in mind. She breathed in the scent of the honeysuckle bushes that lined the street. In that one scent all of her childhood memories came roaring back to her.

"It's funny," she said, "how a smell or a song can set off a string of memories. Every time I smell that honeysuckle I'm reminded of growing up. But not just a specific memory involving Michael, Grace, and I sucking on a honeysuckle flower, but a big umbrella of memories. With the title of 'Happy Childhood Summer Moments.'"

"Do you usually make a mental outline with headings and subsets for your memories?" Nate teased.

"Not on purpose. But, like every time I hear the song, *Sign*, by Ace of Base, I always think about the girls who lived on my floor at college during my freshman year. Not just one night when the song came on, but all twelve of us, at different times, during that year. My mind works in strange and mysterious ways, I suppose."

"That it does." He gave a slight pause and continued on. So, what is it, about three weeks or so before your family comes back to London for all the pre-wedding festivities that are on the schedule?" Nate asked.

"Yeah, that's right. I can't believe how fast time has flown. To be honest, I was a little nervous I would feel like I had been here for an eternity by the time they came back, but I haven't even given it a thought. It's a testament to the lovely manners you Brits show us wayward travelers."

"You make it easy to want to welcome you," was all Nate said in return.

An unruly strand of hair fell out of the butterfly clip, letting Evie off the hook without having to reply. Instead she put the butterfly clip in her mouth and re-twisted her hair and snapped the clip back in place. She risked a sideways glance in Nate's direction, but he was already looking across the street where a slight commotion was occurring. A couple was out walking their dogs, but that wasn't really the problem. The fact that they were out with no less than eight dogs was. The dog parade, with their owners in tow, had crossed the street and was heading right in their direction, towards the dog park on the corner.

Nate laughed quietly and softly in Evie's ear, "I can't imagine what their flat looks like. Do you think the dogs let them have their own bed? Do you think they can even fit a bed in there with all those dogs?"

Evie was too caught up in the sensation of Nate's breath lingering in her ear to speak for a moment. She finally got her emotions in check and was able to speak in what she hoped sounded like her own voice. "Forget a bed. Can you imagine having to clean up the yard after all those dogs?"

The couple passed by Evie and Nate and gave a cheery wave, as they were propelled forward by four leashes each. Nate and Evie smiled back and got a chuckle out of the scene.

"Maybe we should just follow them. That way you can be assured no one will give your p.j's a passing glance."

"You're a prince. I take back all my comments about your gentlemanly manners. They're for shit."

They walked for about fifteen minutes in comfortable silence, one of them breaking it every now and then with a comment about a yard or storefront or restaurant. By the time they were coming upon The Ale House, Evie was ready to retrace their steps and head back to Nate's apartment. She was about to suggest it when two insanely drunk men staggered out from The Ale House's front door.

The larger of the two spied Evie in her pajamas first. "Oh, love, you're all ready to go back to my flat, are you? Glad to see you wore the sexy pajamas. The ones that really show off your cherry." The two of them were so busy laughing at themselves they never saw Nate's fist flying in their direction. It only took two swings to fall the big one who made the comments, and his friend decided it wasn't worth the effort to get his back. While he went stumbling down the street, Nate demanded an apology from his friend, sprawled out on the sidewalk.

"Hey, mate, I'm going to give you a piece of advice," Nate told him menacingly, as soon as he finished groveling to Evie. "I would imagine you don't have a girlfriend, strictly based on the way I just saw you behave. Never, ever, talk to a lady like that. They don't appreciate it, and in case you couldn't tell, neither will whoever they're with at the time."

"Hey, lady, I'm really sorry I offended you. No harm intended." He lowered his voice as he walked by her and continued. "But next time, maybe your boyfriend over here can raise his tolerance level a bit. He's got to expect some comments like that when he's out with a pretty girl in goofy pajamas. Maybe you can tell him he doesn't have to beat the living snot out of the guy giving the next one, just to prove how much he loves you."

If Nate heard the last bit he never let on by his expression. Instead, he just turned to Evie and asked, "You ready to head back?"

If Evelyn thought it was odd that he was acting like nothing out of the ordinary had just happened, she didn't let on. "Yeah. I'm starting to get a little cold anyway."

His reply to that was simply to throw his arm over her shoulder and bring her in tight as they walked down the street together. She decided to ignore all the voices in her head telling her to pull away, and just enjoyed the moment, walking under his protective arm, until they reached the flat.

As they climbed the steps and entered the hallway, she turned to him and said, "You know, that was really sweet what you did outside of The Ale House. But you should seriously be careful. You could've gotten really hurt."

"What makes you think I haven't already?" After a slight pause, he continued. "If you don't mind, I think I'll call it a night and head to bed."

Evie was confused but tried to remain pleasant when she answered him. "Sure, right...I guess that means you forfeit your half of the curry though," she teased him.

Nate already seemed miles away as he strode up the stairs towards his room in the back. "No problems. I think I'm still stuffed from dessert anyway." He had wandered into his room before Evie was able to process anything that had occurred since they had wandered past the pub.

What the frick just happened, she wondered. Back in his own bedroom, Nate was wondering almost the exact same thing. *What the bloody hell was that all about?*

When Evie woke up the next morning, her confusion over the previous night's events had her feeling more foggy and unsure than any of her most debilitating hangovers ever had. *If I didn't know any better I'd say Nate had been acting like a jealous lover. Which wouldn't necessarily be a bad thing, except for the fact we've never even kissed.* Her mind raced around in circles, going over every moment of their evening together. She couldn't remember the last time she had felt so comfortable or had so much fun simply being with another person. The night had gone by in a blur and she wondered how it might have otherwise ended if a middleweight boxing tournament hadn't reared its ugly head before they had gotten home.

She padded downstairs both dreading and hoping to find Nate sitting at the kitchen counter, holding a cup of coffee, asking her if she slept well. She hadn't, obviously, but he always asked, which was nice. It was quite a shock for her to see a note folded neatly in the middle of the counter instead. Her name covered the front of the sheet, written in his strong, but short strokes. He wrote like he talked; fast. She scanned the note and tried to read any hidden meanings behind the completely benign sentences.

Evie,
Got a call from Hannah early this morning. Had to help with a delivery problem. Hope you slept okay. If you get bored and want to visit, you know where to find me.
Cheers,
Nate

"As far as love sonnets go, it's a little lacking," she said to no one in particular, "but I'm still going to keep it." She tucked it into the waistband of her pajamas, so she could toss it in her bag later and reread it to try to dissect it some more when she was feeling more alert.

Twenty-Eight

E vie couldn't believe how the next few weeks flew by. She and Nate seemed to have settled into a kind of routine. On the days that he was working, she'd usually write for a while in a different set of locations. If the weather was nice, she'd stroll down to the park and grab a bench to get some work done. She figured she had to take advantage of the sunny days when they hit so she'd have a fighting chance of not looking like a cadaver next to Grace, who was, no doubt, in full "tanning for the wedding" training.

On the days when the weather wouldn't comply, she'd either stay at the flat or go to the library if she was in need of some outside time, foul weather or not.

By late afternoon, she'd usually find some excuse to grab the Tube and head to the coffee house, and would help with closing up the shop.

When Nate had off, he insisted on playing tour guide and she managed to check off all the places Charlotte's family had insisted she visit, and then some of Nate and Hannah's suggestions, as well. The two of them also found themselves running errands for the bride and groom whenever needed.

"Having you here was the greatest brainstorm I ever had," Michael congratulated himself one night at dinner. Michael and Charlotte had insisted on taking Evie and

Nate out to Flora's to thank them for the set of errands they had finished that afternoon for them, involving the invitations and cake.

"Honestly, it was no problem at all," Nate insisted.

"Yeah," Evie agreed. "I mean, any time you need someone to taste more cake, I am your girl. I almost feel like I should be taking you out to dinner...almost," she laughed.

"So," Charlotte asked, turning to Evie, "are you excited your family is going to be here tomorrow?"

Evie's blue eyes turned slightly troubled as she struggled for the right tone in her answer. "It's going to be great to see everyone. Although I can't believe how quickly this last month has gone by." She tried to keep her voice light as she continued. "But that just means the two of you are going to be husband and wife in no time at all, so that's even more exciting."

Evie let the conversation about the upcoming nuptials wash over here while her mind kept racing around the question she wasn't ready to answer. What was she going to do when the wedding happened and she didn't have a valid excuse to keep staying at Nate's anymore? And how long could she actually postpone booking her return flight home?

———————

Evie first set sight on her family the next night over dinner. They had insisted on checking themselves into the hotel after they arrived and grabbing a nap before they met up with Evie, Michael, Charlotte, and Charlotte's family. It was the first time both sides were together since the engagement party.

After the expected reunion hugs, they were shown their table in the back of the casual pub they had opted for. Lord Futterly looked right at home, but his wife and youngest daughter looked like they didn't relish the location.

Rebecca Dunleavy was looking at her menu and then turned to the waiter in the pub. "You know," she started out with, "I don't see them on the menu, but friends of ours, the Taylors, suggested a couple of different dishes that have local flavor. Could I order off the menu?"

"If the chef has the ingredients, I'm sure it won't be a problem."

"Great, how about something called 'meat and two veg'? Or they mentioned a fish dish called 'wedding tackle,' I believe?"

"HOLY SHIT!" Grace sputtered. "Mom is ordering what amounts to a penis using those crazy phrases from that *Austin Powers* movie. What in God's name is she thinking?"

Evie looked around the table to see if anyone else had noticed. Michael and Jack just sat there looking gob-smacked and trying their hardest not to convulse in fits of laughter. Charlotte was looking back and forth between her parents and Tom and Rebecca, with her mouth agog, looking like the proverbial fly catcher.

Evelyn started to giggle as she listened in. "The Taylor's are the couple that Mom and Dad were helping in the community garden. And if the air quotes around the word helping didn't drive the point home, by helping I really mean hindering."

"...or, oh what was it they said we had to try for dessert, Tom? 'Twig and berries' I think they called it? They said it was a chocolate pirouette cookie with berries on the side covered with fresh shaved coconut, right?"

"Otherwise known as a penis," Michael hissed to his sisters.

"What did Uncle Michael say about peanuts?" Annie asked, suddenly looking up from her menu.

"Just that he's a fan, Annie," Grace answered, shooting a warning shot over the bough (a.k.a. Evie's head.)

"It rather seems like the Taylor's might be really pissed off," Charlotte surmised now wearing a bemused expression on her face.

"Ya' think?" Evie and Grace asked at the same time, equally sarcastically.

"Now you know why I'm so thankful the Dunleavy's go for the semi-annual rather than annual family reunions. It's slightly terrifying and amplified tenfold," was Jack's two cents.

"And they mentioned something called bangers and mash, right hon?" her Mom continued on, looking at her husband.

That one had the whole Futterly clan looking slightly confused. "That actually is something," Charlotte whispered out of the corner of her mouth to the Dunleavy siblings.

Charlotte's mother and sister looked like they couldn't decide whether to strangle Rebecca or drop through a hole in the ground. To Evelyn's eyes she figured they would end up choosing option A if somebody didn't do something quick.

"Hey Mom," she yelled from her seat, "You know I think you should probably just stick with the shepherd's pie. Local flavor *and* it's on the menu."

"Oh, okay, Evelyn. Yes, that does look lovely. I'll have the shepherd's pie then, please."

"Sure thing, love. And maybe we could rustle up the Twig and Berries for dessert," the waiter said to Rebecca.

"Holy crap. Did he just wink at Mom?" Grace whispered. "I think I'm going to be sick."

"Daddy," Annie said to Jack, "can I have the meat and two veg Grandma was talking about for my dinner?"

"No you may not. Now please order some chicken fingers."

"You know," Annie said conspiratorially to her brother, Archie, "he always says we don't eat enough vegetables. I don't know why he'd think it was a bad idea to try them now."

Twenty-Nine

I t was two days later at the bridal luncheon held at the Futterly's manor, that the bottom started to fall out for Evie. It had started innocently enough, with Charlotte reiterating some good news that Michael had shared with his family previously, after Rebecca Dunleavy had tried to order a man's privates for dinner.

"So, I heard Michael told you that we found out we're having a boy. It's so fantastic, isn't it? Granted we wanted it to be a surprise and managed to last until the eighth month before some crazy ass midwife let it slip, but what are you going to do, right?"

Evie looked up slowly from her drink as Charlotte continued to talk. She didn't want to be judgmental, but Charlotte seemed slightly manic at the moment. Her hormones must be having the greatest game of pinball inside her body, she surmised, as Charlotte didn't even seem to stop for a breath.

"I don't know if Michael also mentioned it, but we did manage to come up with a name for him. Finally. I don't know, once we found out the sex of the baby everything just seemed more real and tangible and the name just came from within. We're going to name the baby Monty."

Evie waited for the comedic "ba dum bum" to quickly follow, along with some cheesy lines like, "I just flew in from Vegas and boy are my arms tired." Because there was no way they could possibly be thinking of naming their child Monty.

A few polite "oh's" and "how lovely" were bandied about and Evie looked around at her family completely transfixed. I have no idea who these people are, she thought solemnly. Because my actual family would have a few choice comments about that name.

Someone from the wait staff chose this moment to ask Charlotte a question about toast points, of all things, which led to questions about the cucumber sandwiches. Evie was amazed that there could be more than one way to serve a cucumber sandwich, but apparently there was and to not have an immediate answer from the bride-to-be was going to send the kitchen into great havoc, so Charlotte excused herself and went to check on lunch.

Evie thought this was as good a time as any for her to try and trigger something other than the zombie like responses her family had thrown out regarding the name of the newest Dunleavy.

"Oh my God!" Evie exclaimed. "They're going to name the baby Monty? As in 'Three Card?' Come on. Obviously, Michael didn't have much of a say in that one. Monty is so not the name of a cute little baby...it's the name of someone's dead, great uncle. Or it's what you name a Yorkshire terrier. Not a baby."

Evie was so involved with her ranting she didn't notice Grace start to imperceptibly shake her head from side to side, imploring Evie to shut up. She didn't notice her mother's eyes widen in horror and she would later claim that she never saw her father actually move his hand across his throat in an overt attempt to get her to stop talking. And since she didn't register any of their actions, she continued to say her piece.

"Is her pregnancy that horrible that she would pick a name like Monty? Why stop there? I hear The Prince of

Darkness is likely to become the new John. They could go with that. Give him a fighting chance with his peers."

It was at about this time that Charlotte came into her field of vision. Her wounded eyes were the first thing Evie noticed. *Oh shit*, she thought. *This is so not good.*

"You know, on second thought, I'm not feeling all that hungry. But you all stay and finish lunch." Charlotte left the tray of finger sandwiches on the table and hurried out the door.

Her parents looked at her in disbelief. Grace had telltale red splotches of embarrassment on her cheeks, and she hadn't even uttered a word.

Her usually mild mannered father was the first one to speak. "Well, Jesus Christ, Evie, don't just sit there. Go fix this!"

"But Dad, I don't know what I can do to sort this out. It's not like I can pretend I never said it. She obviously heard every word."

"It's called a sincere apology and it's time you became acquainted with it," he roared.

Evie looked at her Mom and Grace.

"Bloody 'ell, Evie, don't look at us for support. Your father's right. You really look like a bit of a wanker this time, don't you?" her Mom added for good measure.

For the first time Evie did not notice her Mom using the local slang. Or her faux cockney accent. (That was new). She was too busy trying to figure out how she could rectify the situation. The truth was that she felt awful about what she said and the fact it was overheard by Charlotte. She really didn't mean to imply that her choice of a baby name meant she hated her unborn child. Well, technically she did, but just to her immediate family, and just as a joke.

"Fine," she muttered. "I'll go find Charlotte and apologize."

She got up from the table and reached across to grab a sandwich, but her mother's hand stopped hers in its tracks. "You'd have to be mad to think you get a sandwich until you do."

Her head was bowed in shame as she started across the floor, so she was startled to hear Michael's voice break into her thoughts before she had cleared the table.

"Evelyn. I'd like a word, please."

Crap, crap, crap, she thought. "Um, sure Michael. What's up?"

"In private, please," he answered tersely.

The two of them walked out of the room and into the backyard. Evelyn felt a mixture of shame and defiance rise up in her. *Let's get this over with*, she thought.

"I was just talking to Char-Char, who was obviously upset, and she told me what she just overheard you saying."

Evie held up her hand to interrupt. "Look, I'm ready to take my lumps in regards to my actions, but you have to stop calling her 'Char-Char' because every time you do, I throw up a little in my mouth." She filled her cheeks up with air and made a gagging sound to emphasize this point. She hoped some humor would lighten up the situation, but it had the exact opposite effect.

He looked at her with real anger. Anger she hadn't seen since she had used his baseball signed by Reggie Jackson in a game of running bases with some neighbors when she was eight and he was twelve.

"Does every thought that even fleetingly makes its way across the empty expanse that is your mind need to come out in verbal form? Do you have no filter whatsoever? You know what I would like, Evie? For my *BABY* sister to start acting her age and take some responsibility for her actions just once. You're thirty-two years old, for Christ's sake, and you still ask us to call you back so you don't have to pay for your phone calls."

Damn, if Mandy was here, she'd have to tell her the answer to her question of at what point does a thirty-two year old get embarrassed to have her family call her back so she doesn't have to pay for the long distance call, would be right this moment. *It might be time to go on the offensive* she thought to herself.

"Well, Michael, since I think I might have trouble ordering even the simplest cup of coffee with the use of contemporary dance, I'm going to have to keep on using the old fashioned way of communicating. That would be speaking...sorry if what I utter doesn't always suit you."

"It always has to be a joke with you, doesn't it? Sometimes things don't get better with a joke, they get worse. You need to figure out the right time to unleash your humor on everyone, Evie. You know what; I can't even talk to you right now. I've got to go see if Char-Char is okay and make sure all the other guests don't realize how badly you've just ruined this day for us." Michael glared at her, daring Evie to make another joke about his nickname for his fiancé and when he was satisfied she wasn't going to utter a word, stormed off.

That went well, Evie thought to herself. And then she slumped down on a bench in the garden, wondering how she was going to fix all this before the wedding.

Of course, it goes without saying that Nate walked through the backyard at the exact moment she had started to cry.

"This must be one hell of a party if the prettiest guest is left crying outside by herself," he said.

Evie looked up and hastily tried to brush away the tears. A few glistening tears might light up the face of a Hollywood starlet, but crying always made her nose red, runny, and distinctly unattractive. *Let's go with the slightly less than honest approach,* she thought to herself.

"Oh, it's nothing really. I just stubbed my toe against a rock here in the garden. Kind of smarts. I'll be okay in a bit," she added for good measure.

"I just ran into Michael going into the house," Nate threw out. "He does look an awful lot like a rock today, I'd have to say."

Even in her bad mood Evelyn couldn't help the laughter that escaped from her lips.

"You know," Nate said, "you have quite a lovely laugh...it's very infectious. It reminds me of someone."

Please don't say Fran Drescher, please don't say Fran Drescher, Evie quietly prayed to herself.

"Oh, I know...Fran Drescher." Seeing the look of displeasure on Evie's face, he quickly laughed and changed his tune. "Obviously I meant Julia Roberts."

"I suppose I could live with that one. Because, frankly, just so you know going forward, saying someone's laugh is lovely and reminds you of Fran Drescher, is a lot like telling someone they have a lovely silhouette and it reminds you of Quasimodo. And, as you are obviously the Veronica Mars of male, British, coffee house proprietors to have figured out I didn't actually stub my toe, I'll confess. Michael and I had a bit of a row, as I believe you all are fond of saying. And I've got to figure out a way to make amends before this wedding gets under way."

"Did your Mom call you a prat this time? I love it when she uses that one. She says it with such venom," Nathanial laughed.

Evie answered without skipping a beat. "Nah. She went with wanker this time."

"Always a classic," he retorted.

"Well, my Mom's use of British swearing that she finds delightful aside...do you have any suggestions as to a huge mea culpa I could use for Charlotte and Michael?"

"You know, Evelyn, have you thought about just being sincere? I don't know the particulars of what happened, but I don't think any grand gesture would be more appreciated than a simple, sincere apology," Nate said thoughtfully.

"You know...that's exactly what my Dad said. Except his tone was a bit harsher. Apoplectic harsh, to be precise."

"Good man, your father. He obviously knows what he's talking about."

Evelyn brightened for a moment as her brain suddenly wrapped around something he had said earlier. "Did you just refer to me as the "prettiest guest?'" she asked.

Nate looked at her squarely and his glance never faltered. "I absolutely did. And I stand by it." He cautiously raised his hand and brushed away a strand of her hair that had gotten caught on her cheek by a teardrop. His head started to bend towards hers and her heart started to pound uncontrollably. *Finally*, she thought. *I am finally going to kiss Nate. So then why the hell is my Dad's voice now the only thing that I hear? That's not normal.* Evie tentatively opened up her eyes, to see that Nate was doing the same thing.

"Evie, I sincerely doubt that the way to apologize to Charlotte is through Nate's mouth. Last time I checked you two were not a ventriloquist and dummy act." Her Dad was standing in front of the two of them, looking none too pleased.

"Perfect timing," she mumbled.

Nate blushed a little bit, but regained his composure quickly. "Mr. Dunleavy, I apologize. I didn't mean to hijack Evie while she was in the middle of something. Evie, when you're finished, why don't you find me and we can finish our conversation then." With a meaningful glance at Evie, and a smile for her Dad, he strode into the house.

"No offense, Evie," her Dad said, "but you don't deserve a face full of happiness until you make nice with the bride. I think she headed towards the conservatory. That is the place with the piano, right?" her Dad double checked.

———————

Evelyn ran as fast as her kitten heels would allow over the cobblestone courtyard. Her pencil skirt, which she thought was the epitome of class when she was getting dressed for this tea party, really hindered her forward motion. *Which way was it to the conservatory again,* she wondered. She spun around to try to get her bearings and then saw the majestic grand piano encased in the sunroom a little bit to her left. It seemed to her there was a female figure running her fingers over the keys, but she couldn't be sure it was Charlotte, since her back was turned. *You should be able to recognize an eight months pregnant woman,* Evie thought irritably to herself. *Even from the back, you should be able to tell. I am so popping some pastry down her throat once we make amends.*

When she arrived at the conservatory, she slowed down and tried to fix her disheveled appearance. Tendrils of her carefully pinned up hair had escaped and her upper lip was what her Mom would refer to as "glistening" and her Dad as "sweating like a pig."

"Um, Charlotte? Do you mind if I come in?" she asked from the doorway.

Charlotte turned around, surprised to see Evelyn, and hastily brushed away the tears falling down her face. She surprised Evie by saying, "Yeah, kind of." So much for the stiff upper lip of the British she was always hearing about.

"Fair enough," Evelyn answered. "I deserve that. But I'd really like to talk to you."

"Well, Evie, you happen to have caught me at a bad time. I'm about to head out to the stables and take a ride and clear my head before all of the guests arrive. And we both know you're not a horse person. So, unless you're going to give me a lecture about the dangers of riding a horse while eight months pregnant, I'll just excuse myself." Evie took in Charlotte's riding clothes and realized it was the truth.

"Charlotte, please! I really need to speak with you about what happened."

"And I really need to clear my head."

"Please, Charlotte?"

Charlotte gave a 'suit yourself' kind of shrug, and simply said, "Well, follow me then, if you insist. I'll have Charlie saddle up one of the older, gentler mares for you to ride."

Evie hesitated and then figured if this was some kind of test, she was going to have to pass it. How the hell she was going to ride a horse in a pencil skirt and heels she hadn't quite figured out, but she'd cross that bridge when she got to it. Maybe if she talked fast enough, she could have it all worked out before she even had to try to sit on a horse.

But Charlotte didn't give her a chance to start talking and just walked briskly to the stables. Between dodging the cow pats on the trail, and trying to keep up with the fast pace Charlotte had set, Evie didn't have a chance to begin a conversation. *How does a woman that pregnant walk that fast?*

When they got inside the stable, Charlotte simply said, "Wait here. I'll grab some stuff for our ride and get Charlie to help get the horses ready."

Evie bit her lip in thought. She looked down at her clothes. *Obviously can't throw my leg over a horse in this skirt,* she thought. She looked around the stable and found a pair of scissors on the window ledge. She looked down longingly at her beautiful skirt, then took a deep breath and started to cut two long lines up the center of the front and back of the skirt. *That should give me a bit of leg motion range,* she thought to herself, proudly. *Granted, my underpants are going to show a bit, but it'll just be Charlotte and I anyway, so that shouldn't matter too much.*

Charlotte walked back in and gasped when she saw what Evelyn had done to her skirt. "What in God's name did you do?" she asked.

"Well," Evie responded, "I couldn't very well ride a horse in my skirt the way it was, so I improvised."

Charlotte held up a pair of jodhpurs and simply said, "We keep extras in here. That's where I was going. To get you a pair."

"Are you telling me I ruined my elegant ensemble for nothing?"

Charlotte nodded. The two women looked at each other, and then began to tentatively giggle.

"You know, I really loved this skirt," Evie finally managed to say between fits of laughter.

"I know," said Charlotte. "It's so sad."

"Your callous hoots of laughter don't give a whole lot of credence to the fact that you might actually believe that."

"I know. They don't, do they? But it really is sad!" and she howled again.

When their riotous laughter finally subsided, they both looked at each other questioningly. Charlotte was the first to speak.

"You know, I just, I just don't...I, I don't understand why you would be so mean," she finally managed to stammer out. "I thought you liked me."

"I do," Evie answered honestly. "And I truly am sorry." She paused for a moment trying to figure out how to put into words what had prompted her cruel jokes. "Even though Michael and I have the greatest amount of years in between us, we've always been the closest. I think it's because we share the same sense of humor, or maybe it's because I've always put him on a pedestal, or the fact he never treated me like a kid, even when I was one. Whatever the reason, he's always been my first call for sharing silly stories or my sounding board for any of my frustrations and disappointments. And I was his. But I'm not anymore, and I know that. And, believe me, I know that's how it should be," she quickly added. "It's just that I'm terrified of not having that role anymore. It has defined how I see myself, and present myself to the world, and now that has to change. And I'm not quite sure how to change with it. And I feel a little bit alone."

Charlotte looked a bit unsure as to how to respond and seemed to weigh her comments before she started to speak. "Listen, I get how this has been very whirlwind for everyone. Michael and I go through a thousand different emotions every day of the week ourselves. But we're going to be family and I've got one firm rule I'm going to hold you to. Say what you want about me, but say it to my face. I can take a joke, I can take discussions on topics we might not agree upon; I can't take behind my back cruelty."

Evie fought to hold back tears of shame for her behavior as she promised Charlotte vehemently there wouldn't be a repeat performance of what happened that afternoon.

Charlotte looked at Evie and asked, "I just need to know for myself...not that it's going to change my mind or anything," she joked. "Do you really hate the name Monty that much?"

A slow smile spread across Evie's face. "Nah. I probably wouldn't have thought of it for a child of my own, but I don't necessarily equate it to the Devil's name."

Thirty

"So Charlotte, would you mind terribly running some interference for me and letting Michael know we made nice? My apology to him might take a little better if he knew we were okay."

Charlotte looked like she was really giving Evie's request some serious thought and for a moment Evie was afraid she was going to turn her down. When Charlotte saw the stricken look on Evie's face, she couldn't help but laugh before telling her she'd go find Michael and let him know not to be too hard on Evie. The plan was for Charlotte to get a couple of minute's head start and Evie would intercept Michael and basically beg for his forgiveness after Charlotte had finished talking to him. Evie sat down on the floor of the stable—trying desperately not to imagine what might have been in this exact spot at any other given moment—and relived the entire afternoon in her mind's eye. She couldn't imagine any other bridal party luncheon being so wrought with emotion. She had almost managed to completely fuck up what was supposed to be the greatest weekend for Michael and Charlotte, and she was ashamed of herself for it.

She couldn't help but smile, though, when her thoughts turned to Nate and the way he had looked at her when he called her the prettiest guest at the party. She knew he meant it and she couldn't wait to have a second go around for a chance to kiss him. Maybe this could turn into what she might consider to be the greatest weekend ever for herself as well. She was going to give it a try at least, and leave it all hanging out. *Which,* she thought to herself, *is what I'm pretty much doing right now anyway, sitting Indian style on the floor of a stable with my skirt cut up to my v.j. Way to leave a little for the imagination,* she chided herself. Her Mom would die a thousand deaths if she saw how she was lying about.

She figured she had given Charlotte enough of a head start and began to make her way back towards the house via what she now dubbed "Cow Pat Trail," in order to hunt down her brother. Then she was on a mission to find Nate.

Michael was sipping a Heineken, talking to an old friend of his from high school, who was one of the groomsmen. Evie hadn't seen Samuel yet, as she had been told he arrived late last night. She had always gotten along with him and was looking forward to catching up with him later. But first she had to grovel a little bit.

"Michael, do you have a sec?" she asked. "Hey Sammy, do you mind if I steal my brother for a moment. I promise you can have him back shortly."

Samuel gave Evie a once over, his eyes lingering on her split skirt that she tried to hold together as best as she could with her hands. *Awkward at best,* she thought to herself. "I'd rather have you back shortly, to be honest. It's been a while and you're even more gorgeous than I remember." Evie chalked up his leering to the strong smell of alcohol on his breath.

She attempted a bit of levity, seeing as how she felt she had very little dignity left. "I obviously need to change into something a little different before I start mingling, but I'll keep an eye out for you when I do."

"You know I'll be keeping an eye out for you." Sammy's blond eyebrow bulleted up his face in a way that Evie found to be totally creepy and vowed to try to keep her distance. She didn't remember him as a Norman Bates type, and was a little disappointed that he wasn't his old self.

Michael, who had been given the general outline of the conversation that had occurred between his sister and his fiancé, was not holding a grudge, and therefore felt the need to step in and don his usual protective brother armor. "Dude, that's my sister you're talking to like that right in front of me, for Christ's sake. Watch yourself."

Sammy seemed to sober up a bit and decided the best way to get rid of the storm cloud of anger passing over his old friend's face was to use his frat brother rap with his boyhood friend. "Oh man, I forgot how your sisters are off limits. Sorry, bro. I won't mess up again." But the wink he gave to Evie when Michael turned around made her almost physically recoil at the sheer Las Vegas troubadour cheesiness of it all. Note to self: avoid Sammy at all costs for the weekend.

As soon as they were alone she started talking. "Michael, first of all let me start off by saying, you've got the greatest fiancé of all time and I'm so lucky that she's playing the role of her and not me, because I would never have been so gracious to me, if I had been as big of a bitch to myself as I was to her. Did that make any sense at all?" Evie gasped as all her words tumbled out of her mouth without a breath.

"Only if what you were trying to say, and failing miserably at, by the way, was that Charlotte's a bigger person than you could ever be if the situation were reversed."

"Good, you do know what I mean, then."

"Yeah, Evie, I do. Charlotte gave me the gist of the talk you guys had in the stable and she really feels like it was just you not thinking about what you were saying and just trying to be funny in the moment. It would be in your best interest to stop doing that, by the way."

"Oh, God, I know. You're totally right about there being no filter. Sometimes something just pops into my head and it's like I'm physically compelled to utter it out loud. Like my own version of Tourette's. But you have to know how much I love you guys and that I truly think the two of you are an amazing couple and are going to be fabulous parents. You do know that, right?"

"I'd like to think so." That was followed by a slightly troubled pause. "But do you really think I'm going to make a good father?"

"Oh my God, Michael, of course I do. Do you remember that time when I was probably about eight or nine, and I was getting teased and shoved around at the bus stop by Sabrina Potter, who was a year older then me? Mom and Dad were giving me the standard line of "just ignore her and she'll stop," which I tried and it wasn't working. You found me crying in the tool shed at home and asked what was wrong and when I told you, you started giving me boxing lessons that day, on the spot."

"Are you saying I'm going to be a great parent because I'm an advocate of violence?"

"I'm saying you're going to be a great parent because you inspired me to stick up for myself, and be independent. Before you taught me those moves, Sabrina zoned in on the fact that I didn't have any confidence, and knew I was the kid that she could target. When I finally pushed back, thanks to your urging, she knew I was stronger, but not just in a physical sense. Mentally. What a great gift you'll be able to give your children. Confidence in themselves. The belief that they're worthy. Not every kid gets someone who will teach them that. And you will. And let's not forget that you've been to Disney World somewhere in the range of nine times or so, which, let's face it, is a little weird for a grown man without any kids. You've got a built in excuse to go to the Happiest Place on Earth whenever you want to now."

"That will be a convenient excuse. The looks I've been getting have been troubling to say the least."

"It's hard when Mickey doesn't want to take a picture with a grown man without any kids, I know, Michael," Evie consoled with a knowing nod. She then continued, "Listen, in all seriousness...are we okay? You, me, and Charlotte? Because I would hate for there to be any awkwardness or unhappiness because of something stupid I blurted out for the sake of a laugh."

"Yeah, Evie, we're good." Michael put his arm around her and gave her a quick squeeze. "Now why don't you go back to the party and let the family know the seating chart will not be rearranged and you're back in the wedding," he said with a laugh. "For now, at least," he quickly amended. "And I don't know...maybe at least find a safety pin or something," looking pointedly at the skirt she was still gripping.

"Thank you, Michael. From the bottom of my heart, thank you." Evie felt her eyes start to well up and she coughed to stop her voice from choking. "I'll let everyone know things have been worked out," in a voice an octave or two deeper than she normally spoke in, due to the unshed tears. She hurried off to find the rest of the family before she started balling due to the sheer weight of all the emotions that had coursed through her body in the space of a couple of hours.

"Grace, how unusual to find you belly up to the bar," she trilled as soon as she saw her sister.

"It was either this or the carving station and I need to fit into my dress in two days, so alcohol it is." Her gaze took in Evie's sliced up skirt and she placed her drink firmly down on the bar. "Obviously, I need to lay off the wine and coat my stomach because to me it looks like your skirt is cut almost all the way up to your hoo-ha while we stand in the middle of the bridal party luncheon, having a sarcasm contest, and that surely can't be right."

"No, you can finish your drink. My skirt has been destroyed. I'm on my way to change outfits, but I was just trying to find you to tell you that all has been forgiven, I've been reinstated as a sister and the wedding will not be an awkward bomb. At least not due to me and my big mouth. And I'd like your permission to ransack your closet for something to wear that hasn't been mutilated. Please."

"Of course, help yourself to whatever you'd like. See, sometimes it does pay to over pack, doesn't it?"

"I have been wrong so many times today, what's one more? Thanks. I'll be down in a couple of minutes. If you see Mom and Dad, let them know everything's okay, will you?"

"Evie?" her sister called after her before she hit the patio doors that led inside. "You should really wear the red jersey halter dress that's hanging in the closet. It'll look stunning on you, and I wouldn't be surprised if a certain roommate of yours, who, by the way, has been making quite a pest of himself by checking back with me every five minutes or so to see if you'd returned from your talk, would agree. And," she grinned wickedly as she continued, "it's my Stella McCartney and you know that means Emily will approve."

"I love you," Evie mouthed as she hurried up to her sister's room to get changed.

Thirty-One

*G*irl *stuff is silly,* Evie thought to herself while applying a fresh coat of lipstick. *But really kind of fun* her inner princess responded. She had to concede that Grace was right about the dress. The red complemented her dark hair perfectly and the shape of the dress was impeccable. *I actually think this dress makes my shoulders look thin and I don't think I have ever had that thought pass through my head a single other time in my life,* she laughed to herself. She grabbed a pair of red satin Jimmy Choo shoes, and was thoroughly impressed with herself that she had heard of that designer. And then she realized how expensive they were and made a mental note to ask her sister exactly when she started robbing banks and how long of a spree she could conceivably go on before she finds herself being hauled off to the clink.

She skipped down the staircase—in so far as someone can skip in four inch stilettos—in search of Nate. She ran into Samuel first.

"Hey gorgeous," he half slurred when she slammed into him. "Nice shoes. But I'd prefer to see them close up."

She stared at him a minute trying to process that last one. She finally gave up. "Sammy, if that's some kind of come-on...it doesn't make sense. What the hell does that even mean?"

He acknowledged his senseless line with a laugh. "I guess not, but you know what I mean."

"Not really," she breathed out exasperated. "That's why I said it didn't make any sense."

He threw back the rest of his scotch and soda. "I'm trying to say that you look amazing and that it's really great to see you again."

"Well, thank you very much; it's great to see you again, too. Now, if you'll excuse me, I need to find a friend of mine right now."

"Hey, Evie, what's the big rush?" he asked while at the same time planting himself between her and the patio door.

She didn't think she could be much clearer about her purpose, but tried it again, just in case. "I just told you, Sammy. I've got to look for a friend." She spoke slower, not really believing that her speedy speech was the impediment here, but willing to try anything to get away. *My life has become a bad comedy sketch where two people who don't speak the same language start to speak slower in the doubtful hope that one of them will suddenly understand what was being said.*

"Well, I'm sure your friend can wait. You can just explain you got to talking to an *old* friend and just got caught up in the moment." Another unpleasant leer was directed at her. She had an involuntary shudder.

Evie was starting to feel uncomfortable and tried to push her way around Samuel, but he was not to be dismissed that easily. He grabbed her arm and pulled her toward him, giving her a clumsy kiss as he did so. She was so startled that at first she didn't do anything but stand there, trying to comprehend the fact her brother's old friend was kissing her in a drunken stupor. Then the boxing lessons her brother had given her and those fabulous stilettos kicked in both literally and figuratively. She stomped her heel hard into his foot and gave him a quick uppercut to his stomach and calmly walked around him.

She turned to him, completely pissed off. "I'm going to do you a favor, because it's Michael and Charlotte's wedding weekend and I have just been taught a lesson in forgiveness today, and I figure I'll pass it on. I'm *not* going to tell Michael what you just did in here, so he will *not* kick your ass over it. However, if you so much as glance in my direction for the remainder of the weekend or speak to me with some crazy sexual innuendo that only makes sense to you, I will take this heel and pummel you in the balls with it so hard, it will change the way you look at high heels for the rest of your life." *I'm so getting a pair of these shoes, cost be damned,* she thought as she stormed out to the patio and slammed the door behind her. She managed to startle some of the other members of the wedding party, standing around, enjoying their drinks and canapés.

"Sorry," she murmured sheepishly. "I didn't realize it closes so fast," was the best she could come up with at the moment. She took in the scene, hoping to catch Nate's eye in the crowd, but was only confused when she saw the back of his jacket, hurrying up the steps, away from the party.

"Nate," she called out to him, as she tried to catch up. "Wait up a sec," she tried again, when he showed no signs of slowing down. She decided she didn't like the shoes nearly as much as she did two seconds ago. She remembered an article she had read recently on the internet about the second annual foot race that some Russian women had run in high heels and decided they were all mad. She tried to tug them off without missing a step and almost killed herself. "Please, Nate. Can you just hold on for a minute? I'm pretty sure you can hear me," she called out after a moment. "Right?" That seemed to do the trick and he did stop as he neared the top step in the garden, although he had one foot poised on the next step, ready for flight. Evie was out of breath, holding her sister's shoes in one hand, when she caught up to him.

After seeing the look on his face, she knew instantly he was furious. She had no idea what had him so angry, but she felt sorry for whoever did it.

She reached out and grabbed his arm and asked, "Are you okay? What happened? I've been looking all over for you."

She was completely taken by surprise when he roughly pulled his arm out from under her touch and just said, coolly, "You have a very interesting way of looking for me. Perhaps that's just how they do it in America."

Evelyn was completely bewildered and her face must have registered that because he continued on with his explanation. "Your sister was kind enough to inform me you had gone inside to change and I went in to find you, only to see you kissing another one of your brother's friends. Here I had been under the impression, false obviously, that friends of your brother's were off limits, romantically speaking, for you. I was grossly misinformed. I didn't realize you were in the habit of collecting them."

Her face turned ashen with fury and she felt like she, and not Samuel, had been punched in the gut. Could he possibly believe what he was saying to her? She was about to explain the scene he had witnessed, but so completely misinterpreted, and then stopped herself. If that's the only explanation he could come up with, fuck him.

"How dare you," she hissed at him. "If that's what you come up with after sharing an apartment with me for the past three months than I am a poorer judge of character than I could have ever guessed. And you are a complete gobshite." She stormed off before she completely broke down, not even caring that she had fallen prey to her mother's slang game again.

———————

Evie returned to the luncheon, her face a storm cloud, and most people steered clear of her. Eventually, her parents tried to ask her what seemed to be the problem.

"Evelyn, dear, I was under the impression that you and Michael had cleared everything up. Why the long face?" Rebecca inquired.

"Huh? Oh, I didn't realize my face didn't look like its usual self. I'm just a little preoccupied. Bridesmaid's jitters I guess," was all she could think of to say.

"Excuse me you guys, but has anyone seen Nate? I wanted to go over some little details he was going to help me with for the wedding," Michael asked as he and Charlotte walked over to the three of them.

"The last I saw of him, he was heading out towards his car," was all Evie volunteered.

Charlotte looked at Evie quizzically and her brother continued, "That's strange. He doesn't normally forget things like that. I'm going to give him a buzz on his cell and see what happened." Michael wandered off, already dialing his cell phone.

Charlotte continued examining Evie's body language and asked quietly, "Is everything okay with you and Nate? Did you two have a row?"

Evelyn did not want to bother Charlotte with her trivial nonsense right before her upcoming nuptials, so she brushed it off and tried to answer as lightly as she could. "No, everything's fine. Don't worry, we won't be bickering as we walk down the aisle," she promised. What was she going to say anyway? That she had fallen in love with her brother's good friend, which was a no-no in the first place, and he'd jumped to conclusions about her brother's other friend kissing her, and now he was pissed? And that it didn't matter anyway because she was heading home to New York shortly? And since when had she started to admit she was in love with Nate...even in the privacy of her own thoughts?

As all those thoughts raced through Evie's head, Michael had rejoined their group and casually said, "I got through to Nate. He said he was sorry but had forgotten about some repair appointment he had for one of the coffee machines, and that was why he left in such a hurry." He turned to Charlotte saying, "He's going to stop by later tonight and I'll give him the list then. And Evie," he continued turning towards her, "Nate said to let you know he won't be home tonight. He's meeting up with some friends from University and is going to stay in the City tonight, at one of their flats."

Evie tried to hit the right note between chipper and nonchalant with her reply. "Oh, okay. I guess I'll just lock up tonight when I get in." She fell flat.

It took some time to convince her parents and sister that she was better off just going back to Nate's place to sleep.

"Why don't you just stay here at the Futterly's tonight? I'm sure they won't mind. There's plenty of room here. It's such a long ride back to Nate's place, anyway." her Mom kept insisting.

"Mom, I've got to go back anyway since all of my stuff is at the apartment. I'm thirty-two years old and I have slept alone quite a few times. I'll be fine. It's really just easier this way. I was planning on going back there tonight anyway, so it's not like the time factor should be a consideration." As much as she argued that she'd have no clean underwear, or a toothbrush, the fact was she hoping that Nate would change his mind and come home so they could talk about what he thought he witnessed. There was no way in hell that she was going to be sleeping at the Manor two hours away, with her parents in the next room over, if he did. So she kept to her plans and rode back with Michael and Charlotte and tried her best to fall asleep in the back seat. She found it surprisingly easy to do, and woke up as they were turning onto his block.

"Oh, Nate's car isn't in the driveway," she said groggily.

"Remember? He's not coming back tonight?" Michael asked her.

"Oh, yeah, it must've slipped my mind. I'm obviously still waking up," she answered, instantly alert to the facts.

Michael walked in with her and made sure she was alone, as an older brother ought to, and said good night to her at the door. "Are you sure you don't want to come back and crash at our place?" he asked her for the fifteenth time.

"Nah, but thanks. I'll be much more comfortable in my own bed, than on your couch. And you have seen with your own eyes that no one is hiding in any of the corners of the apartment, so go now, and let me get some sleep. I don't know if you've heard, but this is quite a big weekend we've got in front of us. My brother is getting married."

Michael laughed and gave Evelyn and big hug and kiss. "Alright, if you're sure. And try to get a good night sleep. I don't need you uglying up my wedding photos with bags under your eyes."

Thirty-Two

T he next morning Evie threw on her iPod and started walking as fast as she could away from Nate's apartment. How did she find herself in this situation? *I'm a basket case,* she kept repeating over and over. Ironically, it was at this time that Fiona Apple's *Paper Bag* came up in her shuffle. The refrain, sung over and over, with the arrangement changing ever so slightly each time, caught her by surprise. Why did Fiona have to be singing about a guy who didn't want to clean up the mess that was her anyway? Evie was afraid that was too close to how Nate felt about her. And when Fiona sang about not wanting to try because it "cost too much to love?" She should've just threw Evie's name into the chorus and been done with it.

Every time the song ended, Evie started it over from the beginning, like a punishment. The words perfectly captured her raw emotions, and she found she wasn't even embarrassed when the tears started to fall down her cheeks. The fact was, she wished she didn't understand the emotions behind those lyrics. She found it amazing that the song was written by someone other than her, they cut her to the quick so. She tried to gain solace from the fact that she obviously wasn't the only one to feel like she did. Then she grew sad at the fact she wasn't able to be someone who wasn't moved to tears by these words, because they represented her so fully in their four short lines. Of course, that made her sob even harder. Before she knew it, she had been walking and crying and listening to the same song for over an hour. She decided to run into the next store she came across and grab a bottle of water while she got her bearings and headed back to Nate's. Hopefully she could figure out a plan of action before she got home. And she realized she had to, because even in her mind she was referring to this place, where she was only going to stay for a couple of months, as home. She knew with certainty she didn't want to give up on her chance for love. She'd have to figure out a way to steady her shaky hands, as the song said, because she wasn't going to look back on this time in her life and second guess all her decisions. It was time for her to act her age.

The gentleman at the counter looked at her tear-stained face with a mixture of concern and apprehension, as she handed him the money to pay for the water bottle. "Are you okay, love?" he asked.

"I will be," she answered in a hopeful voice as she headed out the door, determined to confront Nate and stop trying to run and hide.

————

She walked down Nate's tree lined street without any hesitancy. She actually ran. She nodded at the dog loving couple that she and Nate laughed so hard about on their Detox Night. She thought about that walk and the way he had casually thrown an arm around her when she mentioned she was getting chilly. And how he had told her he was going to miss her when she left. She thought about all the times she visited him at his coffee house and he kept trying to ply her with their freshly baked treats. She'd say she was afraid she was gaining too much weight and he would tell her she was nuts, she was gorgeous. She always convinced herself he was just being kind, but she realized he meant it every time. She couldn't tell if the gasp she let out when she arrived at the flat and ran up the steps was one of surprised comprehension or exertion from her walk. Probably a combination of both. She had no idea what she was going to say to Nate, but she knew she couldn't hold anything back. She was going to let it all out. It might turn out to be a disaster, but at least she wouldn't spend the rest of her life second guessing herself.

"Nate," she called as she stepped into the hallway and was surprised by how shrill her voice sounded to her own ears. She took a deep breath to steady herself, and called out again, in a more controlled voice. "Anyone home?" she asked. Nobody answered back. She headed into the kitchen to see if he had stepped onto the back patio, and noticed a short note addressed to her in Nate's strong handwriting:

> *Evie,*
> *I headed down to the castle early. Forgot about a prior commitment I had to sort out with Michael. I worked out a ride for you with Emily to the rehearsal dinner. She'll call you to confirm times.*
> *Nate*

Evie sat down on the bar stool at the island with a dejected thud. *So much for coming home and unburdening myself to Nate about my undying love for him,* she thought ruefully. Her fingernails absently tapped the granite on the island as she re-read his note. She was practically begging for some underlying message to jump out at her in an "a-ha" moment; to tell her she wasn't misreading any of the signs she tried so hard to miss.

Unfortunately, the note was cold and she could tell from the terse words he was finished with her.

Crap, I blew it, was the only thought that kept repeating itself, on a loop in her head. She absently hit play on her iPod. The drum machine in her earphones signaling the start of *Paper Bag* finally managed to drown out everything she had been thinking. Then she began to cry again in earnest.

Thirty-Three

E velyn was greeted with a curt nod from Emily who motioned with her head toward the back seat when asked where she should put her dress and weekend bag. Seeing as how the back seat was already piled high with Emily's stuff and five large boxes, that was a harder task than Evie would have anticipated, but she eventually managed to lay her belongings down in what she hoped was a spot that would prove to be wrinkle resistant. She thanked the gods of Bridesmaid Dresses once again for the choice of material Charlotte had opted for, because she would've been totally screwed if the dress had been made of linen.

Emily had already pulled away from the curb before Evie was properly situated in the passenger seat, let alone buckled up, so she hastily strapped herself in before trying to start a conversation with her obviously unenthusiastic driver. "Thanks so much for picking me up last minute. I really appreciate it. I guess Nate had some last minute groomsman duties to attend to. Looks like you drew the short straw." Evie tried to make a joke out of the circumstances surrounding their journey, but only elicited a polite smile from Emily.

"Not a problem. Glad to do it. Anything to make Charlotte's life easier during this crazy time."

Evie waited a moment before trying to tackle some more small talk. "So, what's with all the boxes in the back seat?"

"Oh, didn't Charlotte mention these? They're the bridesmaid hats. It's a tradition for English ladies to wear hats to weddings. The bigger the better. They're quite lovely, too. Huge brims and matching ostrich feathers on each one. They've been dyed to match the dresses perfectly."

Evie didn't know whether or not a joke was being played on her since this was the first time the subject of hats had been brought up. After the Monty debacle she wasn't going to take any chances, though. "Sounds fabulous. I can't wait to see them." It was the right answer since the hats were not a joke. It had merely been an oversight that no one had mentioned them to Evie or Grace before then. Evie was just glad that she wouldn't be the only person at the reception who was going to have hat head. *Safety in numbers* she thought to herself. *Even on the fashion field.*

The rest of the ride went relatively smoothly, in so far as anything with Emily can go smoothly. It wasn't a gregarious laugh-in, but it wasn't a session of Chinese water torture either, Evie admitted to herself. They arrived at the castle with plenty of time to spare before the rehearsal dinner. The two girls went their separate ways after checking in. Emily went to take a nap and Evie tried to locate the rest of her family. Failing to do that, she took her book onto the stately grounds and got comfortable on a cushioned bench under an overgrown willow tree. The portion of the brambles that would have obscured the view was cut back, so Evie felt like she was in her very own tree cabana. She looked around, laughing a little.

"It's like I've been stuck inside an overgrown mushroom or something," she said to herself.

From the safety of what she decided to dub her own personal shire, she watched the comings and goings of the other castle guests, not really even pretending to read. If she was going to be honest, it was more reconnaissance work than Book Club time. From her seat she could see anyone coming in or out of the front doors of the estate and she was hoping to catch a glimpse of Nate in order to talk to him alone. An hour later she had to admit to herself that either Nate had sequestered himself in his room, or he had snuck out the back door or an underground tunnel to get some fresh air. So much for joining the ranks of the super spy. She decided to go for Plan B, which meant she needed to locate Grace before the rehearsal dinner, so she could work her hair and make-up magic on Evie. Besides, she felt it was only fair to warn Grace about the imminent hat situation. She took off at a quick run to try to find her sister and see if she'd be able to salvage anything with Nate before the wedding took place.

The next couple of hours flew by in a blur for Evie. She was so preoccupied with trying to find her family, especially Grace, and getting ready for the evening, that she didn't dwell too much on how she thought things would go when she finally saw Nate.

The wedding party assembled downstairs to grab the bus Michael and Charlotte had arranged for the evening to drive them to the church, the restaurant where dinner was to be held, and then back again to the castle. Her parents were only ten minutes past the set time of seven p.m., and Grace's family only fifteen, which really translated into their being early in their world. Evie couldn't believe it when Nate showed up even five minutes after that, which made him the final person to arrive and jump on the bus. He sat down in the last remaining seat up front behind the driver and started to talk to Charlotte's parents, who were next to him. Evie rolled her eyes at his latest ploy to avoid her. She knew they were supposed to walk down the aisle together, and at this point she wasn't going to rule out the possibility that he had already asked for a substitute bridesmaid for the day. She couldn't decide whether or not she should be annoyed or impressed with how thoroughly he threw himself into his task of ignoring her. She was leaning towards annoyed.

Thirty-Four

L ife seemed to be conspiring against Evie from all fronts. She sat down in a pew with Grace, Jack and the kids only to have the priest announce he wouldn't ask all of the attendants to walk down the aisle that evening. "I figure you all know the drill so I won't take up any time on that front. I'll just go over a couple of notes I have for the bride and groom and you'll soon be off to your dinner."

"So much for trapping him on the altar," she muttered to herself.

Grace looked at her kind of strangely. "Who are you trapping on the altar?"

"Oh, don't mind me. I'm just talking to myself."

"I can see that...it's what you're saying that concerns me."

With Charlotte and Michael being the only two participants involved in the rehearsal, they were through in no time at all. This meant Evelyn was now counting on the dinner to be the spot where she could bend Nate's ear. Of course, he had other plans. He planted a perfunctory kiss on her cheek and asked politely if she had an enjoyable ride to the castle with Emily. Since Emily was standing in close proximity to her at the time, she had no choice but to respond in the affirmative.

"Oh the ride was lovely. It was very nice of Emily to come get me. Listen, if you have a sec, I'd really like to talk to you about..." Evie's voice trailed away, as Nate started to drift into the crowd, his head thrown over his shoulder as he gave a hurried answer.

"Excuse me, please; I've got to grab an old friend of mine that I used to work with at the bank." She barely made out his, "I'll see if I can find you later," since he was running away from her simultaneously.

Grace and Jack looked at each other and back to Evie in confusion.

"Looks to me like someone's starting to wear out her welcome," was Jack's unwanted take on the conversation.

"Who the fuck asked you?" was Evie's unrestrained reply. She startled even herself with her answer and she looked at her sister and brother-in-law sheepishly. "I don't even know where that came from. I'm sorry."

"I do," Grace answered. "You've fallen for Nate, and there's no sense in denying it," she added when she saw Evie start to protest. "The question is, what did you do to get him so pissed?"

Evelyn decided it couldn't hurt to explain the situation to Grace and Jack and get some unbiased feedback about what had transpired at the bridal luncheon with Sammy, and how Nate was under the wrong impression about what he had witnessed. When she had finished sharing all the details, including the threat to Sammy's manhood with Grace's shoes, she looked at the two of them and waited for their sage advice.

Grace did not disappoint. "Well, I think as soon as he's had a little more time to stew, he's going to realize that, if nothing else, he's curious as to what your explanation would be, and then you can get him to see how it was all just one big misunderstanding."

Jack did disappoint. "Or, he's decided that since you're going back to New York soon, there's no sense in even talking about anything, and he'll just try to stay out of your way until you leave."

"Jack, that's just fucking rude," Grace reprimanded her husband.

"For two young ladies, you guys sure do drop the f-bomb a lot. I don't think your Mom would approve."

"Well, for a self proclaimed intelligent man, you're just an idiot sometimes," Evie sputtered.

"I'm going to let that self proclaimed dig go and just say this. Maybe you're going to need to be the one to put yourself out there and not wait for him to give you an opening. Maybe you should make your own," Jack countered.

Evie let that sink in for a moment and asked, "Any suggestions as to how to do that?"

"No, I'm tapped out."

"Surely we can figure something out," Grace said in her most optimistic, can do tone.

"Don't call me Shirley, and I don't think so," Evie responded, sotto voice.

———————

The wait staff was trying to usher the guests of the rehearsal dinner into the dining room, without much luck. People were reluctant to leave their spots at the bar, even if coating their stomachs with food was probably a good idea.

"It's like trying to herd cats," Evie overheard one waitress complain to another. They finally implored the priest to help them get folks seated at the tables. Because really, who's going to tell a priest to go to hell?

Evelyn and her parents were talking to the best man, Dave Kerns, who had literally just arrived at the restaurant. He was Michael's best friend since grade school and his wife had delivered their third child four days earlier. He laughed about it with the three of them. "Honestly, if it had been the first, or maybe even the second, I don't know if Tracy would've let me come over for the wedding. But by this point, she's got this whole motherhood thing down to a science so I wouldn't be surprised to find out he's sleeping through the night and potty trained by the time I get home. She tells me I don't really add much to the family dynamic, except for being eye candy."

"Dave," Rebecca said tenderly, "It really is bloody marvelous to see you again. You haven't changed a bit." She heard the priest requesting that folks find a seat and added, "Oh, it looks like the vicar wants people to head into the dining area, so why don't we all go ahead and do that."

Dave looked at Evie, obviously confused, and she just mouthed, "Don't ask."

She heard a smooth voice say hello to her parents and turned around to see Nate greeting Rebecca and Tom on his way into the dining room. When Tom asked Nate if he had met David, the best man, yet, his response was simply, "Ahhh, another old friend of Michael's made it into town. Evie, it must be really great for you to get to catch up with so many old faces. I'll let you finish your conversation and just excuse myself. David," he added with a shake of his hand, "very nice to meet you, and I'll obviously see you tomorrow."

"Nice guy," David said simply while heading into the dining room, not realizing the innocuous comments he heard were daggers to Evie.

"Plan B is now officially in effect," Evie told Grace and Jack while grabbing a glass of white wine off the nearest server's tray. "Keep the wine coming so I can just get through these next couple of days and get my ass back to New York City. You know what, Grace? Jack was right. It was just a crush that I let get out of control without any thought to the consequences. Seriously, I live in New York, he lives in London. What was I thinking? Mom loaned me too many of her Sophie Kinsella books before coming over here and I became caught up in the idea of a storybook romance. But that's not real life and that's especially not *my* life. I just have to get the hell out of here as soon as possible." She looked at her sister who was about to say something, and continued on with her rant before she was able to. "And don't say one word until I've finished at least two of these," and held up her wine.

Grace raised her arms in acquiescence and said nothing.

———

Evie assumed the meal was delicious, not because of any taste sensations exploding on her tongue, but because everyone around her kept saying it was. She figured she'd play along and claim to enjoy it as much as the rest of the group, but frankly, she couldn't even say what exactly she was eating. She was putting on a show, plastering on the smile and partaking in all the small talk that was expected as sister of the groom. Midway through her second glass of wine, though, she had switched over to Coke. She figured it would be in very poor form, even for her, to be grossly hung over at her only brother's wedding.

Grace came over and started to speak. "Listen, about Nate," was as far as she got before Evelyn cut her off. She pointed to her half empty wine glass and said, "That's still my second and you know the rule."

Grace looked at her with her eyes narrowed into slits and shrugged her shoulders, feigning defeat. "You're not going to finish that are you?"

Evie nodded in assent.

"Fine, so you don't want to talk about this tonight, I get it. But just because I can't bring the topic up doesn't mean I can't slap some sense into you," she said as she swatted Evie on the back of her head. Hard. "Let me know if you change your mind and want to talk." She smirked at her sister. "That was kind of fun. Thanks."

———————

After dinner, people once again congregated by the bar. That was where Evie caught up with Grace and Rebecca, who was urgently rifling through her evening bag. "Blimey, I totally thought I threw in a couple of quid with my fags when I was getting my purse together tonight. Bullocks." Rebecca said with feeling.

Evie and Grace just stared at their Mom like she was some kind of school science experiment gone terribly wrong. They could not have stared harder if she had suddenly sprung into a potato with toothpicks stuck all over her, sitting on a sunny windowsill.

Grace was the first to speak and did so without breaking eye contact with Rebecca, although her comments were directed at Evie. "I know she's putting words together, presumably in some sort of sentence, but for the life of me, I can't figure out what she's trying to say. Can you?"

"Not so much," was Evie's reply.

"Oh for God's sakes, girls, use your heads. I was just saying I thought I threw some money in my purse with my cigarettes. Apparently, I didn't."

"We should use *our* heads?" Evie laughed. "Aside from the fact that the words you've chosen are not really used in Connecticut, at least with those meanings attached to them, I ask you to remind yourself that you don't smoke. Making that sentence ridiculous on multiple levels."

"I know," Rebecca said conspiringly to her daughters. But in all the books I read to prepare myself for this trip, it seemed like most of the characters smoked, so I figured I could use them as a prop, if you will. Or offer them around to break the ice if needed."

"Sort of like a cancer breath mint?" Grace asked incredulously.

Evie couldn't help the snort of laughter that escaped her, while Rebecca ignored her daughter's sarcasm. "Just doing my part to try to fit in and bridge differences," was how she justified herself. "I'd like get a real feel for the culture while I'm here."

"Yeah, Mom, I'm just not seeing the connection between cigarettes and culture. That's quite a leap of faith you're making. And I highly doubt that England's Chamber of Commerce would really want you equating them to the land of ciggies. They'd probably rather you visit The Tower of London and see the Crown Jewels, or go to Buckingham Palace, or St. Paul's Cathedral. Visit Shakespeare's Globe. Places of some historical significance. I'm just guessing," Evie ended lamely with, seeing her Mom's annoyed face.

Evie got a good natured swat at the back of her carefully curled tresses. "Well, you two laugh all you want, but I don't want to embarrass your brother in front of his future in-laws."

"Hey, that's the second time tonight one of you have hit me in the back of the head. Enough already with the fists of fury."

Grace chose to ignore Evie's remarks and went on to reassure their mother. "Mom, that's sweet, but I don't think you have anything to concern yourself with. Just look towards the bar," Grace said. And there was Michael, with a bunch of his friends around him, and a pint of ale on his head, trying to do a Russian dance without letting it fall to the ground, which he very nearly accomplished. Very nearly...which is a nicer way of saying very unsuccessfully.

"What the hell was I worried about?" Rebecca asked her daughters. "But now, back to the couple of quid I thought I had thrown in my bag...I was checking to make sure I had some because I wanted to get some vinegar chips before we head back to the castle later. Those are actually French fries and not potato chips," she threw out as an aside. "Can I borrow some from one of you girls until tomorrow, since I'm so skint right now?"

"Yeah, Mom, just find me when you head to the fish and chip shop and I'll give you some money," Evie said. "In fact, I'll go with you and have some myself."

Thirty-Five

Michael and Charlotte's wedding day dawned perfectly, natch. Emily had gone around the previous night joking with whoever would listen that she had "talked to the Big Guy himself and he promised only glorious weather for her sister on her wedding day." Evie allowed herself a moment to imagine what the weather for Emily's wedding would end up being when it was her turn to get married. She envisioned choirs of heavenly angels swooping out of the sky with sunbeams in their pockets and arranging dollops of puffy white clouds on her veil. Emily would accept nothing less.

She forced herself out of her reverie just as a swarm of ladybugs and butterflies were doing a synchronized dance in the air above Emily's cumulus veil and landed on planet Earth once again.

"My new mantra will be 'I will not become a crazy cat lady.'"

"I think I'd give 'I will stop talking to myself' a whirl and see how that one works out for you first," Grace said, bursting through Evie's unlocked door.

"Jesus, Grace, you scared the piss out of me."

Grace looked at her sister's pajama bottoms pointedly. "Well, lucky for you there are no tell tale signs of that. That would be embarrassing for you." She held up her flat iron and make-up bag, dangling the latter in front of Evie's face like a hypnotist's pocket watch.

"Yes or no to hair and make-up today?"

"That would be a resounding yes."

"Fine, just know going into this that I now hold all the cards and as such will be making the rules. The first of which is...we talk about Nate."

"Never mind, I'll do it myself."

"Suit yourself then. Oh, did I tell you I picked up this new mousse foundation in just our color from the Elizabeth Arden salon before heading over here? You will not believe how flawless it makes your skin look. But you won't have to just take my word for it...you'll be able to see the magic it can work when you view it on me. Do you even have foundation? Never mind, I'm sure you'll look just lovely regardless of your foundation, or lack thereof."

The two sisters stared long and hard at each other before Evie sighed in resignation. "You are a make-up mercenary, you do know that, right? Fine, pepper me with all the questions and/or advice you want. Just make me gorgeous."

"Believe it or not, Evelyn," Grace began, "but I'm not planning on assaulting you with a bunch of well intentioned but annoying sisterly advice, even if everything I say is usually spot on and quite pertinent. That's beside the point. And I'm certainly not asking you to spill the beans to me at this precise moment. All I'm going to say on the matter is probably something you'd be thinking yourself if you were thinking clearly. It's very simple really. How do you feel about Nate? And not about the fact that he's one of Michael's best friends, or that he lives in England and you live in New York City or any other sort of obstacle you can contrive...but how do you feel about him as a person? Period. Because as soon as you can answer that, all the other shit should fall away and I think you'll know what you have to do."

Evie just stared at Grace and started to blurt out how much she cared for Nate, but Grace interrupted her. "Jesus, Evie, I didn't ask you to spill your guts to me without the courtesy of a little "heads up, emotional baggage coming through" traffic sign or something. You need to noodle on this yourself, not be looking to set up some sort of community forum on the subject. Now, I'm going to do your hair in a low chignon so as to avoid any hat head later on in the day, since I'm pretty sure you'll want to take the hat off at some point during the reception. Please God; say we're allowed to take our hats off at the reception."

Thirty-Six

T he lobby had filled up by the time Evie arrived to take her place amongst the bridesmaids, and her whole family had the good sense not to be late. Michael and his groomsmen had taken a separate limo to the church, so Evelyn was able to keep the butterflies in her stomach to a minimum, since it would still be awhile before she'd set eyes upon Nate. She looked down at herself and wondered briefly what he'd think when he saw her. Grace had once again done an outstanding job in the hair and make-up department and Evie counted her blessings on that front. Her parents beamed at her when she trotted across the tile floor on her precariously high heels.

"You look gorgeous, sweetie," her Mom trilled when she caught up to them. "A bit like a three year old who has stolen her mother's shoes and is trying to walk in heels for the first time, but really gorgeous, nonetheless."

"Really pretty," her Dad seconded. "Both my girls are knockouts," he added, as Grace joined their group. "But they have always tended to take after their mother in that regard," and he gave Rebecca a quick squeeze, admiring her in the pink cocktail dress with suit jacket she had chosen, appropriate enough for the title of Mother of the Groom, but looking way too young for him to believe she could have a son getting married today.

"Always the charmer, Tom. You may be smarter than you look, after all," Rebecca teased her husband. "And still quite the handsome devil in a tux," she added, acknowledging the dashing figure her husband still cut in his formal wear.

At that moment Emily departed the elevator and gave a short clap to get everyone's attention. "Okay, here's the situa..." and then stopped herself short, looking around in a horrified manner. She was obviously scanning the crowd for Evie in fear that she would have to contend with a repeat performance from the bachelorette party and the Will Smith song catalog. Evie just smiled at her with a "Don't Worry, Not Happening" shrug and Emily continued.

"Here's what's going to happen now, people. The photographer will be coming down with Charlotte and my parents in just a few minutes and we'll take some group shots of the bride with the bridesmaids, flower girl and ring bearer before we head out to the church. Following the ceremony, we'll head to the grounds of the castle where Michael and Charlotte, along with the entire bridal party, will have some additional photos taken before heading into the reception."

Showing a crack in the armor of Most Organized Maid of Honor Ever and the slightest bit of humor, she added, "I've been in a wedding party before that used this photographer and I feel the need to warn you all that he's prone to not learning the names of the people he's taking pictures of, and refers to them by nicknames he gives them himself, based entirely on physical traits or tidbits he's learned about you." She looked squarely at Jacquelyn with her Brenda Starr red hair and said, "I'll bet you five quid he's going to call you Red."

Two minutes later the photographer jumped out of the elevator with Charlotte and her parents following closely behind. He clapped his hands even sharper then

Emily had done moments ago and everyone stood stock still. He was like a terrifying drill sergeant with a camera slung around his neck. Everyone was slightly nervous he would get angry and make them "drop and give me twenty" or something equally ridiculous while he photographed the scene. So they just stood there and waited for him to say something.

"You, over there," he said pointing to Grace. "Who are you and what is your relationship to the bride or groom?"

Grace seemed to be at a slight loss for words, but was able to blurt out, "My brother is the groom. I'm Grace."

"Great, don't be offended, but I'm just going to end up calling you Groom's Sister Number One. Where's the other sister? I know there's one more."

Evie held her hand up, knowing before he spoke what she would be known as for the rest of the day.

"Fabulous, you, obviously, will be Groom's Sister Number Two. Now Red, come here next to the sisters, and I'd like you to stand next to Charlotte here, and I'm going to check my lighting..." and he was off, mumbling to himself like a mad Ansel Adams.

Emily looked at Jacquelyn and laughed. "You can pay me later."

Thirty-Seven

The soft palette of stained glass window shadows danced across Annie's face while Evie watched in delight. Annie was looking decidedly grown up with her soft blond hair up in a cascade of tendrils and her brown eyes soberly taking in her surrounding area. She touched her niece's cheek gently, and whispered, "Right here is a purple smudge and over here," she tapped Annie's earlobe for emphasis, "is a blue-ish green-ish halo. Overall, you should know that these colors look good on you. Literally." The two laughed softly, wary of disturbing the calm in the church foyer they were standing in. In just a few moments, the bridesmaids would begin the procession that would end with Charlotte. Shortly after that, her brother was going to become a married man. Just like that.

Twinges of nerves shot through Evie when she thought about having to walk back down the aisle with Nate, but she found a way to push them aside when they tickled her stomach. She realized it was much easier to put all her energy into being excited for Michael on his wedding day than work herself up into a state of agita over Nate.

"Can you believe he's actually going to do it?" Grace whispered in her ear. "Our brother is really taking the plunge. Am I a horrible sister to admit I bought travel insurance on our flights because I was always half waiting for the other shoe to drop?"

"Nah, I was too, to tell you the truth. Until I moved here and saw how happy they make each other. I think Michael just had us conditioned to view any girl he brought home as transitory and we, in turn, learned not to get attached. But this," Evie said, tossing her head in the direction of the altar where Michael was nervously pacing, "is the real deal."

Grace nodded in agreement. "He's going to make a great husband and father. I can't even believe I'm saying those words and referring to Michael," she giggled.

The wedding coordinator had begun to line the girls up by height and set Constance, as the shortest, down the aisle first. Three hundred pairs of eyes turned backwards at the exact moment the soft click of her high heels hit the ground and the organ started to come to life with music.

"Thank God I'm not first," Evie said to Jacquelyn, who was the next one to be shoved out of the starting block, as Evie was beginning to picture the doorway. She started to imagine a mechanical rabbit plodding along for the bridesmaids to chase, like in the Bugs Bunny cartoon. Evie laughed a little to herself at that thought while being pushed out the door by the wedding coordinator and into the line of vision of what she considered to be roughly all of London. *With great power comes quite the mofo guest list* she thought, and tried to slow her gait down to an unnatural crawl. Especially for a New Yorker used to keeping pace with slow moving vehicles on a gridlock alert traffic day. (The coordinator had threatened bodily harm to any girl making it to the altar before the count of twenty. But there would be bonus points to anyone who stretched it out to a twenty- five count. Evie decided it would be unwise to challenge the coordinator on her rule. Besides, the rumor was that the bonus points were to come in the form of some Cadbury Flake bars, so Evie was willing to walk in reverse for a couple of those.)

And for that count of twenty, walking serenely to the front of the church, Nate found himself spellbound by Evelyn. The dress fit her perfectly, just as Wendy the seamstress said it would, and the blue coloring set off her eyes remarkably. Even the hat seemed to be working, and Evie looked more Audrey Hepburn in *Breakfast at Tiffany's* than fool in a wide brimmed hat with ostrich feathers. Nate couldn't help it and found himself grinning at her as their eyes connected when she reached her final destination, and she felt her heart lift just the slightest bit. Then he remembered who he was smiling at and his face settled into the detached indifference that he had been wearing since walking in on Sammy manhandling her a few days prior.

So much for mending fences and building bridges, she thought, and then decided to let it all go. Her brother's wedding day was not going to be ruined for her. This was her brother who went frog catching at the pond with her, and taught her how to roller skate before in line skating was a fad. The same guy who never told the "Easter Bunny" that he hated Cadbury Crème Eggs and always gave her the ones in his basket because he knew she loved them with an obsession that was borderline eating disorder-ish. He deserves my full involvement and utter attention.

She smiled in her brother's direction, noting how handsome he looked up on the altar waiting for Charlotte to make her entrance. His dark, curly hair was not as unruly as usual; probably from the piles of product (as the *Queer Eye* guys were fond of saying) he bought for the occasion that would most likely never be used again. His dark eyes strained down the aisle, waiting for his bride to show herself at last. And when she did, those same dark eyes widened in joy and a huge grin spread over his face.

For good reason, also, as Charlotte was absolutely breathtaking. The combination of bridal and pregnancy radiance was in full effect on her, and soon the entire congregation was following her movement with their eyes, goofy grins on every last face.

Her blond hair was loosely piled on top of her head and she had one huge fuchsia peony stuck in one of the intricate locks. The one bold make-up choice she had gone with was the deep pink lipstick that matched the flower in her hair, and those she carried down to the altar. Her blue eyes twinkled as she smiled at both sides of the church as she made her way down to Michael. Her dress was the simplest Empire waist silk concoction that Evie had ever seen. The square neckline, which was adorned with bevel cut jewels, was the only ornamental part of the dress. She looked pure (ironic Evie had to admit, since she *was* eight months pregnant) serene, and absolutely lovely.

For the rest of the ceremony Evie was able to compartmentalize Nate and keep him out of her thoughts. She listened to the sermon the priest was giving about the beauty of love and friendship and the roles they each play in a marriage and she was genuinely happy that Michael and Charlotte had found each other. She watched her parents beaming from their pew as their only son recited his vows while keeping a protective hand on Charlotte's pregnant belly throughout. She laughed at the solemn faces that Annie and Archie wore, if only to receive the bribe of two huge Flake bars waiting in the limo for their return. She hoped for their sakes the air conditioning had been left on, since it was a humid August afternoon.

Before she knew it, the bride and groom had sealed the deal with a kiss (and a whoop from Michael) and the groomsmen were lining up to escort their pre-assigned partner back to the limos.

Nate and Evie smiled awkwardly at each other and began to head towards the back of the church. After a short pause, Evie was the first to speak up. "You look quite nice in your tuxedo." Nate waited longer than what most people would have considered to be polite and responded, "You too."

"I'm not wearing a tux," Evie couldn't help but quip.

"You know what I mean," was all Nate would add.

They came to a stand still as the photographer was taking shots of each couple before they left the church and there was a bit of a bottleneck as he did so. They waited for him to finish with the two couples ahead of them and Evie found her eyes darting around all the corners of the church, just to avoid looking at Nate.

"You know, Nate," she began at the same moment the procession started up again and got no farther. Nate tugged at her arm like she was a misbehaving puppy on a leash instead of an elegantly dressed bridesmaid of thirty-two; which she found to be insulting. She half stumbled and grabbed onto his arm tighter then she was originally holding it, which wasn't difficult to do, since before he tugged there was actually some air in between her hand and his arm.

"God damn it, do you have to be so rude?" she glowered at him as she righted herself.

"You might want to watch the expletives in a house of God, especially those that take His name in vain," he whispered angrily, as several older matrons (with ridiculously large hats, Evie couldn't help but notice) were looking at her in a disapproving manner.

"Maybe I wouldn't have to if you weren't jostling me all over the place like an inexperienced pickpocket or something. Fagin would not be proud!"

"Just smile for the photographer," he muttered as they approached the end of the aisle.

"Okay, Coffee Guy and Groom's Sister Number Two...show me those pearly whites."

Evie turned in the direction she thought Nate stormed off in, although it was hard to tell as she had become momentarily blinded by the flash bulb the photographer set off, and sneered, "Ha, you're Coffee Guy."

She guessed his area correctly because his response came from the same spot she shouted into. "Better than a number."

Thirty-Eight

T hey continued to follow the itinerary Emily had laid out to them earlier and arrived on the castle grounds for a bunch of different photo ops. From there they would head directly to the reception.

The photographer started to assemble the rest of the wedding party for their photos once he had finished the ones of Charlotte and Michael with Emily and David. While those pictures were being posed, Evie had managed to avoid Nate by staying with Grace, Jack and the kids. She was feeling out of sorts and out of her element. It was made worse by the cameraman's next request. "Alright, then, gang. I'm going to need you to partner up with whomever it was you walked down the aisle with. Gentlemen, if you would kindly stand behind the ladies, we'll try that first." He stared thoughtfully at the group standing in front of him, the large brims and ostrich feathers mostly obscuring the faces of the guys standing in the back. "Yeah, that's not really going to work. Ladies, why don't you remove your hats for the moment and hold them gently in front of you, please?"

The whole time Nate stood rigidly behind Evie, not saying a word. *This is just ridiculous*, Evie thought to herself. *I've got to do something.*

She half turned to Nate and hissed through clenched teeth, "Are you seriously not going to talk to me throughout this entire wedding? You don't even know what actually happened and you're willing to write me off like that? What is wrong with you?"

"Excuse me, Groom's Sister Number Two? I'm going to ask you to face forward, please, so I can get this shot. Can't have you all turned around over your guy behind you for the photos now, can I?"

Evie glowered at Nate and faced the photographer as requested. She did her best to paste on an appropriate bridesmaid smile.

"I'm sorry," Nate hissed back. "I really don't think there was too much to figure out about what happened. I walked in to see you snogging one of your brother's friends. How far-fetched could my conclusion be?"

The photographer seemed to be losing patience. "Um...Coffee Guy? What I need from the back row is not a lowered head in deep conversation, but eyes up at me, with a smile on your face. Can we get this please, people?"

Nate looked up with more of a grimace than a grin, but this time Evie just spun around and snapped, "You never even asked me for an explanation. And there was one."

The exasperated photographer looked from one to the other. "I'm only going to ask the two of you one more time to please face front and smile for the camera. If not for me, then for the other eight people who have had the same smiles frozen on their faces since your bickering began, or for Michael and Charlotte who are paying me quite a bit of money to see their friends and family captured on film on their big day."

This last speech seemed to stop Evie and Nate in their tracks, and they looked around to see all the other members of the wedding pretending to look elsewhere and not make eye contact with either of them. Even Emily seemed embarrassed for them.

Both of them were quite contrite and started mumbling apologies to the group and the photographer.

"Hey, don't mention it guys," Sammy bellowed. "Personally, I've been fine standing here with Connie."

"It's Constance," she corrected him quickly, all the while trying to push his roving hand off her ass. "And I for one would love to finish up with these photos, sir," she pleaded with the photographer.

The photographer got what he wanted from the wedding party after a couple of shots where they were all miraculously looking at him, and then he headed over to the bride and groom with their parents. Nate pulled Evie roughly away from the group and stared at her. "So?"

"What?" she asked, defensively.

"So, what's the big explanation that's going to clear everything up for me?" Small raindrops had started to splatter around them, and Evie heard Jacquelyn complain, "Bloody hell. Typical weather for an English wedding. It was bound to start sometime, I suppose."

"It's not that big a deal. Sammy cornered me, he was drunk, and he kissed me. I was shocked for a moment, but when I came to my senses, I punched him in the stomach, while stepping on his foot with my high heel. I guess you had left before that happened, though." The rain had really started to come down now, and the bridesmaids and groomsmen had started to race towards the limos. Michael and Charlotte stayed under the gazebo with their parents and the photographer, trapped, but dry. The only concession Evie made to the rain was to put on her fancy, wide brimmed "it's a tradition" hat.

Nate still stared down at her, trying to read her face. "So you really don't have feelings for him?"

"Sammy? Are you crazy? He's one of my brother's oldest friends, I could never like him."

Nate's face closed down instantly and he answered her with a crisp, "I see."

Evie figured it was now or never. This wasn't exactly the private setting she imagined confessing this in, but if this was the only opportunity she was going to be given, so be it. She was going to have to follow Jack's suggestion and make the opening for herself...not just wait for one.

"Nate. I'm going to be completely honest with you. My lack of feelings for Sammy has nothing to do with the fact he's friends with my brother. They have to do with the fact that I've fallen in love with another one of Michael's friends."

Nate stood there with a hesitant smile that quickly turned into a huge grin as he absorbed her words. "Do you have any idea how said friend of your brother's feels about you?" he teased.

Evie suddenly felt self conscious and unsure of how to respond. "Well, I was hoping he might feel a little bit of the same way. To be honest, we haven't openly discussed it before."

"Maybe this can give you some idea as to how he feels," he said, his voice deep with emotion, lifting her off the ground and kissing her soundly and thoroughly. Evelyn never even gave it a moment's thought that there was a limo full of family and friends watching. Or a gazebo that included her parents and her brother catching sight of her first kiss with Nate. All she cared about was that Nate was kissing her and nothing had ever felt this perfect before.

When they slowed down and stopped for breath, she coyly asked him, "Does this mean he might possibly feel the same way?"

Nate, still holding her aloft, looked up at her face and simply said, "He most certainly does. And he has wanted to tell you for quite some time now." Evie bent her head down and started kissing him again.

"I'd appreciate it if you stopped using my sister and her hat as your own personal umbrella, Nate," Michael called out from the relative dryness of the gazebo.

Evie started to giggle a little bit. "You know, he sounds a lot calmer than I would've expected him to, after witnessing that. I guess marriage has mellowed him."

It was Nate's turn to look a little sheepish. "Actually, he might've had some time to adjust to the idea of you and I being together. When I mentioned a commitment in my note to you, I really came down early to tell Michael that I had fallen for you, and that I needed him to get a grip on whatever it was that would make him oppose that. I told him I would like his blessing, but I didn't need his permission. There was no way I was letting you go back to New York without telling you how I felt."

Evie was more then a little shocked. "And he was fine with what you said?"

"Well, he was pretty surprised at first. And more than a little pissed. But he called Charlotte and started to rant a little on the phone to her, and she managed to get him to calm down pretty quickly. She was more than a little great on our behalf, to be honest with you. She told him he was probably the only person in the world who couldn't see that we've been falling in love with each other right under his nose these past couple of months, and he was going to have to trust both his sister and good friend to know their hearts. She also warned him he was just going to have to stay out of it, and worry about his own wedding that was about to take place the next day. It obviously did the trick because when he hung up with her, he gave me a hug, and promised me all sorts of bodily harm if I ended up hurting you."

"That sounds about right. More like the Michael I grew up with."

Nate started to head to the safety of the limo while still carrying Evie in his arms. "Any chance I could convince you to delay your departure? Stay a little while? Maybe even forever?"

"You would need to do some pretty powerful convincing," Evie teased.

"Would this do?" he asked, starting to kiss her again, amidst the groans and catcalls emerging from the limos.

"It's a start. It's definitely a start."

From: <Evelyn.Dunleavy@TheOldeGrind.com>
To:<RTDunleavy1@aol.com>;
<Gracie.Mullane27@comcast.com>; <redkelly@PS131.edu>;
<Maura@NYCHotelcorp.com>; <Amanda-95@GHFD.com>

Subject: MIA

Hi all,

I'm sorry I haven't written any of you in a couple of weeks. I know I mentioned to you all that Nate and I were taking a two week vacation to Greece, which was amazing. Add that to the fact that right before I left I had to finish polishing the latest article I just sold to London's version of *Town and Country*. (That makes four sold these last nine months, plus I'm making great progress on my novel. But who's counting?) This time you guys will actually get a chance to buy it right off your local newsstand, because they're printing it in the U.S. as well. (You know I'm totally going to expect all of you to write letters to the editor, with comments such as "I will continue to support your magazine if you continue to publish such articulate writers like Evelyn Dunleavy, it was a truly enlightening piece" etc, etc, etc. But not those exact lines, because that's how my letter reads. That being said, I belatedly realize I probably shouldn't have already

posted aforementioned letter, because the article hasn't actually gone to print yet. Even though I used a fake name, I don't think it's going to take much for them to get from point A to point B and figure out who actually sent the note. Damn. But I'm completely digressing.) Anyway, this article is the one I did on the subtle differences in urban living between New York City and London. And they're already lined up to purchase sort of a companion piece I just pitched to the editor the other day when I got back from Greece. This one is going to be on the differences in weddings between the two cities. I figure I'll be able to do quite a bit more research on the topic since NATE PROPOSED TO ME WHILE WE WERE IN GREECE. I'M GETTING MARRIED!!!!!!!!!!!!!!!!
After I hit send, I'll be starting the countdown and waiting for your calls. (Some habits die hard, even if it's no longer a necessity! Ha.)
I love you all!
Evie

From: <Amanda-95@GHFD.com>
To: <Evelyn.Dunleavy@TheOldeGrind.com>

Subject: MIA

Evie,
Why the hell would you lead with the sale of an article? Frankly, I find your sense of storytelling in both the written and verbal form lacking, especially when you consider your trade. I'll call you in a sec.
Love,
Amanda

P.S. Apropos of nothing whatsoever, I feel I must take back my snarky remarks about your comparison of Amy Winehouse to Britney. I guess they really are both complete train wrecks.